WINGS OF FIRE

BOOK ONE
THE DRAGONET PROPHECY

BOOK TWO
THE LOST HEIR

BOOK THREE
THE HIDDEN KINGDOM

BOOK FOUR
THE DARK SECRET

BOOK FIVE
THE BRIGHTEST NIGHT

BOOK SIX
MOON RISING

BOOK SEVEN
WINTER TURNING

BOOK EIGHT
ESCAPING PERIL

BOOK NINE
TALONS OF POWER

BOOK TEN
DARKNESS OF DRAGONS

BOOK ELEVEN
THE LOST CONTINENT

LEGENDS
DARKSTALKER

WINGS OF FIRE

THE LOST CONTINENT

by
TUI T. SUTHERLAND

SCHOLASTIC PRESS
NEW YORK

Library of Congress Cataloging-in-Publication Data available

ISBN 978-93-5275-691-9

First printing, July 2018
Book design by Phil Falco
This edition February 2022
Reprinted by Scholastic India Pvt. Ltd., 2020, Feb. 2021, 2022
Printed in India at Shivam Offset Press, New Delhi

For Mum and Dad —

I love you, and thank you for being nothing like any of these dragon parents!

Tsetse Hive
Beetle Lake
Vinegaroon Hive
Hornet Hive
Cicada Hive
Mantis Hive
PANTALA

OF PANTALA
Yellowjacket Hive
Wasp Hive
Bloodworm Hive
Lake Scorpion

HIVEWINGS

Description: red, yellow, and/or orange, but always mixed with some black scales; four wings

Abilities: vary from dragon to dragon; examples include deadly stingers that can extend from their wrists to stab their enemies; venom in their teeth or claws; or a paralyzing toxin that can immobilize their prey; others can spray boiling acid from a stinger on their tails

Queen: Queen Wasp

SILKWINGS

Description: SilkWing dragonets are born wingless, but go through a metamorphosis at age six, when they develop four huge wings and silk-spinning abilities; as beautiful and gentle as butterflies, with scales in any color under the sun, except black

Abilities: can spin silk from glands on their wrists to create webs or other woven articles; can detect vibrations with their antennae to assess threats

Queen: Queen Wasp (the last SilkWing queen, before the Tree Wars, was Queen Monarch)

LEAFWINGS

Description: wiped out during the Tree Wars with the HiveWings, but while they lived, this tribe had green and brown scales and wings shaped like leaves

Abilities: could absorb energy from sunlight and were accomplished gardeners; some were rumored to have unusual control over plants

Queen: last known queen of the LeafWings was Queen Sequoia, about fifty years ago, at the time of the Tree Wars

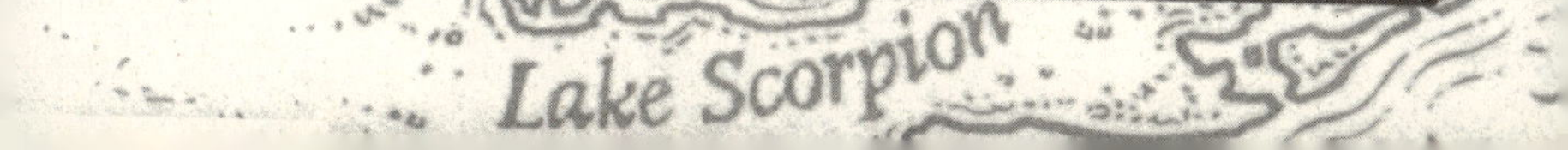

Tsetse Hive
Beetle Lake
Vinegaroon Hive
Hornet Hive
Cicada Hive
Mantis Hive

THE LOST CONTINENT PROPHECY

Turn your eyes, your wings, your fire
To the land across the sea
Where dragons are poisoned and dragons are dying
And no one can ever be free.

A secret lurks inside their eggs.
A secret hides within their book.
A secret buried far below
May save those brave enough to look.

Open your hearts, your minds, your wings
To the dragons who flee from the Hive.
Face a great evil with talons united
Or none of the tribes will survive.

PROLOGUE

About two thousand years ago . . .

If you are flying directly into a hurricane, it is probably useful to be a dragon who can see the future.

Then again, if you are a dragon who can see the future, you are most likely far too smart to fly directly into a hurricane.

And yet, according to Clearsight's visions, that was exactly what she needed to do.

She shook out her black wings, which were already tired from how far she'd flown all morning and the day before. Her talons clung to the slippery wet rock below her. Her scales felt itchy with salt from the ocean spray. Above her, the sun peeked wearily through cracks in the dull gray clouds.

She closed her eyes, tracing the future paths ahead of her.

In one direction — south and a little east — there was a small island with a warm sandy beach. Two coconut palms nodded toward each other and there were lazy tiger sharks to eat. The hurricane would pass it by completely. If she went there, Clearsight could rest, eat, and sleep in safety. Then she could continue on in two days, after the storm was over.

But in the other direction — a long flight west and slightly north — the lost continent was waiting for her.

She knew it was real now. When she'd left Pyrrhia to find it, she'd half expected to fly all the way around the world and end up back on Pyrrhia's other coast. No one was sure another continent even existed . . . and if it did, everyone knew it was too far away to fly to. Any dragon would tire, fall into the sea, and drown before reaching it.

But Clearsight wasn't any dragon. She had something no one else did: the ability to carefully trace the paths of multiple possible futures. Standing on the edge of Pyrrhia, she could see which direction would take her to an island where she could rest. And then the next day: to another island. Shifting her course slightly each day, guided by her visions, she had found a trail of small islands to take her safely across the ocean.

A gust of wind roared over her, splattering a handful of raindrops onto her head.

The hurricane was almost upon her. If she didn't leave right now, dragons on the lost continent would die. Dragons who might one day be her friends, if she saved them. Dragons who had no idea what was bearing down on them, because there was no one there to warn them.

Yet.

Clearsight took a deep breath, vaulted into the sky, and pointed herself west.

Her mind immediately started flashing through all the ways she could die in the next two days. This was why she hated flying in storms. They were too unpredictable; the smallest twitch of the wind in the wrong direction could send her plummeting to the rocks below, or drive a stray palm branch into her heart.

Don't think about that. Think about the dragons who need you.

The other vision was fading; the one where she flew southeast and hid. In that one, she'd arrived on the lost continent in the hurricane's aftermath. The images of the devastation and dead bodies would be hard to shake off, even if she prevented them in reality.

Will they believe me? Will they listen to me?

In some of her visions, they did; in some, they didn't.

All she could do was fly her hardest and hope.

The hurricane fought her at every wingbeat, as if it knew she was trying to snatch victims from its claws. Rain battered her ferociously. She felt like she'd be driven into the endless sea at any moment. Or maybe she'd drown up here, in the water-logged sky.

But this was only the outer edge of the storm; there was far worse still to come. Clearsight was trying to reach land before the really terrible fury behind her did. She couldn't stop, couldn't slow down for a moment.

At one point she glanced back and saw a spout of water sucked into the air. In the middle of it, an orca flailed desperately, before the storm flung it away.

A while later, after the sun had apparently been swallowed for good, Clearsight saw an entire hut fly by her, then splinter apart. She had to duck quickly to a lower air current to avoid the debris. Where had it come from? Who had lived in it? She would never know, her visions told her.

And then, when Clearsight was beginning to lose all feeling in her wings, she saw a shape loom out of the clouds ahead.

A cliff. Land. A lot of land.

A whole continent, in fact.

She canted her wings and soared toward the top of it, where she could see a never-ending line of trees tossing violently in the wind. The hurricane made one more effort to throw her back into the sea, but she fought with her last reserves until she felt earth beneath her talons. She collapsed forward, clutching the wet soil for a moment, grateful to be alive.

Keep going. They're not safe yet.

Clearsight pushed herself up and faced the trees. They were coming. The first two dragons she would meet in this strange new world.

What would it be like to face unfamiliar tribes, completely different from the ones she knew? There wouldn't be any NightWings like her here. No sand dragons, no sea dragons, no ice dragons.

She'd glimpsed what these new dragons would look like, but she didn't know anything yet about their tribes . . . or whether they would trust her.

They stepped out of the trees, eyeing her with wary curiosity.

Oh, they're beautiful, she thought.

One was dark forest green, the color of the trees all around them. His wings curved gracefully like long leaves on either side of him, and mahogany-brown underscales glinted from his chest.

But it was the other who took Clearsight's breath away. His scales were iridescent gold layered over metallic rose and blue, shimmering through the rain. He outshone even the RainWings she'd occasionally seen in the marketplace, and those were the most beautiful dragons in Pyrrhia.

Not only that, but his wings were startlingly weird. There were four of them instead of two; a second pair at the back overlapped the front ones, tilting and dipping at slightly different angles from the first pair to give the dragon extra agility in the air.

Like dragonflies, she realized, remembering the delicate insects darting across the ponds in the mountain meadows. *Or butterflies, or beetles.*

She sat up and spread her front talons to show that she was harmless. "Hello," she said in her very least threatening voice.

The green one circled her slowly. The iridescent one sat down and gave her a small smile. She smiled back, although her heart was pounding. She knew she had to wait for them to make the first move.

"Leefromichou?" said the green dragon finally, in a deep, calm voice. "Wayroot?"

Take a breath. You knew it would be like this at first.

"My name is Clearsight," she said, touching her forehead. "I am from far over the sea." She pointed at the churning ocean stretching way off to the east behind her. "Anyone speak Dragon?"

The two strangers exchanged surprised glances.

"The old language," said the shimmering dragon, awkwardly and slowly, as if pulling the words from his memory bit by bit.

"You do know it!" Clearsight said, hope darting through her veins.

"Some little," he said. "Much old." He smiled again.

The green dragon said something in their own language and nodded at the ocean. The other answered and they spoke for a few moments. If they had been a pair of NightWings, Clearsight would have guessed they were arguing, but their tone was so peaceful that she couldn't really tell.

"The old language" . . . I wonder if their continent and ours had more contact in the past. Maybe we will again in the future. I could teach them all Dragon, especially if some of them already know it. That way if any more Pyrrhians ever come this way, they could communicate.

It was hard to imagine other dragons making the journey she'd just made, though. It was so far, and depended on finding those small islands in such a vast sea.

But maybe she could help with that. *Not soon, though. Not while I feel any temptation to wake Darkstalker. I can't go back to Pyrrhia until I've forgotten him.*

So, probably never.

"Whyer you here down?" the gold-pink dragon asked her.

"There's a *really* bad storm coming," she said as clearly as she could. "*Very* bad."

He spread his wings and looked up, smiling into the raindrops. "See that," he said with a shrug.

"No." She shook her head. "*I* see." She pointed to her head. "I see the future. Tomorrow and tomorrow and the next day. I see all the days. This storm kills many dragons." She waved her talons at the dripping forest around them. "Rips up *many many* trees."

Both dragons were frowning now.

"Treeharm?" growled the green dragon. "Twigheartlots splinterfall?"

"But you can save them," Clearsight pressed on. The visions were crowding into her head; she was running out of time. She couldn't be diplomatic and patient any longer. "We have to move everyone. All dragons, far far far inland, as far as they can fly, right now. And wait there until the storm is over." She turned to the metallic dragon, her talons clasped together. "Please save them."

The moment teetered, two paths waveringly possible.

Finally the shimmering dragon nodded. "Move all. We will do." He said something in their language to the green dragon, who nodded as well.

The relief hit Clearsight so hard, she nearly had to lie down again. But the dragons beckoned her to follow them, and they all took off, flying cautiously through the storm-tossed treetops.

Dragons appeared between the leaves as she swept through the forest with her two companions, all of them watching her with startled curiosity. Most of them were dark green and brown with leaf-shaped wings. *That's their name in Dragon,* she realized from a new cascade of visions. *LeafWings.*

But about a quarter of them were the other tribe, the one Clearsight didn't have a name for yet, and those glittered like jewels on the branches: gold and blue and purple and orange and every color of the rainbow.

She saw a tiny lavender dragonet clinging to a branch, and for a moment Clearsight was alarmed to see that she didn't have any wings. Then she spotted little wingbuds on the dragonet's back and remembered—or foresaw, or remembered foreseeing—that the glittering tribe grew their wings a few years after hatching. *Growing up wingless . . . that must be so strange.*

Clearsight's mind flashed to that other vision, the horrible one, where this dragonet had been one of the many bodies left in the hurricane wreckage.

But instead, tomorrow the little dragon would wake up and chase butterflies in the sunlight, complaining that she wanted blackberries for breakfast.

I saved her. I did something right.

The green dragon called out in a booming voice like a bell tolling. Whatever he said, the dragons around them repeated it, passing it along. Clearsight could hear the echoes of other dragon voices rolling through the forest. She felt the drumming wingbeats behind her as both tribes rose into the air and followed them to safety.

"You save us," said the shimmering dragon, looping around to fly beside Clearsight. He smiled at her again. "You safe now, too."

Maybe I am, she thought. *I stopped Darkstalker. I saved Fathom, and the NightWings, and my parents. And now I've found a new home, with new dragons to save. I can help them with my visions. I can do everything right this time.*

New futures exploded in her mind. She might marry this kind, funny dragon, whose name would turn out to be Sunstreak. Or she could end up with a dragon she'd meet in three days, while helping to clean up the forest, whose gentle green eyes were nothing like Darkstalker's. She could move in with an affable, very old LeafWing named Maple, who spoke the old language, or she could find her own tree hollow to live in, or she could explore the new continent first, then come back here to build a home.

And there would be dragonets, if she wanted them. Clearsight felt a sudden, dizzying rush of love for dragons who weren't even eggs yet: little Jewel, and whip-smart Tortoiseshell, and cuddly Orange (who names their dragonet Orange? Sunstreak, apparently. They might have to have some conversations about that plan), and Commodore, the king of giggles.

She would always miss the dragonets she should have had with Darkstalker, but she would love the ones that were coming with all her heart. And nothing bad would ever *ever* happen to them. They would all live the longest, happiest lives, because she would be here, tracking their paths, keeping them safe.

She would get it right this time.

"Your rootplace," Sunstreak said, gently interrupting her thoughts. "Where?"

She pointed back out to sea. "Pyrrhia." She waved her claws at the continent around them. "This? Where?" she asked.

He smiled again. "Pantala," he said slowly and clearly, and with evident pride.

"Pantala," she echoed back.

The lost continent is real, and it has a name. And it's my home now.

Pantala, here I am.

Tsetse Hive
Beetle Lake
Vinegaroon Hive
Hornet Hive
Cicada Hive
Mantis Hive

PART ONE

IN THE COCOON

Two Thousand Years Later . . .

CHAPTER 1

Blue was a dragon who liked things the way they were.

That is, if he didn't exactly like *everything* about life as a SilkWing, he had to admit that at least he was safe, and, you know, things were fine, really. It wasn't perfect, but at least his tribe and the HiveWings coexisted peacefully. The HiveWings protected them from outside threats. And everyone followed the rules and the Hives were beautiful and spotless and there were always enough yams and okra to eat, so wasn't that the kind of world everyone wanted to live in?

Blue wasn't sure how everyone else felt, but he wondered about it all the time. He often tried to imagine himself as other dragons — were they all as content as he was, or was he luckier than most? Did they want the same things he did? What did they worry about; what did they hope for? If they seemed unhappy, why was that?

His guesses were probably mostly wrong, he was sure, but Blue couldn't stop thinking about it. It felt like a constant tugging on his imagination.

What was the fidgety dragonet next to him in math class thinking while she drew hexagons in the margins of her test? What did their rose-pink neighbor worry about while he cleaned the dead bugs from his webs? What about the HiveWings — how were their lives and hopes and lunches and morning aches and nightmares different from his?

The other lives drew him like a flame, or the scent of nectarines.

He spent the night before his sister's Metamorphosis as her, winding himself deep into the dream of being Luna.

Perhaps her wingbuds had started to flutter open as she fell asleep. Perhaps she lay awake for a while, gazing up at the shrouded stars, thinking of the moment she could leap from the top of the Hive and race the skylarks to the sea. He thought she might also be looking forward to the moonsilk dark she would spin herself and the days of emerald-tinted sleep inside the Cocoon. No one could yell at her or assign her extra work while she was in there, growing her wings.

He knew Luna wasn't scared, like he would be in six days when his own Metamorphosis time came. Luna had always felt ready for life with wings. Blue was not, and most of all, he was not ready for life with *her* wings, which meant everything changing.

Once she had wings, Luna would be assigned to a work order. Soon she'd be paired up with whichever partner the queen chose for her and given another cell to live in. She might even be moved to another Hive.

It was normal; it was the way life always was for SilkWings. Everyone had a Metamorphosis. Everyone had a new life chosen for them. Everyone moved on.

But now that it was happening to his family, Blue found it extremely nerve-racking.

He was already awake when Luna bounded across the web and started shaking him, shortly before dawn. He wasn't sure he'd slept at all. For a while he'd been watching the glow of tiny lights moving far below them in Cicada Hive, imagining himself as one of those early-rising dragons on their way to work, awake before the sun. In the distance he could see Hornet Hive in one direction and Mantis Hive in the other, although the webs that connected them were mostly invisible in the dark.

He'd never been to any of the other Hives, but he knew they were spread out in a wide circle around the plains of Pantala. The enormous dragon cities rose from the grassland and reached for the sky like towering, dragon-made echoes of the trees that used to dominate the land. Their roofs arched out like branches, and the dense silvery threads of SilkWing webs created a canopy tying those branches together, so even wingless SilkWing dragonets could travel between Hives far above the ground, if they wanted to (and were allowed to).

He yawned and batted Luna's talons away, pretending he'd been in a deep sleep. Dewdrops glittered all across the web around and above them, as if it had rained tiny diamonds in the night. He could see the silk-bundled shape of Luna's mother on the outer edge of their cell, still fast asleep. His own mother was on a night crew these days and had been gone since midnight.

"It's today, it's today!" Luna whispered. Her pale green tail flipped back and forth, sending tremors through the silken threads. She bounced closer to Blue to poke his shoulder again and sent his hammock rocking perilously.

"Hey, watch it," he teased, nudging her away. "Some of us won't have wings for another six days." There were layers and layers of other strong webs crisscrossing below his family's web, ready to catch any falling dragonets . . . but even so, it was hard to forget how far down the ground was. He always felt safer in the Hives than he did out on the webs, which he worried was not a very normal SilkWing attitude.

"And some of us," she sang, "will have them todaaaaaaaaaaaaaaay!" She sat up and flexed the tiny wingbuds on her shoulder blades.

"Well, not exactly," he pointed out. "Today is only your cocoon-spinning day. It'll take another five days for your wings to actuaaaaAAAAH!" he yelped as she upended his hammock and dumped him onto the web.

"Don't you 'actually' me," Luna said sternly. "I'm your older sister and I've been to, like, twelve Metamorphosis days, plus I have the highest grade in our class in silk studies. I can 'actually' you under the table."

"Yes, all right," Blue said, stretching his legs one by one. "You're the smartest dragon in the family, I know, I admit it." He snuck a glance over his shoulder at his own wingbuds. They looked the same as yesterday: small, tightly curled, and iridescent violet, a brighter, more purple shade than the gemlike azure of the rest of his scales.

Luna's wingbuds were starting to unfurl, so he could see whorls of cobalt and gold inside the pale green exterior. There were also signs of her silk coming in; already her palms and wrists were glowing a little, as though tiny fireflies were waking up under her scales.

That'll be me soon, he thought, tamping down a wave of panic. *After my own Metamorphosis, I'll have wings and silk, too.*

Maybe the changes would be small. Maybe he'd be assigned to live right here to help his mother strengthen the bridges between Hives. Maybe Luna would stay, too, and be a Hive drone like her mother, working for one of the upper-class HiveWing families.

She wouldn't like that, though. Luna wanted to be a spinner. She was hoping to be paired with Swordtail in an artist's cell near the sunny heights of the web. She wanted to make a weaving so beautiful it would have to be given to the queen of the HiveWings, who ruled both tribes — or at least to one of the queen's sisters.

Blue had seen the queen only once, when she visited Cicada Hive. Queen Wasp had come through to inspect their school with twenty HiveWing soldiers marching in impressive exact unison behind her. Her scales glittered in perfect black and yellow stripes and her eyes were large and completely black, surrounded by an oval of yellow scales.

Imagining himself into her was almost impossible; it was like trying to imagine life as the sun. But he couldn't help trying. He thought about how she must wake up in the morning and eat breakfast like anyone else. (Although if the rumors were true, she ate as rarely as possible, and only predators: the head of a lioness for lunch one day, slices of black mamba in squid ink soup for dinner twelve days later.)

He wondered if her wings felt strong or heavy as she flew from Hive to Hive to check on her subjects. Was she relieved to have sisters to share her responsibilities with — or did she worry that they might covet her throne? How often did she check the Book of Clearsight? If he were queen, with two tribes full of thousands of dragons depending on him, Blue guessed he'd read it every day until he had it memorized.

At one point during her visit, she had spotted Blue and Luna and stared at them for approximately a century and a half, by his internal clock. He'd gotten the distinct feeling that she was trying to decide between adopting them or eating them.

Queen Wasp was as breathtaking and superior as all the

stories said. After that, her sister Lady Cicada, the ruler of their Hive, had never seemed quite so terrifying to him again.

And maybe that was the point of the queen's visits: to remind everyone whose claws held the real power.

"So?" Luna said, taking one of his talons in hers. "My last day as a dragonet! What are we going to do?"

"Lie around on the web in the sunlight?" he suggested hopefully.

"No, you lazy banana slug," she said. "All my favorite things! That's the correct answer."

"This isn't fair," he pointed out. "By the time it's *my* Metamorphosis Day, nobody will be left to do all *my* favorite things with me. You'll all be too busy flying around with your big flappy wings doing fancy busy wingish things."

Luna managed not to make a face, but Blue instantly felt guilty anyway. He knew she wished Swordtail could spend the day with them, too. But Swordtail was on construction duty on the west side of Cicada Hive all day — probably getting dusty and frustrated and missing Luna like crazy.

"Sorry," Blue said.

"Don't be," Luna said. "Once I have my wings, Swordtail and I can be partnered, and then I'll see quite enough of him." She grinned, as though applying for the partnership actually meant they'd get it, which Blue thought was far from certain. He didn't know any adult SilkWings who'd been given the partner of their choice. His mother and Luna's mother hadn't even known their father, who had been whisked away to another Hive once there were eggs. Blue knew his name — Admiral — and nothing else.

Better this way, though, he thought. Burnet and Silverspot ended up loving each other much more than they could ever have loved Admiral. They were a good family, the four of them. It had all worked out for the best. Queen Wasp and her sisters knew what they were doing with the partner assignments. If Luna and Swordtail weren't matched up, it would be for a good reason.

"So where do we start?" he asked. "No, wait, let me guess. Honey drops."

"Honey drops!" Luna sang, bouncing the web again and fluttering her wingbuds. "Move your tail and maybe we'll beat the line at the checkpoint."

He dipped his snout into their dew collector, washing his antennae and the dry scales under his eyes, as Luna darted across the web to her mother. Silverspot sat up and wrapped her wings around Luna — quickly enough that Blue wondered whether she had been awake all night, too.

"Have a wonderful day, my darling. I'll try to make it to the Cocoon," Silverspot promised. "But —"

"I know," Luna said. "It's all right." Silverspot's mistress was bad-tempered and frantically insecure about her place in the Hive hierarchy, and she tended to take out her rage on Silverspot with thousands of small cruelties. Keeping

Silverspot from her only daughter's Metamorphosis would probably be the highlight of her year.

"Just think," Luna said brightly, "next time I see you, I'll have wings! We can go flying together!"

"I can't wait," Silverspot agreed. But when she hugged Luna again, Blue caught a strange expression crossing her face.

Anxiety? Fear?

He felt a weird chill run through his scales. Silverspot looked as though she knew something they didn't.

As if, for some reason, Silverspot suspected she would never see her daughter again.

CHAPTER 2

The creeping sense of foreboding followed Blue as he clambered along the webs after Luna. The sun was rising, sending shafts of filmy gray light through the silken strands around them. The soft hum of insect wings rose from the tall, waving grasses of the savanna below.

Luna was a reckless climber, leaping from one level to the next like a monkey . . . or like a dragon who already had her wings. Blue was more sensible, relying on the slight stickiness of the silk to keep him anchored as he ascended. Even so, today he felt more airsick than he normally did. Each tremor along the silk seemed to vibrate right into his bones, making his antennae twitch nervously and his teeth ache.

He was relieved when they reached the Hive entrance, where the webs connected to the uppermost tier of the city. There was already a line twenty dragons long, but at least here they could wait on the solid ground of the entrance tunnel. He stepped off the web onto the papery dry surface and flexed his talons.

The walls of the tunnel were painted with a mural of SilkWings and HiveWings flying together in a bright blue sky, all of them looking as happy as Luna on a honey drop spree. Much of the mural was covered up, though, by the posters that lined the walls.

BE VIGILANT!

WE ARE ALWAYS IN DANGER!

BEWARE OF LEAFWINGS!

REPORT DISLOYAL SILKWINGS TO A HIVEWING AUTHORITY IMMEDIATELY!

QUEEN WASP SEES EVERYTHING. QUEEN WASP PROTECTS US ALL. ALL HAIL QUEEN WASP!

LEAFWINGS: GONE . . . OR LYING IN WAIT?

REPORT ANY SIGHTINGS OF POSSIBLE LEAFWINGS TO A HIVEWING AUTHORITY IMMEDIATELY!

That last one had a drawing of a snarling dark green dragon on it, complete with bloodstained claws and teeth. It seemed as if a new poster appeared on the walls every other day, and half of them were about the threat of LeafWings.

Luna caught him studying the picture and snorted.

"What?" he said.

"Come on," she said. "You're not really afraid of LeafWings, are you?"

"Why not?" he asked. "They nearly wiped us out half a century ago. Or has my genius sister forgotten all our history lessons already?"

"But they failed," she pointed out. "And now they're

extinct. So there's nothing to worry about. It's not like they can attack us if they're all dead."

"We don't know that they are," he argued. "Tussock said his uncle saw one flying overhead a couple of years ago. And what about that section of Mantis Hive that collapsed last year? Everyone said that was LeafWing sabotage."

"Pffft," Luna said scornfully. "What Tussock's uncle saw was a green SilkWing. He's just hysterical. And that collapse was caused by shoddy workmanship. The sabotage story was so obviously a cover-up."

"Shhhhhhh," Blue said, glancing at the HiveWing soldiers up ahead. They looked busy checking IDs, but they might still overhear Luna's treacherous talk.

"Look," Luna said, lowering her voice and rolling her eyes. "No one has *really* seen a LeafWing in over fifty years. And we cut down all their trees, so where would they even be living, if they were still alive? Slithering through the tall grass of the savanna? No, they're gone, thanks to Queen Wasp, so all of this is totally unnecessary." She waved her claws at the warning posters.

"The Hives don't cover the *whole* continent," he suggested, but she was already talking over him.

"The queen just needs us to have a — what's it called — a common enemy, you know? So the SilkWings don't start complaining or asking for their own queen or anything like that."

"Our own queen?" Blue was startled. He'd never even thought about the SilkWings asking for a separate queen before. It was kind of alarming that Luna had. That seemed like the kind of dangerous idea Swordtail might have put in her head.

"I mean, not that *I* think we should," Luna said hurriedly, and this time she was the one to glance over at the soldiers. "But, you know, someone might, if they were unhappy with the way things are."

Blue shook his head. "I don't think so. I don't know any unhappy SilkWings." The poster behind Luna read LOYALTY ABOVE ALL, with a giant drawing of Queen Wasp's huge dark eyes. Sometimes they were a comforting sight, but in the middle of this conversation, they were making him uneasy. "Everything is great in the Hives. We're safe, and we all work together, so I don't see what anyone would have to complain about."

The line moved them within earshot of the soldiers, and they both stopped talking instinctively. Blue gazed at the long, pale blue wings of the dragon in front of him, imagining where she might be going, until finally it was their turn.

"Names?" said one of the soldiers in a bored voice.

Every HiveWing had at least a few black scales, inherited from their common ancestor, Clearsight, but this dragon was almost entirely black, with only a few orange flecks here and there. Blue and Luna had seen him here at the checkpoint nearly every day for three years, and yet the soldier never gave any indication of recognizing them or caring that they existed beyond their IDs. His name was Hawker, not that he'd ever told them that. Blue had picked it up from listening to the guards grumbling at one another.

"Blue," he said, holding out his right arm. The soldier studied the letters that had been carved into Blue's palm when he was a newly hatched dragonet: *B* for his name, forming a triangle with a smaller *B* and *A* for his parents' names. Luna always said she was glad the marking happened while they were too young to remember, but Blue was pretty sure he *did* have memories of that day . . . a bright light, a searing pain, and, most clearly, a sense of betrayal.

Hawker grunted and moved on to examining the wrist cuff on Blue's other arm. It was a dull bronze color and annoyingly heavy, although Blue was mostly used to it by now. It indicated that he was a student at one of the schools in the Hive, so he was permitted to go in and out through this checkpoint. The name of the school was inscribed in the metal: Silkworm Hall.

"And I'm Luna," said his sister.

"Ah," said the soldier, turning to consult a list on a small rectangle of paper. "Metamorphosis today."

"That's right," Luna said. Blue could tell she was trying so hard not to smile. Smiling at soldiers was always risky. You never knew if you'd get a rare smile back, or if you'd end up spending an afternoon on Misbehaver's Way for "taunting a figure of authority."

Blue imagined that the soldiers had to be that alert and

suspicious — if dragons didn't respect them, how could they keep the peace and control the Hive?

But he also believed that Swordtail hadn't deserved it any of the three times he'd wound up on Misbehaver's Way. Swordtail had wild ideas and talked a little too freely, but he wasn't a danger to the Hive.

"You'll have a new one of these next time you come through here," Hawker said, tapping Luna's wrist cuff, which matched Blue's.

"I know," she said, as Blue's heart sank. One more change: Luna was done with school now. He'd have to go without her.

Not for very long, though. I'll be needing a new wristband soon, too. How would it feel to have this one cut off and exchanged for something else? Surely it would be a bit like having one of his toes casually replaced.

"Well," said the soldier. He looked at his list and then back at Luna again. "You may go." Hawker cleared his throat gruffly as they started forward. "Hrm. Good luck."

"Oh — thank you," Luna said, startled. She dragged Blue forward, managing to hold on until they were far down the tunnel before she burst into giggles.

"He said so many words to us all of a sudden!" she cried. "I didn't know he knew so many words!"

"Maybe he likes you," Blue suggested with a grin. It was a joke — but then, what if he did? Blue felt himself slipping into visions of the HiveWing's possible life. Did Hawker go home and dream of the SilkWing he saw every day but couldn't ever be with? Did his friends tease him about his dedication to his work? Did he like being a soldier, following orders all day long, or did he ever wish the rules were different?

"Oooo, maybe we'll have a *forbidden love*!" Luna gasped, falling into Blue and knocking him back into reality.

"Well, I am *not* going to be the one to tell Swordtail," he said.

Luna laughed and started telling a story about something funny Swordtail had said the night before. Blue padded beside her, glad to be off the topic of SilkWing-HiveWing relationships. Forbidden was putting it mildly. Whatever the strongest word for illegal was, that was the right word. Prohibited? Outlawed? Punishable by death? All of those times a million.

They reached the end of the tunnel, where it widened and forked into several other tunnels. The path to the right led to the Mosaic Garden, but they'd go there later, Blue was sure. It was Luna's favorite place in the Hive.

First, though, they made their way down three levels, through two more checkpoints. It was warm, as always in the Hive, with sunlight filtering through the walls to cast an amber glow over everything. All the Hives were made of treestuff, which was a particular mix of wood pulp and silk and clay and other things Blue would learn about if he was assigned to a construction crew. It looked paper-thin and allowed light to filter through, but it was solid as rock. Under his talons, the treestuff floor was dry and mostly smooth, apart from a few lumps where workers hadn't been careful enough.

The problem was, the Hives had been built back when there were plenty of trees all over Pantala. Now that the trees were all gone (or mostly gone), the only wood pulp came from the shrubby little bushes that fought their way out of the dry soil of the savanna. So the only way to expand a Hive was to take the treestuff from somewhere else in the Hive and reshape it where you wanted it. It was hard, back-breaking work, usually given to the SilkWings who caused the most trouble in school.

Such as, for instance, Swordtail.

Blue was really, really hoping he didn't get assigned to a construction crew. A silk work detail would be different — what his mom did in the sky between Hives was half architecture, half art. He wouldn't mind a job like that. Blue had been a good, quiet, obedient student at Silkworm Hall his whole life. Surely he'd earned a better assignment than treestuff construction.

Finally, Luna took a path to the right instead of the left, and they came to the open market of Cicada Hive. This was a huge, vaulted space that hummed with activity. The best shops had permanent six-sided cells around the outer wall; everyone else had to scramble for stalls in the labyrinthian middle. Overhead, yellow and orange lanterns hung along silk filaments, crisscrossing the ceiling like necklaces of tiny suns.

And, as always, soldiers perched on balconies above the market, keeping a sharp eye on the hustle and bustle of the dragons below. Some of them held long, needlelike lances that looked like bigger versions of the stingers that could spring from the tips of Queen Wasp's claws. Not that Blue had ever seen her use them, but they were featured in several of the posters. Some of those in here, in fact — her face loomed over the market in murals and posters until he almost felt as though he had a hundred lenses in his eyes, each of them reflecting her back at him.

Luna led the way confidently through the maze, until Blue realized she was aiming for the best nectar store in the Hive: a tall, imposing cell-front with delicate sugar confections arrayed in the window.

He jumped forward and stepped on her tail, yanking her back.

"Ow!" she yelped. "What was that for?" Three haughty-looking HiveWings nearly ran into them, and he tugged Luna out of their way, mumbling apologies. They wrinkled their noses and spread their wings, making a few other SilkWings duck to the side of the path to give them space, and then they swept away.

"Luna, SilkWings don't go into The Sugar Dream," he said. "Let's go to Droplets, like we always do."

"It's my Metamorphosis Day!" she objected. "We've only never been there because we usually can't afford it, but today is different. Mother gave me enough scales for it. *She* said to have the best last day ever."

Blue shivered involuntarily. The phrase "last day" really wasn't helping his anxiety about Silverspot's face this morning.

"Stop worrying," Luna said, nudging his shoulder. "They'll take our scales no matter who we are. And these might be the best honey drops we ever get."

She bounded off again and he followed, unconvinced, but aware that arguing with his sister would get him exactly nowhere.

There was only one other customer in The Sugar Dream when they entered: an older lemon-yellow HiveWing with black stripes on her wings and ruby scales freckling her nose and tail. She peered over a pair of spectacles at them, then went back to squinting at the shelves of pale pink and lavender candies.

But the HiveWing behind the counter stiffened and flicked his long red tail disapprovingly, his brows arching as high as they could possibly go.

"Hello!" Luna said cheerfully, ignoring his expression. "We'd like two honey drops, please." She touched the soft gray silk pouch around her neck as she spoke so that the scales inside jingled.

"Who's your mistress?" the clerk asked. "Is she new to this Hive? She should know that shopping for luxury items is not a task traditionally entrusted to servants."

"We're nobody's servants," Luna said indignantly. "We want them for ourselves!"

"Nobody's servants yet," Blue added quickly. "We're still in school." He pointed to their wingbuds. "It's her Metamorphosis Day today, actually, so, we'll know our assignments soon, and then I'm sure our . . . uh . . . the dragons we work for will . . . uh . . ." He made himself stop talking. Judging by the frown on the shopkeeper's face, it was clearly not helping.

"Indeed," said the salesdragon. "Well, as you can see, I am currently assisting another customer. I'm afraid you will have to wait." He narrowed his eyes and tipped his chin at the spectacled dragon.

Blue and Luna glanced over at her. The elderly dragon had her snout down close to a box of honey sticks. As they watched, she nudged a bag of sugar cubes closer to her and tapped it with a claw, mumbling as though she was counting each cube.

Luna shot the clerk an "are you kidding me?" look. He pretended not to see it.

"We can wait," Blue whispered to her. Causing trouble would only get them kicked out with no honey drops.

Several long moments passed. Blue studied the beautiful spun-sugar artwork behind the clerk: an elegant pale green praying mantis, a glittering blue-and-white dragonfly, an array of different jewel-colored beetles, and several miniature wasps. He wondered if it felt disrespectful to any of the HiveWings to eat something their queen was named after.

Was this clerk the one who had made the delicate sugar insects? Did he spend his early mornings in the back room of the shop, carefully pouring honey into frozen teardrops and lacing chocolate stars with speckles of orange peel? Did he love coming here every day, or was he so sick of sweetness that all he could stomach anymore was the saltiest gazelle jerky?

Blue guessed that the shopkeeper had hoped his rudeness would drive them away — and now he was regretting his choice, because it meant two SilkWings were lingering in his precious store, right where anyone might wander by and see them. He probably wished he had taken their money and gotten rid of them quickly, but now he was stuck waiting for his other customer to make up her mind, just as they were.

The door swung open, letting in a burst of noise from outside as two HiveWings entered. Their giddy chatter dropped away abruptly when they saw Blue and Luna standing by the counter.

"Oh," said one of them. "Chafer, what . . . interesting new customers you have."

The other one giggled and edged past Blue, keeping her wings canted away from him.

"Don't worry, Weevil, sir. I'm sure they'll be leaving soon," Chafer said, somehow managing to be oily and tense at the same time.

"Yes, we will," Luna piped up. "As soon as we get our honey drops."

Chafer twitched his snout at her as if she were an actual moth he'd found nibbling on one of his rugs.

"By the Hive, what a bore it must be to be wingless," Weevil said, pacing around the two SilkWing dragonets. "I bet you feel like half a dragon. Hardly a dragon at all. Such cute little wingbuds, though. Can I touch one?" He reached out toward Luna's back.

"No!" Luna cried, jerking away from him.

Blue wasn't sure which dragon was the most horrified: himself, Chafer, or the rude HiveWing.

"You can touch mine," he said quickly. "It's her Metamorphosis Day, so she's — they're — it's, um, better not to touch them right before the change." That wasn't true at all. Luna was just being difficult and impertinent to dragons who could really get them in a lot of trouble if they wanted to. Those soldiers outside could be summoned at a moment's notice by any HiveWing.

"Ohhhhh," said Weevil. "Right, of course," he added, as though he obviously knew everything about Metamorphosis. "How exciting for you, little SilkWing." He reached out his talons and poked Blue's wingbuds roughly, as though Weevil was trying to unfurl them by force. Blue tried not to wince.

He tried to make it better by imagining Weevil's life—a family who loved him, perhaps, who hugged him good-bye in the morning. Maybe he'd desperately wanted to be a soldier but hadn't qualified for the academies. Maybe he'd been reassigned to a management or gathering job instead, which made him bitter and imperious with anyone he could safely push around.

It was difficult, though, to slide into sympathy with this particular dragon. Possibly he was just a jerk and had always been that way.

The old HiveWing with the spectacles suddenly appeared at Weevil's side. "There's no need to be a brute, Weevil," she said to him. "Could you help me with these nectar vials over here? I'm always afraid my old claws will drop one."

"Of course, Lady Scarab," Weevil said deferentially. He let go of Blue and followed her to the other side of the shop.

Lady Scarab? Blue thought. If she had a title, she must be related to the queen. A sister or an aunt, perhaps, but not one with her own Hive. Still, she would be *way* up the hierarchy of the HiveWings, which explained Weevil's behavior toward her.

"Mmmm, someone said honey drops, and now I must have them," said Weevil's friend, who had been blissfully pretending not to see Luna or Blue. "We'll take eight of those, six of the little sugar wasps, and a box of apricot taffy. Make it pretty."

"Of course," said the salesdragon. He took a pale pink

box out from under the counter and started packing her order into it.

"Don't say anything," Blue whispered to Luna, who was giving Chafer her best murderous glare. "It's just the way it is."

To her credit (and Blue's surprise), Luna bit her tongue until the two HiveWings were gone, sailing out of the shop with their candy and a few loud whispers about poor wingless street urchins cluttering up the place.

"So," Luna said to Chafer, with strained politeness. "May we please have our honey drops now?"

"After I serve the Lady Scarab," he said sniffily.

"But — those — you just —" Luna protested.

"I beg your pardon." Blue turned and saw Lady Scarab eyeing Chafer like a bone she'd already chewed on. She had moved on from counting sugar cubes to checking nectar vials under one of the lamps, but her talons were suddenly still and her tail was coiled up like a snake. "Am I to understand that you are delaying these little no-wings on my account?"

"It's no trouble, Lady Scarab," Chafer oozed. "They can wait. You are my first priority."

"Well, I don't want to be," she snapped. "Serve them right now."

Blue poked Luna with his tail to try to get the smug look off her face.

"My lady," said Chafer. "I quite insist. We do not serve second-class dragons before royalty in *this* establishment."

"Even if *I* insist?" she said coldly.

They stared at each other for a long moment, and Blue suddenly got the feeling that there was something more complicated about Lady Scarab's place in the Hive than he'd realized. Something that made this salesclerk willing to test the edges of her dominance.

And then the air shifted. Blue's nose twitched and twitched again. It was some kind of . . . *smell.* It started small, a faint hint of rottenness, but slowly grew stronger and sharper and more horrible. Luna covered her snout with a gagging sound.

"My lady!" Chafer cried, stumbling back as though the odor had punched him in the face. "Please don't! I'll have to close my shop for the rest of the day! This isn't necessary!"

"I *said,*" she hissed, "serve them *right now.*"

He scrabbled frantically behind the counter, grabbed a small white box, and dumped two honey drops into it. "Here," he gasped at Luna. "Take it."

"How much?" she asked through her talons.

"Just get out of here," he begged.

Blue took the box, but Luna stopped to pull a pair of scales out of her pouch. She dropped them on the counter and darted toward the door.

"Thank you, I think," Blue said to Lady Scarab, trying not to breathe through his nose. She looked serene and supremely unbothered by the smell.

"Choose an establishment friendlier to SilkWings next time," she suggested.

He nodded and escaped out into the market behind Luna.

"Was that *her*?" Luna asked as they hurried between stalls. "Did *she* make that awful smell?"

"I've heard some HiveWings have that power," he said. "But I didn't think anyone would ever actually *use* it. I mean, why would they?"

"To terrorize their enemies!" Luna answered. "Moons, I sure would! If I had super stink powers, I'd have blasted that Weevil guy right in the snout the moment he got anywhere near our wingbuds. Oooo, that would have been awesome."

"For about two heartbeats," Blue pointed out. "And then it would have been the opposite of awesome, because you would be in jail forever."

"Blue," she said. "Don't you think it's unfair that HiveWings can use their weapons on us anytime they want, but we can't do anything to fight back?"

"No!" He looked around quickly, but none of the nearby dragons reacted as if they'd just heard treason. It was loud enough in the market, and they were moving so quickly between stalls, that he could hope no one would overhear them. "The HiveWings saved us, remember? Our tribe agreed to accept their queen. Besides, there's a reason why the universe gave them weapons and not us. That's why they're in charge."

"But maybe if we fought back, they wouldn't *be* in charge," she pointed out.

"*Luna.*" He herded her into the tunnels that led to the other levels of the Hive. His voice dropped to a whisper. "For the love of silk, what's gotten into you today? I know Swordtail is full of crazy ideas, but please don't let him drag you into prison along with him."

"Those are *my* ideas," she said crossly. "He got them from *me*."

"Well, then leave me out of it." He covered his ears. "La la la, everyone's a good Hive citizen here."

His sister rolled her eyes. "Oh, Blue." She hesitated, studying his face, and then shook her head as though she hadn't found the answer she wanted there. "All right, I'm sorry." She flexed her claws and looked down at her wrists. "It's probably because of my silk coming in. It hurts a lot more than I expected it to."

Her palms and wrists were glowing even brighter than before. Blue hadn't noticed in the well-lit market, but here in the dim tunnels it was impossible to ignore. She seemed to have little balls of fire clustered under her scales, bubbles of molten orange and gold.

"That doesn't look normal," he said anxiously. "I've never seen anyone's silk glands do that before Metamorphosis. Have you?"

Swordtail and his sister, Io, had gotten their wings not too long ago. He remembered their palms glowing a little bit, but not like this — and they hadn't mentioned anything about it hurting.

Does Metamorphosis hurt? Why wouldn't someone warn us about that?

"I'm sure it's nothing," Luna said with a shrug. "Everyone Metamorphoses a little differently."

"Should we take you to a doctor?"

"No WAY," she said. She swiped the box of honey drops out of his talons. "I'm not spending my perfect last day getting prodded by some HiveWing who thinks we're all weird and revolting. I'm totally fine! To the Mosaic Garden! Let's go!"

Luna darted away up the tunnel. Blue rubbed his own wrists worriedly and then followed her. He could see the glow from her scales reflecting off the tunnel walls.

Is she going to be all right?

If everything has to change, could it at least be ordinary predictable change?

Spirit of Clearsight, if you're listening: Please take care of my sister. Please let her Metamorphosis be normal.

And if you have time, please could you also make sure she's not arrested for treason? That would be great, thanks.

CHAPTER 3

The Mosaic Garden glimmered in droplets of amber and gold, cobalt and jade, obsidian and pearl. Fragments of dragons prowled along the walkways underclaw and coiled around the columns. In the pavilions, claws and teeth roared across the ceilings, ancient battles captured in bits of glass forever.

Here at the top of the Hive, the sky was allowed to run free. It was the only space where HiveWings could look up and see no roof, unless they wanted to climb to the top layers of the webs (which HiveWings never did) or venture into the dry savanna below.

Across the garden, sunlight drenched the grassy slopes and hedgerows, soaking into the obedient faces of the flowers that marched rose-carnation-marigold-violet in orderly lines beside the path. The scents were heavy and warm, like the drowsy buzzing insects that browsed the floral options. The path itself seemed winding and random, branching and wandering back, but it eventually spiraled everyone in to the central feature, the Salvation Wall.

This morning the garden was busy with dragons, but Blue and Luna found a spot on the grassy slope where they could sprawl with a view of the Salvation mosaic.

"I'm not sure why you like this scene so much," Blue said as Luna passed him his honey drop. "It has a few too many dead SilkWings in it for me." His wingbuds twitched and he glanced around, double-checking that there were no HiveWings in earshot. He didn't *think* it was treason to criticize the Salvation mosaic, but it certainly might be.

"But even more dead LeafWings," Luna pointed out. "Isn't that reassuring?"

Blue didn't argue with her, but he'd always found the mosaic sad instead of triumphant. He knew it showed the end of the war, so it made sense that there were dead dragons in it. It should make him glad that these were supposed to be the last dragons ever killed in the war with the LeafWings. He also knew they should all be grateful to the HiveWings for saving the SilkWings from the vicious green tribe.

But it just made him wonder why there had to be a war at all. Why didn't the LeafWings give up and go away, or agree to be ruled by Queen Wasp? Why did they fight so hard instead? They must have known they couldn't win . . . there were so many more HiveWings, and, of course, there was the Book, which was guaranteed to guide the HiveWings to victory.

So why did the LeafWings bother fighting, knowing so many dragons would die for no good reason?

It was their own fault their tribe was wiped out, if Luna was right and they were really gone. Queen Sequoia should have given up her throne and accepted Queen Wasp's protection, like Queen Monarch did. Then the LeafWings could have lived alongside the SilkWings, all three tribes under one queen, working together. Maybe Queen Wasp would have left them some trees to live in, between the Hives. So what made them fight instead of accepting that? Had their queen really thought her tribe had any chance of winning?

Blue studied the blocky dark green shape that was meant to be the queen of the LeafWings. It was so hard to imagine being Queen Sequoia, leading an entire tribe into a doomed war. He didn't even like arguing with other dragons. If someone offered Blue peace and stability and all he had to give up was a little independence, he would say yes in a heartbeat.

"I hope I get to see it one day," Luna said, licking honey off her claws.

"What?" he said, startled out of his reverie.

She pointed at the mosaic, at the central yellow-and-black striped figure holding a rectangular shape over her head, the only object in the mosaic made entirely of gold tiles so it caught the sun like a fragment of fire.

"The Book of Clearsight," Luna said softly. "Don't you ever wonder what it says? What the next big disaster will be, or what's going to happen to all of us next?"

"Of course," Blue said, "but nobody gets to read it except the queen and the Librarian."

"I could *see* it, though," Luna said. "From a distance, if I get to visit the temple one day."

"Well, Wasp Hive's not that far away," Blue said. "It'll be easy to visit the Temple of Clearsight once you have wings." *If you're assigned a job with travel permission and time off,* he thought, but didn't say out loud. Luna had enough to worry about.

He stole a glance at her wrists, which she kept rubbing and then resting in the cool grass. Would the quiet lavender scales on his arms glow like that in six days? Was Metamorphosis really more painful than anyone had warned them? He'd expected his wings to hurt a little as they came in, but he hadn't even thought to worry about his silk.

They heard the chatter of approaching dragonets, enough voices that it was probably a field trip from one of the fancy HiveWing schools. Blue scooped up the empty Sugar Dream box and they retreated to a less crowded section of the garden, where they played hide-and-seek until the sun reached its highest point and began to slant back down the sky.

They ate lunch at Luna's favorite café and then wandered through the Lady Cicada art gallery on one of the lower floors of the Hive. Blue found all the different portraits of Lady Cicada a little intense, but Luna liked the tapestry rooms. Weavings were the one kind of art that was left entirely to SilkWings. A HiveWing could probably buy dyed silk threads from one of the market stalls and a loom, like the ones SilkWing dragonets used for practice, but none of them would bother with learning to make a low SilkWing art. Which Blue thought was a bit silly; they certainly didn't mind buying the results and hanging them all over their walls.

He left Luna gazing at her favorite tapestry — the one where Lady Cicada is flying with a long trail of radiant SilkWings behind her in the sky — while he checked out the sculpture rooms. Lady Cicada was old enough to have been alive when there were still trees to spare, so there was one small wooden carving of her in the middle of the clay and metal and marble statues. The wood was a shade of brown close to her actual red color, and Blue liked to look at it and wonder about the artist. What did woodcarvers do when there were no more trees to carve? Did they still get to make art, and did they have to learn all new techniques, or did the queen give them new jobs? Did they ever wish all the trees weren't gone?

"Let's get to the Cocoon," Luna said, appearing behind him. Her pale green scales looked white in the dim light of the gallery, and it was hard to see the gold flecks along her back and tail. Her wingbuds were definitely more unfurled than they had been this morning, though, and her wrists were glowing as brightly as the lamps.

"We have a little more time," Blue said, seized with a sudden panic. "We could get another honey drop? Or —"

"No," Luna said. Her expression was strange, as though she was already drifting into the Metamorphosis trance. "I think I need to get to the Cocoon as . . . as quick as we can."

"All right," Blue said. Should he have made her see a doctor after all? But someone at the Cocoon would know what to do if there was anything wrong, surely . . .

They hurried to the outer spiral and down, down, level after level getting darker as they descended in strange silence (for Luna — Blue couldn't remember a time when she'd stopped talking for this long). Blue wasn't sure if he was imagining that the hum seemed louder down here, as if the insects outside were closer to the Hive, busily swarming around it.

The Cocoon wasn't on quite the lowest, ground-floor level of the Hive, but it was close to it. Here the streets were dimmer and emptier, the lamps fewer and farther between. A few lower-class HiveWings lived down here, in the small cells near the outer spiral. There was one hulking building that Blue thought might be a training center for guards. The courtyard around it was open for a few levels up to give them space to fly their exercises. Blue glanced up as they went by, watching the dragons moving around the streets above them. Occasionally a flutter of black and red wings broke the quiet as a HiveWing flew from one side of the Hive to the other to save walking time.

But the main thing on this level was the Cocoon: a long oval dome, two levels tall, which was swathed in so many beautiful weavings it almost seemed to be made out of silk itself. Every SilkWing in Cicada Hive came here for his or her Metamorphosis, and according to tradition, afterward each one made a silk weaving for the dome as an offering of thanks.

Some of the weavings, especially the older ones, were simple: shimmery silver-gray silk in the shape of cobwebs or sunbursts or clouds. Other dragons had used dyes to add brilliant colors — here a silver dragon spangled with emerald green wings and matching green eyes all around her; here a swarm of tiny orange butterflies. Someone had even been able to afford two colors, weaving a midnight black shape of a Hive behind an iridescent blue web.

There were no trees, of course; it was forbidden to include trees in art ever since the LeafWings had been driven out. Even the Hive shape was dangerously close to that of a tree, and Blue wondered if the weaver had been worried about that.

But for the first time — maybe because anxiety was sharpening his attention — Blue noticed something on one of the tapestries that looked like a leaf. No, wait — was it a teardrop? A single, autumn-red shape, somewhere between a leaf and a teardrop and no bigger than his claw tip, gleamed in the middle of the butterfly swarm. Was he seeing that right? Why spend the money on a second dye color and only use it in such a small way?

Wait, there was another one! He blinked, startled. This one was slightly darker red, hidden against the black backdrop of the Hive weaving.

His eyes scanned the dome. There was another, veiled among a spray of escaping diamonds from a waterfall.

Blue wrinkled his snout, puzzled. Now that he was looking, there were little red "leafdrops" hidden in half the weavings he could see. Why had so many SilkWings decided to include *that* shape in that color? If it meant something, why didn't he know about it?

Blue realized that Luna was staring up at the dome weavings, too, opening and closing her talons nervously. He thought about asking her if she'd noticed the hidden red shapes. But it wasn't worth it to start a conversation that might stress her out . . . what she needed was distraction and calming down.

"What's your weaving going to look like?" he asked. "Have you decided?" She'd been talking about nothing else for weeks, so Blue had heard all her ideas. But he was mostly trying to get her to smile, or blink, or do anything to reassure him that his bubbly sister was still in there.

Luna winced. "I don't know," she said. "I have to . . . get through this first."

"You'll be fine," Blue said, taking her front talons in his. "I've never heard of anything going wrong during a Metamorphosis. I'm sure what you're feeling is totally normal. All of this is normal. It's going to be all right. Everything is always all right in the end, you know? You're going to wake up with awesome wings and cool silk and fly everywhere and be the greatest spinner in the history of the Hives."

Luna closed her eyes and whispered, "Everything is always all right" as though he'd just said "The sun is always shining" or "The bees would absolutely love for you to take all their honey" instead.

Blue was relieved to see a cluster of dragons gathered near the low arched entrance of the Cocoon — maybe one of them could get through to Luna.

"Look how popular you are," he joked, but his smile faded as they got closer and he realized that most of the gathered dragons were HiveWing guards.

Why are there so many guards? He was sure that normally there were only two. He remembered the two extremely bored-looking guards who had fallen asleep by the exit during Swordtail's Metamorphosis while he and Luna called encouraging words to their friend.

But today there were at least five outside, and they all looked anything but bored. Black and yellow and red scales shifted and caught the dim lamplight as the HiveWings scowled and stamped their feet. Two of them carried weapons, but the other three looked menacing enough without them. Most likely they had venom in their claws or shot poisonous darts from their tails, or something along those lines.

Blue shot a worried look at Luna.

First Silverspot. And Luna's weird glowing scales. Now all these guards . . .

What does everyone know that we don't?

CHAPTER 4

Blue had to keep Luna calm. Whatever was going on, he didn't want her to go into her Metamorphosis feeling scared or anxious.

"Why are there so many guards today?" Luna whispered to Blue. "Weren't there only two at Swordtail's Metamorphosis?"

"Oh, I don't remember," he said brightly. "I'm sure there are always this many and we just never noticed them."

"Hm," she said doubtfully.

"Luna!" Swordtail cried, emerging from the group and bounding toward them. His scales were dark blue with a small pattern of white triangles along his spine and snout, and then dappled all over with orange splotches, as though someone had melted a sunset in a cauldron and flung it at his wings. Blue always thought of his friend as one of the shiniest SilkWings around, bright and gleaming, the way Swordtail had been when they first met on the school racetrack five years ago. But lately Swordtail was always covered in dirt, with splinters of treestuff caught between his claws and tangled in his long, elegant horns.

And all too often he wore *this* expression — this worried, grim look that was really the last thing Luna needed today.

"Happy Metamorphosis Day!" Blue said to him, perhaps a little too loud. He widened his eyes significantly at Swordtail. "Isn't this *exciting*?"

"Are you all right?" Swordtail asked, gathering Luna into his wings. She leaned into him as though she'd been flying for days and he was the island she'd been searching for. He took one of her front talons in his, and soft gray silk spun out from his wrists, gently wrapping around hers to wind them together.

"I can't believe you're here," Luna said. "I thought Grasshopper would never let you come."

Swordtail made a face. "He didn't. I finished all my work and asked — yes, *very* politely, Blue, I promise — and he still said no." He shrugged. "So I snuck off when he wasn't looking."

Blue's idea of "politely" tended to be quite different from Swordtail's . . . but Blue had met Swordtail's boss once and was not at all surprised that Grasshopper had tried to keep Swordtail from attending Luna's Metamorphosis. Silverspot's mistress would do it out of spite; Grasshopper most likely said no because he was still trying to teach Swordtail obedience and good behavior.

If Swordtail would quit picking fights with HiveWings and

expressing unpopular opinions all over the place, Blue thought, *perhaps figures of authority would be a little less annoyed with him, and his life would be a little bit easier.*

"Oh, Swordtail," he said ruefully. "You're going to be in so much trouble."

"Doesn't matter. This is more important." Swordtail turned Luna's palms up and frowned at the glowing embers under her scales. "Whoa."

"Does it look weird to you?" Luna said anxiously.

"Of course not," Blue said. "You're totally fine."

"I remember a little bit of light where my silk came in, but not this bright," Swordtail said, completely trampling over Blue's efforts to calm Luna down. "I'm not — I'm not sure this is normal. Io, have you seen anything like this before?" He turned to his sister as she came up to join them. Directly behind her was Blue's mother, Burnet, who stepped around the others to give Blue and Luna quick hugs.

"No," Io said, sounding even more alarmed than he did. Her wings had come in several months ago, huge and dark purple with shimmers of aquamarine green. She was only a year older than them, but she had long, aristocratic-looking bones and horns, and she towered over Luna. "You don't think . . ."

They both glanced at Burnet, for some reason, but she wouldn't meet their eyes. "Oh," she said carelessly, "I've been to so many of these, and there's always something surprising. Never anything serious, though. Nothing to worry about."

Blue had never heard his mother lie in his own stretched

"everything is fine here" voice. It made him feel as if his nice, normal world was as thin as paper and as easy to stab holes in.

"Are you Luna?" one of the HiveWing guards said roughly, slithering up to them. He muscled Swordtail aside, breaking the slender threads that bound him and Luna together. "You're late. Time to get inside."

"Sorry," Luna said, which was what she was supposed to say, and yet so unlike Luna to actually say it that Blue shivered. The ground felt unsteady below him.

Also, they were *not* late, not even by a heartbeat. All HiveWings and SilkWings had a precise internal clock that always kept their days on schedule and warned them when the rainy season was coming. Blue's told him they were right on time . . . but of course he wasn't about to argue with the guard.

"I love you, Luna," Swordtail said fiercely.

"We do, too," said Burnet, and Blue nodded, although his sister wasn't looking at them and didn't seem to hear them either.

"You lot, up to the balcony if you must stay," the guard said, waving one of his crimson-and-black dappled wings at the side entrance. He gave Luna a small shove in the direction of the archway and she went, with only one last nervous glance back at them before she disappeared inside.

"Should we do something?" Io asked Swordtail. "Tell someone?"

"There's no time," he said. His long blue antennae

unfurled, twitching, and he turned to stride toward the dome. "And it's probably not . . . I mean, it's so rare . . . "

"What?" Blue asked. "Tell someone what? What are you so worried about? Io, what's so rare?"

Io looked as though she might be about to tell him, but —

"Nothing," Burnet said, putting one wing over Blue's shoulders. "Don't worry, sweetheart. Let's go cheer for Luna."

He let his mother steer him through the side entrance and up the stairs, their footsteps muffled on the ancient silver-silk carpets. The gallery was a long, open balcony that ran around the entire dome, overlooking the dim, quiet floor below. The only light came from small candles floating in the central pool of water.

Blue started toward their usual spot, on the far side of the dome, but Burnet gently tugged him back.

"Let's stand here this time," she said, choosing a spot not far from the stairs. Swordtail and Io joined them, the faint glow of candlelight rippling along their iridescent scales. Swordtail rested his front talons on the thick stone railing so he could lean over the edge, as though trying to get as close to Luna as he could. Blue wouldn't do that until he had wings; it wasn't far to fall, but it would still hurt if he did.

All around them, SilkWings were gathered in the shadows of the balcony, friends and family to the three other dragonets undergoing Metamorphosis today. Blue recognized many of their faces, lit from below like eerie moons all around the dome. Most of them were whispering to one another, but a hush fell as Luna was escorted onto the floor.

Like the others, her wrist band had been cut off by the guards. Now, in the twilight room next to the other dragons, and with her scales more visible, it was terrifyingly clear that something different was happening to Luna. Where the others had a pale silvery light coming from their wrists, Luna seemed to have fireflies on fire, startling spots of molten gold.

Blue felt Io grab Swordtail's arm, but he couldn't look away from his sister, all alone on the Cocoon floor.

I'm the one who was with her all day. I should have noticed that something was wrong. I should have made her ask someone for help.

One SilkWing, a starved-looking turquoise dragonet from their class at school, had already entered her Metamorphosis trance. Two long seamless strands of moon-colored silk spiraled out of her wrists. Her eyes were closed and her talons moved automatically, weaving the silk into a cocoon around her.

As Luna glanced around nervously, a second dragonet drifted into his trance and lifted his talons, silk threads spinning out. His cocoon looked like the first dragonet's; like every SilkWing's, it would shelter him for five days and nights while his wings came in.

Swordtail had promised Blue that he wouldn't remember a thing about the trance time. But Blue found that almost scarier: the idea that he'd be unconscious to the world for that long, and then he'd come out looking totally different. ("Not totally different," Swordtail insisted. "I still look like me, don't I?" Which he sort of did, except that the wings made him look quite a bit bigger and more dramatic.)

The third dragonet was eyeing Luna's wrists with concern and taking small, sidling steps away from her. Whispers were gusting through the watching SilkWings, like the sweeping winds that shook their webs before the storms of the rainy season. There were even more guards now — at least seven of them, most standing unsettlingly close to Luna and pretending not to watch her, while their eyes darted constantly from her to the balcony to the pool to the others and back to her.

Luna held out her front talons, and the whole world seemed to hold its breath for a moment.

Then suddenly she let out a sharp cry and silk began to spiral out of her wrists.

But it wasn't normal gray silk. Luna's silk flared like threads of lava erupting from under her scales. It hissed as it hit the air, lighting up the room with sudden bright-star brilliance. It was like the fire of the sun twisted into filaments that snaked back to clutch at Luna's talons, her legs, her whole body.

"Oh no," Io whispered. She looked at Swordtail, whose face was transfixed with horror.

"Flamesilk," he breathed.

CHAPTER 5

"What's flamesilk?" Blue asked frantically as the guards advanced toward his sister. He shook Swordtail with trembling talons. "What's happening? What's wrong with Luna?"

The third dragonet down below bolted for the far side of the dome and tried to scramble up one of the side walls, away from the guards and the burning light. Luna shrieked with fear and leaped away from the fiery silk spilling out of her, but there was nowhere to go. It clung to her like a real cocoon would, winding around her talons and legs even as she tried to claw it away.

"Is it burning her?" Blue cried. He turned to Io, his voice high and desperate. "Io, is she all right? *What is flamesilk?*"

"It won't hurt her," his mother said, but her voice was as sad and soft as the splash of a silk-wrapped corpse slipping into the bay.

"Did you know?" Io asked Burnet fiercely over Blue's head.

"Silverspot and I suspected," Burnet answered. "Their father didn't say anything, and you couldn't tell by looking at him . . . but he was watched so carefully and taken away so quickly, we knew there had to be something."

"You could have *warned* us," Io hissed. "We could have hidden her!"

Burnet shook her head.

Luna let out another, fainter cry, collapsing forward with her eyes closed. The flamesilk spun on and on, and everywhere it touched her she went still, as though it was tranquilizing her.

"Everybody, please remain calm," one of the HiveWings said smoothly, spreading his wings to address the horrified audience of SilkWings. "We are well prepared for SilkWing diseases like this. Everything is under control."

"Diseases?" Blue echoed in a choked whisper. Io scowled.

His sister wouldn't be left to transform quietly on the floor of the Cocoon, like the other two small silken bundles beside her. Already she was surrounded by all the guards, spears lifted, swords and claws and tail spikes all pointed at her as though her flamesilk cocoon might sprout fiery wings and try to escape.

And a dark metal cart was rattling through the door, yawning mouth ready to swallow her up.

"Luna!" Swordtail shouted, shaken out of his horror by the sight of the cart. He vaulted over the balcony railing and plummeted to the floor below, with barely enough time to spread his wings to break his fall. His legs were already moving as he landed, galloping across the floor toward the guards.

"What do we do?" Blue asked Io and Burnet. Should they all jump down and try to save Luna? But there were so many guards — and maybe they were trying to help her. They did say they were prepared, so they'd seen this before — maybe they could take her somewhere to cure her? Maybe they could fix her silk and make it normal . . .

"*You* run," Io said. She dragged Blue away from the railing and shoved him at the stairs.

"Me?" Blue said, astonished.

"He can't escape," Burnet argued tiredly, following Io. "There's nowhere he can go. It would be safer for him to turn himself in."

"No way!" Io cried. "We can't just *let* them take him!"

"Why would they take me?" Blue yelped in alarm. His talons scrabbled on the stone floor as Io pushed him forward again. "I didn't do anything! I'm not sick!"

"Neither is Luna," Io pointed out. She herded him along in front of her, talking fast as they stumbled down the steps. "Flamesilk is something you hatch with. She must have inherited it from your father, which means you have it, too. Which means they'll come for you next."

"But why?" he said. One of his claws snagged painfully on the carpet. He paused to unhook it, looked back up the stairs, and saw his mother watching him go with a bleak expression. Watching, but not following. She'd already given up. "What are they going to do with Luna?"

"We don't know," Io said. "We've never been able to find out. Flamesilks are very rare, and the HiveWings make them vanish immediately."

"Vanish?" Blue echoed. "Like . . . forever?" His insides felt as if they'd all leaped off the top of the Hive and were currently plummeting toward the distant ground.

"Do you see why you have to run?" Io pushed open the door at the bottom of the stairs and looked out. "All clear. Quick, while they're busy with Luna and Swordtail."

Blue dug in his claws as she tried to throw him out the door. "Wait, wait! Run *where*?" he pleaded.

"Anywhere!" she said. "Run, hide, and don't let them find you!"

"But I'll get in trouble!" he said. "I can't hide from the HiveWings! Mother's right; if they want me, I should turn myself in. They won't hurt me." His voice wavered, thinking of flamesilks vanishing forever, disappeared so thoroughly that he'd never even heard of them. "M-Maybe they can fix me so I w-won't have flamesilk."

Io groaned softly. "Why did it have to be you?" she said. "The one SilkWing who thinks HiveWings have any good in them? Listen, Blue. Stop trusting them *right now.* They've let you go about your ordinary life so far, but now you look dangerous to them, and they're not going to let you have that life back. It's gone."

"But it doesn't have to be," Blue protested. "If I'm good, if I do what I'm told — I mean, I'm *not* dangerous. I could *never* be dangerous."

"I know," Io said, rubbing the spot on her forehead between her horns. "Unfortunately, I think that's true." She took his shoulders and shook him. "But they don't care. Please promise me you'll hide from them, Blue. Don't let them catch you."

"For how long?" Blue said. "Where can I go? What about my Metamorphosis? It's really soon and then I'll have to come back here."

Io sighed. "Let's hide you first and then figure that out," she said. She shoved open the door, flung him outside, and bolted after him. Blue found himself running even though his brain was shouting at him to go back, to ask the guards for help, to make sure Luna was all right.

Was she still terrified? Or had the silk entranced her, taking her into peaceful darkness even as chaos swarmed outside her cocoon? What had the guards done to Swordtail? He could never fight so many; a SilkWing didn't stand a chance against even one HiveWing. Was he lying beside Luna on the sand now, bleeding and swollen with venom?

Blue shuddered, his claws wobbling underneath him.

They had just reached the edge of the outer courtyard when he heard shouts behind them. "Stop! You there! SilkWings! Stop at once!"

His feet obeyed instinctively. Guards were talking to him;

guards were to be listened to. You never argued with HiveWing guards, or else you'd get sprayed or stabbed with something; everyone knew that.

But Io didn't stop. Io threw her talons around his chest and hurled up into the air, her spectacular wings pumping desperately.

"Io!" Blue yelped with fear as his claws left the ground. Suddenly they were flying along the narrow streets, flashes of startled faces peering out of windows at them. The indigo whirl of Io's wings beat around Blue's head and he covered his eyes.

"Stop! Queen Wasp orders you to stop at once!"

Where did Io think they were going? There was nowhere in the Hives where Queen Wasp wouldn't find them. Nobody ran from the queen's guards. And she would surely kill them both for disobeying her orders.

Io let out a small roar of frustration, and Blue peeked through his claws. They were nearly at the exit that led to the tunnels spiraling up — but guards were closing rank in front of it, spears crossed, teeth gleaming.

That's the only exit, Blue thought frantically. There weren't even any windows or ledges to the open sky on this level of the Hive.

Oh, he realized with a fresh burst of terror. *That's probably intentional.*

So there's no way for a flamesilk to escape.

Io whirled in the air and shot down one of the avenues toward the training center. Which, frankly, seemed like a poorly thought-out plan: Blue could see a small army of eager-looking HiveWing trainees swarming out of the front gate. Yellow-striped wings flicked and buzzed; sharp white teeth snapped at the air as the dragons spread out to search the streets. *For us. They're searching for us.*

But then Io banked suddenly left and up — up through the open courtyard toward the higher Hive levels. Blue yelped again as the ground dropped even farther away, and then really wished he hadn't even thought the word *dropped*.

Shouts of fury rose from below, followed by the sound of buzzing, beating wings as all the guards and soldiers took to the air.

We're going to die, Blue thought. *There's so many of them, and they have — wait — why aren't they shooting at us?*

He knew some of the HiveWings behind them had dart weapons and spears. So why hadn't they thrown them?

Dragons on the surrounding levels rushed to the edge of the ledges to watch the chase. Blue had never had this many eyes on him before. *What do they see? What do they think? Does anyone want to help? Or are they all hoping we'll be caught and it'll be exciting to watch?*

Suddenly, Io was jerked backward and Blue felt himself slip through her talons for just a moment, until she dug her claws in (*ouch!*) and gave a mighty heave of her wings, kicking backward at the HiveWing who'd grabbed her tail.

They struggled in the air, Blue dangling between them, and then Io swept her wings in a huge arc and *threw* Blue up toward the highest open level.

"YAAAAAAAAAAH!" Blue screamed. He flung out his claws and felt them catch in the rough treestuff walls. His body slammed into the side with a bone-jarring thump and he dug in his back talons desperately.

"Up!" Io shouted to him as she swung her attacker like a club, smashing other HiveWings away. "Climb, Blue! Go!"

He tried to imagine he was out on the webs, having a perfectly normal climb with lots and lots and lots of secure webs below to catch him. He pushed himself up, and up again, and in a moment he felt the ledge above. He clutched at it, his wingbuds churning as though they could help.

Two faces peered down at him — SilkWings, ones he didn't know. But he could guess what they were thinking: *Should we help this wingless dragonet? Will the HiveWings punish us if we do? What has he done to make the guards chase him? He must be a very bad dragon to be running from the guards . . . but if we let him fall, he'll die . . .*

Talons reached down and circled his wrists; strong arms pulled him up to safety. He sprawled on the treestuff, gasping more from fear than exhaustion. This was a residential level, full of HiveWing homes a bit smaller than the one where Silverspot worked, and he'd landed in their school's practice vegetable garden. All around him were garden boxes full of dirt and little tendrils of maybe-one-day-I'll-be-a-plant, labeled with optimistic scrawls on flat wooden sticks.

The two SilkWings, watching him with confusion, were the only dragons nearby, but he could see HiveWings running toward him along the streets and others spreading their wings on the far side of the city.

"Io," he panted, scrambling up. "Is she —"

"Are you all right?" asked the gray-blue SilkWing with speckles of yellow across her scales.

"What's —" began the other, but he broke off as Io landed on the ledge behind Blue.

"The seeds will grow again," Io said to them. She shoved Blue forward without waiting for a response, but he saw a look of recognition cross their faces.

"What?" he said to her as they plunged down the nearest empty street. He glanced back and saw the SilkWings casually blocking the road behind them, their wings spread wide as they started arguing about something.

"There are SilkWings who will help you," Io said rapidly, "if you can find them. A group called the Chrysalis."

The houses they ran past were narrow but elegant, made of treestuff that flowed straight into the street below and into the roof above them, as though they had grown with the Hive. Most of them had intricate patterns of seashells or glass tiles embedded in their outer walls, spirals of pearl-pink coral or zigzagging diamonds of aquamarine. Streetlamps that hung from the ceiling above cast a warm glow over everything, deceptively calm and cozy, like a shroud of silk around a wasp nest.

"The Chrysalis — what — why don't I know about them?" Blue asked, breathing hard. He'd never run this much for this long in his life. His sides ached and his talons hurt and his eyes were blurry and his heart felt like a beehive about to explode.

Io snorted. "Because every time someone says to you, 'Hey, wasn't that mean what that HiveWing did?' you say, 'Oh, maybe she's tired or frustrated with work or just lost something important or is having a fight with her sister,' and then it's kind of hard to follow up with 'Well, so, care to join a movement to take her down?'"

"A movement?" Blue sputtered. "To take *who* down?"

The street abruptly ended, spilling them out into a HiveWing park — or at least, it looked a bit like a park, but without any grass or flowers. Instead the vast circle was full of playground structures carved from real wood, dark and smooth, like the abandoned bones of ancient trees. Many of them arched all the way to the roof, which was probably a lot of fun if you were a dragonet with wings and a chance of surviving a fall from that height. A HiveWing school, shinier and much bigger than Silkworm Hall, loomed along one side of the park, and in the center of the circle was a pool of water lined with silver-bright mirror tiles.

On the far side of the park, Blue caught a glimpse of slanting sunset light through one of the openings where dragons could fly in and out of the Hive. Out that window were the savanna and the open sky.

But how could they get there? The park was full of HiveWings: dragonets playing, parents gathering water from the pool, guards and families and teachers who'd finished school for the day, all strolling the paths, filling the space between here and escape.

He'd wondered why the houses they ran past seemed to be empty. Apparently this park was the place where the entire neighborhood gathered at the end of the day.

"Duck your head," Io said. "Pretend to be a servant. Walk quickly but not too fast." She folded her wings in close and darted out onto one of the more crowded pathways, weaving between dragons. With her head bowed submissively, she blended in with the other SilkWing servants Blue could see here and there, many of them carrying heavy water jugs or keeping an eye on young dragonets while HiveWing parents chatted with each other.

This is never going to work, Blue thought as he ducked his head and followed her.

And yet, for a moment, it seemed as if it might. The HiveWings barely glanced at two more lowly SilkWings. They were so busy with one another, it was as though the SilkWings didn't exist. Many of them were watching a group of young dragonets leap from a climbing structure, their tiny wings pumping to help them drift down. One little black-and-orange dragonet crashed into Blue as she ran across to her friends, but she just yelped, "Oops! Sorry!" and kept going.

It looked like a nice place to live — perhaps not as huge and impressive as the higher level where Silverspot's mistress had her mansion, but a place where families were friends with one another. These dragons made one another laugh, worked hard, cared about their dragonets. They were happy to be safe. They weren't so different from Blue and his family.

Surely they wouldn't let him be dragged away by guards to . . . whatever happened to flamesilks. Did they even know about flamesilks?

Behind him he heard clanking and running talonsteps. He tried to duck his head even farther, following Io around a tall, fortlike playhouse where three HiveWing dragonets passed pretend honey tea out the windows.

The open air wasn't too far away now. In a moment Io could swoop him off into the grassland. HiveWings didn't like going out too far into the savanna, so they should be able to find somewhere to hide out there. And then Io could explain everything to him and they could figure out a safe way to make this right.

They were passing behind a cluster of tiny dragonets in a sandbox when the silence fell.

It fell so suddenly, like a wall of nothingness, that Blue found himself pausing to touch his ears in bewilderment.

Why did everyone stop . . . talking . . .

He glanced around uneasily. They hadn't just stopped talking; every HiveWing in sight was frozen, right in the middle of whatever they'd been doing. The dragonet halfway up the climbing structure had one claw raised; the twins in the sandbox were scowling at each other, mouths open, but no sound coming out.

Io slowed to a stop in front of him, spreading her wings slightly to keep him back. Her gaze nervously darted around at the silent dragons. Blue realized that the other SilkWings in the park were looking around, too, many of them just as bewildered.

And then the HiveWings lifted their heads, all of them at once, and tilted their chins toward the east.

Blue felt a scream building in his throat.

All of their eyes had gone pure white.

"Find the flamesilk dragonet," the HiveWings said in unison. **"Capture him. And bring him to me."**

CHAPTER 6

A shriek of terror ripped through the heavy air, but it wasn't coming from Blue.

It came from near the pool, from a young SilkWing with pale blue-and-pink wings holding a baby HiveWing in his arms. The tiny dragonet glared up at him with its fathomless eyes.

"Aphid," the SilkWing cried. "What's wrong with you? Aphid, can you hear me?"

Aphid bared small teeth and twisted his body fiercely, struggling to get free.

"Let him go," said an older SilkWing softly, touching the younger one's shoulder. "They're not themselves right now."

The dragonet snapped at his caretaker's talons as the SilkWing set him gently on the ground.

"Where is the flamesilk?" Aphid said in spine-chilling unison with the other HiveWings. **"Who can see him?"**

The HiveWings all slowly, eerily, began swiveling their

heads, staring in turn at each SilkWing in their line of sight, like snakes studying a herd for the weakest prey.

"Io?" Blue whispered as softly as he could.

"I think . . . run," she whispered back.

They bolted for the exit, Blue's legs screaming in protest.

Every head snapped toward them. A black-spotted scarlet dragonet, no taller than Blue's wingbuds, threw herself off a slide at them, hissing. She landed on Io's back and sank in her claws, but Io dove into a roll and knocked her off.

Blue felt pinpricks of pain stab into his ankle. He glanced back as he ran and found an orange dragonet with his teeth embedded in Blue's back leg, too small to do much damage, but hanging on grimly.

How do I shake him off without hurting him? Blue thought frantically.

There was no more time to think. Two much larger HiveWings blocked their path, wings spread and claws gleaming.

"Give up, wingless," they said. **"You cannot escape me."**

Blue skidded to a stop and the dragonet tumbled off his ankle. There were HiveWings in every direction, all focused on him. The voice was right; there was no —

Io barreled into the two dragons in front of them. Her wings flapped huge and purple in their faces, driving them back for a moment, clearing a path.

And there was the sky . . .

Blue darted through the opening and ran pell-mell toward the ledge. It was close now. He could see two of the three moons rising. He could see small twisted trees and a distant giraffe and the long yellow grass waving far below.

Too far below.

He reached the edge and froze.

The wall of the Hive plunged down before him, impossibly steep, impossibly terrifying. This level was far below the webs, but still a long way from the ground. Blue couldn't possibly jump from here; he would break his neck and die.

If only I had my wings!

He turned and saw Io fighting off three full-grown HiveWings. Their talons slashed at her side, and one had his tail raised to stab her with the stinger at the end.

"Io!" Blue cried.

"*Go,* Blue!" she shrieked. "Get out of here!"

"I can't!" He felt tears finally start to flood his eyes. "I can't go without you!"

In a way he meant, "I can't fly from here; I need your wings," but in another, deeper way, he really meant that he couldn't leave her at the mercy of these zombie dragons. He couldn't keep running, alone, knowing she would be caught and punished, and punished worse if he *did* escape.

"You *have* to!" she shouted. But she must have realized he couldn't take that leap. As he took an indecisive step back toward her, she kicked a HiveWing in the face and broke free for a moment, just long enough for her to grab a twisted ladder structure and knock it over between her and her attackers. In the breath that gave her, she shot a twist of silk from her wrists up at the ceiling and another that coiled around Blue's ankle. A heartbeat later, he was hurled toward the roof.

His claws caught the webs that Io was shooting across the top of the cavern. Instinctively he swung to the next one and then the next. He jumped swiftly, like they'd learned to do in school during emergency drills: What if the web is falling, what if you have to get to a Hive quickly for safety, what if you only have a few strands of silk to escape along.

But those drills had been about the threat of LeafWings attacking the webs. They were practiced so that little wingless dragonets would be ready to flee to a place where HiveWings could protect them. Never once, despite his overactive imagination, had Blue ever imagined using these skills to run away from HiveWings.

He shot over the heads of the families on the playground, so fast that they lost track of him for a moment. As they whipped their heads around, buzzing and hissing, he reached the end of Io's silk, shielded by a tall slide near the walls of the school, and looked back.

Io was almost at the ledge . . . and with the HiveWings distracted, looking for him, she might be able to get out and fly away.

But not with him. She'd only be able to escape without him.

He gouged a chunk of treestuff out of the ceiling above him and threw it as far and hard as he could. It landed with a scattering thud halfway across the playground, and all the HiveWings spun toward the sound.

Blue let go of Io's silk and dropped to the top of the school wall, then over it and down into the small courtyard beyond. Triangles of lime-colored chalk marked out the games young HiveWings played here during recess. For a moment, Blue thought about grabbing one of the pale blue metal practice spears that leaned against the wall, but the truth was that he'd be more likely to hurt himself than anyone else with one of those — and he couldn't even *begin* to imagine stabbing another dragon on purpose.

Where do I go? He glanced around the courtyard, trying to catch his breath. It was surrounded on all sides by the school, except for the wall behind him, which had the neighborhood park and a horde of white-eyed zombie dragons on the other side. *They'll follow the trail of Io's silk and figure out where I went in a moment.*

Even if I can get out of this school somehow, where would I go after that? I can't go back to Mother. I'm sure Swordtail will be on Misbehaver's Way by morning, if he's still alive. And I have no idea what they've done with Luna.

He pressed his talons to his mouth. He didn't have time to cry. He didn't have time to be sucked into imagining how Luna and Swordtail and Burnet and Io must be feeling right now.

He started across the courtyard toward one of the school doors, although at this time of day he was afraid they'd all be locked.

"Pssst! Over here!"

Blue whirled around. A small equipment shed was built along the side of one of the school walls; the door was open a crack, and a pair of golden-yellow talons was reaching out of it, beckoning to him.

He could hear the HiveWing voices issuing commands on the other side of the wall. There wasn't time to be worried and indecisive. He bolted toward the shed and let the strange talons yank him inside.

The door snicked shut behind him, leaving them in pitch-darkness. Blue tripped over a ball under his claws and the other dragon caught him, strong arms holding him up. He felt the brush of wings against his side. This was a SilkWing who had already gone through Metamorphosis, then — but it must have been recently; this dragon was smaller than he was.

"Who —" he whispered.

"Shhhhh," she said. She wrapped her front claws softly around his snout.

The shed was small and packed with paraphernalia; there was barely room for Blue and the other dragon to stand. His claws felt clumsily entangled with hers; his neck kept bumping against cool scales, and her tail lightly rested over his. But she was so perfectly still that he couldn't pull away — or at least, he feared that if he did, he might knock over a wall of armor or something.

He wondered if she could feel his heart slamming around his chest. Did she work at the school? Cleaning HiveWing classrooms or preparing their snacks? Had she ever seen the HiveWings act like this before, as though their minds had all melded into one? Did she know what was happening, and how dangerous it was to protect him?

"Don't move," she whispered, apple-scented breath in his ear. She let go of his face and in the dark he felt her crouch beside him, reaching for the inner wall. Her wings were like a cloud of butterflies against his scales, touching down and taking off in a thousand little brushes.

Maybe she was scared, too. Or had she rescued other SilkWings like this before? He tried to imagine being that brave — brave enough to see a dragon in trouble and an entire tribe turned terrifying and still reach out to help.

Maybe if he imagined it hard enough, he could make himself a little braver, too.

She took one of his front talons and touched it to the wall, or rather, to a spot where the wall disappeared: an opening, a trapdoor into a tunnel.

"Stay close to me," she whispered. "The tunnels can be confusing."

"Are you with the Chrysalis?" he whispered back, his nose bumping hers as he turned toward her.

She touched his mouth again, a "hush" gesture, before ducking into the tunnel. He followed as close as he dared, trying not to step on her tail.

It was like crawling through an ant farm, following the tunnels in a winding maze through the walls of the school. Here and there chinks of light shone through the cracks and Blue caught glimpses of the buttercup yellow scales of the dragon in the dark. Through the cracks he could also see fragments of the school: even rows of tables, a blackboard covered with neat columns of numbers, an easel divided into narrow lines of blue and black paint.

At last she stopped and peeked through a small hole just at eye level. After a moment, she unlatched a trapdoor, pushed it open, and climbed out, beckoning for him to follow.

He had to duck his head as he came through, since the trapdoor opened out of the wall under a long table. Blue's eyes were dazzled for a moment as he crawled out, although the room they were in was not particularly bright. It had no outer windows and was lit only by a few small lamps.

The first thing he saw as his eyes adjusted were the books — shelves and shelves of books reaching floor to ceiling, all around the room. He stretched his aching legs and turned in a slow, wondering circle, thinking of the students who were lucky enough to attend a school with so many books. Had anyone read all of them? Did the librarian love handing them out, or did she wish she could keep all of them safely within the circle of her wings?

"This is our library," said his rescuer, hopping up onto the table and curling her tail around her back claws. "I know, it's pretty small. But it's closed most of the time — we share our librarian with a bigger school uplevel — so it's a good place to hide when the rest of the tribe goes all creepy-eyes."

Blue turned slowly toward her, his heart thumping like mad.

Her claws were small and sharp, like a leopard's, and her four wings swooped down from her back in beautiful smooth folds. She had an open, curious face, gold-rimmed spectacles, and warm, dark brown eyes that made him think of owls and tree hollows. In the glow of the lamplight, her scales were gold and tangerine, but speckled here and there with black scales that looked like tiny inkblots.

Black scales. The unmistakable sign of a dragon descended from Clearsight.

SilkWings never had black scales.

His rescuer was a HiveWing.

CHAPTER 7

Blue inhaled sharply.

"I — I thought —" he stammered.

"Wow, you're *beautiful,*" she said wonderingly. "I've never seen a SilkWing in those shades of blue and purple before. Is that what your parents look like, too?"

"Um," he said, looking down at his azure talons. "Not exactly. Or, I mean, I'm not sure. I've never met my father. Shouldn't you —"

"Really?" she said. She tipped her head at him, catching sparkles from the lamps in her glasses. "Why don't you know your father? Is that normal for SilkWings? Don't you live with your parents? Or, I'm sorry, is that a question I'm not supposed to ask? I ask a lot of questions I'm not supposed to ask, apparently, according to most of my teachers — also my parents — actually, according to pretty much every grown-up HiveWing. *Too many questions, Cricket! Don't you know what happens to nosy little HiveWings? They lose those noses!* Which is silly; I've never seen a dragonet without a nose and

I'm *sure* I can't be the first one with this many questions. What's your name? Oh, that's another question. Sorry. I'm Cricket."

"Blue," he said. "I'm Blue."

"You sure are," she said, and giggled. "Oh dear, I'm sorry, I bet you've heard that one before."

He took a step closer to her, trying to rearrange his understanding of what kind of dragon she was. A HiveWing who helped SilkWings — that wasn't a thing. "Um — shouldn't you —"

"Be all mind-controlled, too?" she finished for him, and hesitated. "Yes, I should be. Every other HiveWing is. I have no idea why I'm not." She flicked her wings and settled them again with a little laugh. "I can't believe I've kept that secret for six years and the first dragon I'm telling is a strange SilkWing. Katydid is going to be so mad."

"Is that what happened to everyone? Mind control?"

"You didn't know about that?" she said. "I mean, I suppose I didn't either, until I saw it happen the first time. She doesn't do it very often, but Queen Wasp can control every HiveWing in the tribe — one at a time, or just one Hive, or everyone at once if she wants to."

"Whoa," Blue said, reeling a little.

"I know," she said.

"Except you?" he said.

"Except me. Isn't that fascinating?" Her face lit up like all three moons rising at once. "I can't figure it out! There's *nothing* in any of these books about how she does it. Is it genetic? Am I some kind of mutation? Or could it be something we eat? But I eat everything, and, like, a lot of everything; I'm always hungry. It's so mysterious. There's seriously nothing about me that's different from all the other HiveWings."

Blue thought there was. He'd never met another HiveWing like her — first of all, willing to talk to a SilkWing as though they could be friends. Second of all, looking at him as if he was a real dragon, not a wingless curiosity or nuisance to be stepped over.

"That must be such a weird feeling," he said, "having someone take over your body like that. Making you say things and do things you wouldn't say or do yourself. Do you think they remember it afterward? Are they in there, feeling trapped, while it's happening?"

"They *do* remember it," she said. "They remember pretty much everything. My sister, Katydid, says it's not a trapped feeling, though . . . it's more like, suddenly you *really* want to do exactly what everyone else is doing. There's no struggle. She says it's kind of peaceful, having someone else make all the decisions for you for a bit."

"Maybe." Blue thought of the tiny dragonets attacking him and shivered. "Except then later you'd feel like everything you did was still your choice, and you'd probably feel guilty about it, even though it wasn't really you at all."

She looked surprised, and then her gaze drifted up the

shelves of books as she thought about what he'd said. "That's true," she said after a moment. "I don't actually know if it ever bothers them. I wonder how I can find out." She flicked her tail thoughtfully. "You know, without getting my nose cut off. I think 'do you ever feel bad about what Queen Wasp makes you do?' is *definitely* one of those questions I'm not supposed to ask."

"Especially if you don't want anyone to know that the mind control doesn't work on you," he said.

"Right." Cricket fiddled with the earpiece of her glasses. "Katydid is the only one who knows. I'm worried Queen Wasp might be angry if she found out. So I hide whenever it happens and hope no one notices."

"I won't tell anyone," Blue promised.

She gave him a sweet, slightly sad smile, and it occurred to him that he might never have a chance to tell anyone anyway. He felt a sharp prickle of pain under his wristband.

"So what did you do?" she asked. "Why is the whole Hive looking for you? What kind of criminal enterprise have I gotten myself involved in?"

She kept smiling, but Blue noticed a shiver tremble across her wings. He guessed there was a part of her that had suddenly realized she was alone with a dragon who might be dangerous. Him, of all dragons, scaring a HiveWing!

"Nothing!" he said quickly. He looked up at her and put one talon on the table, palm open. "I promise. I'm totally harmless. The most harmless. Thoroughly utterly completely incapable of harm doing."

"Oh," she said. She thought for a second. "That is reassuring. Thoroughly utterly completely reassuring, except for how it's exactly what a dangerous criminal would say."

"Is it really?" he asked, wide-eyed.

Cricket laughed. "I don't know. I guess I'll have to ask all my dangerous criminal friends."

He liked the way her laugh made sun-colored scales ripple all down her long neck. His head was starting to feel strangely woozy. "What would the least dangerous dragon in the world say?" he asked.

"Why would the least dangerous dragon in the world be running away from HiveWing guards?" she countered. "What could he possibly have done that's so terrible, it made Queen Wasp bust out her mind-control powers?"

The question hit Blue like an entire Hive collapsing on his chest.

What did *I do? I've always been a good dragon. Why is this happening to me?*

"Oh no," she said, slipping off the table and crouching beside him as he folded to the floor. "Why did that make you look so sad? What happened?" She unfolded her wings to shelter the curve of his back.

"I don't know," he said. It was splendid having her wings over him, like being hugged by the sun, although actually it would probably be terrible to be hugged by the sun; this was much cooler. What was he talking about? Oh, right: the worst day ever. "One moment it was a normal Metamorphosis Day, and then suddenly Luna was on fire and Swordtail was attacking guards and Io was carrying me and I don't even — I mean, I would *never* disobey a HiveWing — it all just happened so fast and I was so scared." Were the books blurrier from this angle? Or were his eyes losing focus?

"It's your Metamorphosis Day?" Cricket said. She tipped her head at his wingbuds but politely didn't touch them. (*A polite HiveWing? How did she get so weird and perfect?*) "Are you sure? They don't look ready yet." She picked up one of his talons and examined his wrist scales.

"No, no," Blue said. "It's Luna's Metamorphosis Day. My sister."

"The one on fire," Cricket said. "Is she all right? Why was she on fire? Lightning? I think I'd have noticed lightning striking the Hive today. How would fire even get into —" She stopped suddenly, staring at him with her mouth open.

"Did you get frozen?" he said in a panic. "Are you being mind-controlled right now?"

"Your sister's a *flamesilk*?" she whispered in her own voice. "A real one? That's *amazing*!"

"It is? You — you know about those?" He tried to get to his feet, discovered that his knees had chosen an entirely different life goal, staggered a little sideways, and fell into her.

"Uh-oh," Cricket said, wrapping her wings around him. "Let me see your wristband."

He could barely move his arm over to where she could catch it. She tugged on his wristband, trying to slide a claw underneath it, but it was heavy and snug.

"Why is my —" he tried to say, but apparently words were too hard. Really it was just unreasonable to expect entire word sentence groups arranged in order.

"Shhh," she said, helping him lie down on his back. "Don't be scared, but there might be a toxin in your wristband. I read a study about the idea once, but I didn't think they'd implemented it yet. Did you feel anything? Like a needle poking you, kind of? I bet they rigged it to inject you if they ever couldn't find you."

"Whyyyy," he mumbled. He wanted to ask if it was going to kill him; he thought he should probably be worried if he was about to die. But it would be much easier to close his eyes, wouldn't it? And stop thinking about it? It would be much easier to think about how sparkly Cricket's glasses were. And how they made her face all interesting, as though there were lots of unexpected angles and layers to it, like a prism. Prism. Words were funny.

"They're hoping you'll flop over somewhere and be easy to catch," she said, wiggling a folded piece of paper between his wristband and his scales. "Joke's on them, though, because you've got me to hide you." The paper caught on something hidden, tearing a little gash in his skin, and he yelped with startled pain.

"I'm sorry." Cricket cupped his face in her talons and caught his eyes with hers, like her gaze was amber and he was safe inside of it. "Don't conk out. We might have to go back into the tunnels if they start searching the school."

"Can't . . . move . . . " he slurred.

"I'm going to take off your wrist cuff," she said. "Is that all right? Blue, can you hear me? Blink if that's all right with you."

"No *way,*" he managed around his numb tongue. "I'll be in . . . so much *trouble.*"

"Oh, beautiful dragon," she said sympathetically. "Don't you know how much trouble you're already in?"

He closed his eyes. Something wet was leaking out of them. Apparently the toxin had affected his tear ducts, too.

Cricket scrambled up and disappeared from his side. He opened his eyes again, afraid that she'd be gone completely, but she was only across the library, carefully unscrewing one of the lamps from the wall, with a dust rag wrapped around her claws to protect them from the heat. Soon she had uncovered a small, glowing glass ball from inside the globe of the lamp. It shone bright enough to make Blue's eyes hurt. She folded the cloth over the ball and carried it to the librarian's desk, where she cleared away the books and papers, then set down a metal plate from a side drawer.

"Whrm?" Blue mumbled.

"Don't worry, I've done this before," she said. "I mean . . . never anywhere quite so . . . flammable. But I'm sure it'll be fine." She dug through the rest of the drawers until she found something that looked like a long, thin pair of tweezers. Blue had seen tools like that before; he'd even used them a few times, to untangle particularly messy snarls of silk.

Cricket took a deep breath, unwrapped the ball, and caught it between the tweezers, setting it down on the metal plate. She threw the rag into a far corner, still holding the ball steady, and then picked up a marble paperweight shaped like a coiled python.

She moved so confidently and efficiently that it didn't occur to Blue to be afraid — until the last moment, when she looked up at the ceiling and whispered, "Please help me not set the library on fire, Clearsight." He couldn't have stopped her anyway, as she brought the pale gray snake smashing down on the light ball.

Glass splintered across the desk and a powerful burnt-metal smell filled the air, but Cricket pounced forward with the tweezers and lifted something up.

It looked like a filament of silk, as long as one of Blue's claws, but alight with fire from end to end.

That was the source of light in all the lamps in the Hive. Flamesilk.

How had he never known that before? He'd never even wondered how the lamps worked. He'd assumed it was a HiveWing skill. If he'd had to guess, he would have imagined that perhaps some of them could create fire, like the dragons from the old stories who'd once lived across the sea.

Scarcely breathing, Cricket eased across the room toward him, holding the flamesilk thread in the tweezers.

Could she really set the whole library on fire with that little thing? he wondered. *If so . . . she's taking a big risk for me.*

She crouched beside him and lifted his left arm gently in her free claws.

"Don't move," she said. "I mean, I know you can't, but really don't." With infinite caution, she traced the flamesilk across his wrist cuff. It seared a smoking black line in the bronze, right across the *w* in *Silkworm Hall.*

Hawker is going to kill me, Blue thought deliriously. *When I get to the checkpoint, he's going to make that very stern frowny face and* tut-tut *and check his list and grumble about paperwork and then stab me with his spear thingy.*

Cricket traced the line again and then again with the flamesilk thread, burning it a little deeper each time. The smell of blacksmiths and melting chains filled the room, swamping the scent of old paper.

And then, a few careful passes later, the metal gave way and fell off his wrist, brushing against his scales and leaving a small scorch mark that hurt like a viper bite. Blue bit back a whimper.

"Oh, shoot," Cricket said. She jumped up and ran back to the librarian's desk, grabbed a small watering can, and poured water from it over his burn. Then she dropped the flamesilk thread into the water that was left in the can. A sizzling, hissing sound and a cloud of steam billowed out of the top of it.

Blue's arm felt as though it was floating . . . like maybe it would drift right up to the roof and bump around between the books on the top shelves. He felt untethered from the earth, a feeling that was tangled up with how close he was to Cricket and how she maybe had superpowers or at least the absolute very best brain in the world.

Cricket laughed. "I don't know about that," she said, and he realized that he must have said something out loud. "My teachers seem to think my brain is terribly annoying."

"I like it," Blue said. Everything still felt blurry, but his mouth was working a little better, or at least, words were coming out of it in order, even though those words didn't seem to be waiting for approval from the rest of him. He managed to sit up and smile at her. "It's my new favorite brain."

And then the world kind of tipped sideways and went dark, and Blue slipped quietly into the nothing.

CHAPTER 8

Blue had the impression that he should wake up. That it might be a good idea. That the reason it was a good idea might have something to do with how wherever he was sleeping wasn't swaying in the breeze, the way it was supposed to. This web hammock he'd fallen asleep in was weirdly still and hard underneath him.

And there was someone shaking his shoulder. Someone whose wings brushed his face sometimes. Mother? Mother never smelled like books and apples, the way this dragon did.

"Are you awake?" the dragon whispered. "Blue? If you're not, could you be? Please? Now-ish?"

"Yrmrft," Blue said, which was odd, because he'd been trying to say "You bet," but apparently "yrmrft" was good enough for the dragon with all the questions, because she started trying to nudge him up to his feet.

Oh, questions — it's Cricket.

"What are you smiling about?" she said curiously. "I hope that's a good sign. Do you think you could smile and stand up at the same time? I would love to let you sleep more, but I think we really need to move." She froze for a moment, with him leaning heavily against her shoulder.

Now the library was coming into focus around him. The glow of the lamps, the rows and rows of books, the sound of tramping talons from the hallway outside.

Um. The what?

He pointed at the door in alarm and she nodded. "That's why I woke you," she whispered. "Quick, into the tunnels." She bundled him under the table and through the trapdoor. His arms felt all wobbly and his tail seemed to be entirely in the way, but he somehow managed to crawl into the dark space beyond. He dragged himself forward so Cricket could scrunch in behind him.

The glow from the library lamps vanished as Cricket pulled the trapdoor shut. Blue started to retreat farther into the shadows, but she caught his nearest talon and put one claw to her mouth in warning.

Blue froze, and in that instant he heard the library door slam open. Three sets of talons thundered in, shaking the room so that a couple of books toppled off tall shelves and a small cloud of book dust wafted through the cracks in the trapdoor. He twisted his neck to peek over Cricket's shoulder. In the glimpses he could see as they moved around, the HiveWings' eyes were blank white pearls.

So the queen was still mind-controlling them. He wondered how long he'd been unconscious. He wondered how long she could keep it up. He wondered if she planned to keep them all as her zombies until she found him, no matter how long that took.

And then his heart stopped in his chest as he remembered the wrist cuff Cricket had burned off him. He couldn't see it from his angle, but wasn't it still lying out there on the floor? Wouldn't they see it and know immediately that he'd been here?

But several agonizing moments passed and the searching dragons didn't cry out or roar for backup or hiss in triumph. They moved mechanically, soundlessly, through the room, checking every obvious hiding spot. One crouched down to look under the table, and Blue closed his eyes in fright, not daring to breathe. But the trapdoor must have looked like part of the wall, because the HiveWing — jet-black with flecks of red along his ears, wings, and claws — only grunted and moved on.

Cricket twitched suddenly, as if startled, and Blue realized he was leaning against her side, their tails entangled, their talons touching. He had been too terrified to notice, and he was afraid that pulling away would make a noise the searchers might hear. He checked her face, or what little of it he could see in the tiny bars of light. She had her gaze fixed on one of the HiveWings, a yellow-orange dragon freckled all over with black spots, but he couldn't quite interpret her expression. Dismay? Regret? Anger?

What is she feeling? he wondered. *Hiding from her own tribe, in the dark with a stranger, risking her queen's wrath to help a SilkWing.*

He wondered about the HiveWings out there, too. Their sweet family evening of slides and seesaws and zebra meat snacks had abruptly turned into a dragon hunt. Everything they'd been planning to do tonight had been ripped out from under them. They didn't even know where their own dragonets were because, right now, finding Blue was all they cared about. The giggling little dragonets had gone from playing tag to prowling the shadows of the Hive with snarling teeth, every scale ready to attack.

How could they all go back home after this, back to family dinners and wing aerodynamics homework, knowing that someone could take over their minds and change their whole lives at any moment?

The three HiveWings touched their foreheads with one talon, all at the same time with exact mirrored movements. "**Nothing in the library,**" they said in unison. A ripple of fury crossed each of their faces simultaneously. "**He must be here somewhere. Keep looking.**"

They marched out the door, but Blue could hear their talonsteps in the corridor for a long time after they were out of sight. Cricket opened her mouth to say something, and this time he was the one to shush her. His antennae unfurled softly, feeling the vibrations in the air. Now that he was calmer and more awake, he could sense at least twenty other dragons searching the school.

He could also feel Cricket's heart beating, very close to his and almost as fast.

Don't be scared, he tried to think to her. There was no reason not to be; if they were caught, he was sure she'd be in awful trouble. But he'd do everything he could to keep her out of it. He'd let them catch him first.

He reached out carefully through the dark and took one of her talons, pressing it to his own heart.

I'm so glad you're here with me.

She looked up at him, small cracks of light dappling her face in gold and shadow, and he felt her pulse jump to match his.

Oh, this is the thing that's forbidden, Blue realized. *This feeling. Looking at a HiveWing like this. Her looking back.*

If they could be in more trouble than they already were, this was how.

But maybe that wasn't what she was feeling. Maybe he was still woozy from the toxin and confused by his life being upended. Maybe he was just imagining the flutter in their twining heartbeats.

His antennae twitched quietly, following the vibrations of dragons moving away from this section of the school.

"I think they've all gone upstairs," he whispered. "Is there an upstairs?"

"Yes. How can you tell where they are?" she whispered back. "Your antennae?"

He nodded.

"I found some old biology books that said HiveWings used to have antennae, too," she said softly. "But when I asked my science teacher about it, he said not to be impertinent, and then the books disappeared from the library." She sighed. "Everything interesting is off-limits. Why can't we study our own evolution? Don't you want to know what the tribes were like two thousand years ago, when Clearsight arrived?"

"I never thought about it," he admitted. But she was right — if HiveWings were all descendants of Clearsight, what had they been like before she came to Pantala?

They stayed there, quietly, in the dark, with their talons and tails entwined, for a long time as the sounds of the search tramped above them, around them, in and out and along the halls and every room of the enormous school. Blue felt the jarring thumps of tables being overturned, the rattling clatter of closets being emptied, all their contents clawed out and thrown on the floor. He felt tremendously sorry for whoever had to clean up all this tomorrow. He guessed Queen Wasp wouldn't helpfully brainwash them into doing that.

At last all the vibrations faded, and Blue tested the air until he was sure the school was empty again.

"They're all gone," he whispered.

"That's a pretty cool superpower," she said, smiling at his antennae as they curled back in.

"Not quite as cool as knowing everything about everything," he said.

She blinked. "Are you talking about me? I hardly know anything! There's so MUCH I don't know! I mean, yet. One day I will, I hope. I'm working on it." She wrinkled her snout as though the existence of unanswered questions was one of the greatest trials of her life. "Like how Queen Wasp's mind control works. I *really* want to know that."

"Do you wish —" He hesitated, then plunged into his question. "Do you wish you were like the other HiveWings? If you could make yourself, um, mind-controllable, would you?"

"No!" she said, her wings brushing his sides as they flared out and hit the walls of the tunnel. "Would you? Who would? No, I'd fix it so it didn't work on *anyone*, if I could. That's what you would do, too, isn't it? At the very least I'd fix Katydid."

"Oh," he said. "Was that your sister? The yellow one with the black spots you were watching?"

She exhaled. "Yes. She's my sister and my best friend. She normally looks much . . . kinder . . . than that."

"It must be awful," Blue said, studying her face. "Seeing someone you love transformed. Like her brain and soul were stolen. She looks like her, but she's not, and you don't know what she might do or how she might treat you, but you know you can't reach her."

Cricket tilted her head at him. "That's right," she said. "That's exactly what it's like. Katydid says it's fine and she doesn't mind, since it happens so rarely . . . but she can't see herself all creepy-eyed. She doesn't know what it feels like for me to have to hide from her." She shivered slightly and Blue realized he was still holding her talon. He let go of it reluctantly.

"I hope you do find a way to save her," he said. "And all of them."

"I know the grunting one who checked under the table, too," Cricket said quickly, as though she was trying to change the subject so she wouldn't cry. "His name's Bombardier. But he's awful, so there's not much difference between regular him and brain-dead him. He thinks I'm in love with him, if you've ever wondered what the most enormous arrogance looks like. I guess I'd still save him, but maybe, like, last."

"Why didn't they see my wrist cuff?" Blue asked. "Or the broken glass and the flamesilk thread in the watering can?"

"I cleaned it all up, of course," she said. "You didn't notice, in between your snores?"

"I wasn't — did I? I didn't, did I?"

Cricket laughed. "No, you're a very polite sleeper, don't worry." She glanced out at the library again. "The only thing I couldn't do was replace the missing light globe. But those burn out or get stolen all the time, so hopefully no one will connect it to you."

"So every light globe in the Hive has a bit of flamesilk inside it?" he said tentatively.

"Of course," she said. "Every light globe in *every* Hive. It would be tough to live the way we do without flamesilk. We'd all be bumping around in the dark, treading on everyone's claws. Plus we need it for everything else that's made with fire: metalwork, glass . . . " She touched her spectacles self-consciously.

"Do all the HiveWings know about flamesilks?" he asked. "Because I'd never heard of them until today."

"I think they know the queen has a source of flamesilk," she said thoughtfully, "but most of them probably don't think about where it comes from very much . . . it's just something you order when you need it."

Blue opened and closed his mouth on his next question. He remembered the eerie golden lava erupting from Luna's wrists and weaving around her scales. Her silk was a . . . a *commodity* to the HiveWings. Something to be ordered and bought and sold and used.

"If your sister's a flamesilk," Cricket said, reaching for his wrist, "does that mean you're going to be a flamesilk, too?" She traced one claw over the spot where his silk would come out, and he shivered.

"I don't know," he said. "Io said I would be, but we weren't taught anything about flamesilks at Silkworm Hall."

"But that must be why they're chasing you, right?" she said. "Queen Wasp would never let a flamesilk wander around her Hives unguarded."

"I've never been guarded before," he said. "I've never done anything wrong. I'm really good at following the rules. She doesn't have to worry about me." He frowned, touching the spot on his forehead that was starting to hurt. "Maybe she just doesn't know that. Maybe I could go to her and explain that I'm a loyal SilkWing. Maybe if I promise I'll be careful, she'll let me go back to my normal life. And Luna, too. Luna isn't dangerous."

Cricket hesitated. "I think . . . I think HiveWing policy is that all free flamesilks are dangerous, no matter what they say." She unlatched the trapdoor and crawled back into the library. Blue followed her as she pulled a book off one of the high shelves, fluttering her wings a little to lift herself up to where she could reach it. She flipped through the pages, then slid it under his nose.

Scarlet colors leaped off the page, assaulting his eyeballs. The picture was of a Hive on fire, burning from top to bottom, with screaming HiveWing faces dimly visible through the smoke. At the top, huge dark letters proclaimed: THE CONSEQUENCES OF UNCHAINED FLAMESILKS.

"Yikes," he said.

"I guess that's supposed to be you," she said, pointing to a SilkWing standing in the middle of the burning Hive with fire pouring out of his wrists. The illustrated dragon had a gleeful, unhinged grin on his face as he torched the city.

Blue shuddered. "I would *never*," he said. "Why *would* anyone ever — that's just *horrible*."

Cricket tugged the book back over to her and turned to the next page, studying the words. Her eyes darted so quickly across the text that Blue couldn't believe she was actually absorbing any of it, until she said, "OK, here.

Flamesilk genetics. A dragonet with one flamesilk parent has a fifty percent chance of being a flamesilk, too. So we know Luna is, but you might or might not be." She looked over the top of her glasses at him. "Do you think you are? Do your wrists ever feel like they're burning? What symptoms did Luna have?"

"She didn't have any!" Blue said. "I mean, not until today, when her silk started coming in all arrrrrgh-now-there's-lava-everywhere. But she's been totally normal before now."

"So there's no way to know if you are or not until your Metamorphosis Day," Cricket said. "Hmmm. They must want to keep you locked up until then anyway, in case you try to run away."

"My friend Io's the one who made me run away. It wouldn't have occurred to me to run," Blue pointed out, "at least, not until they started *chasing me*."

"What's the Chrysalis?" Cricket asked.

"The — what?"

"When we first met, in the shed. You asked if I was with the Chrysalis."

Blue felt a twist of guilt in his chest. He was *pretty* sure that whatever the Chrysalis was, HiveWings weren't supposed to know about it. Even smart, sympathetic HiveWings with interesting glasses. Io would be furious if she found out he'd blurted it out to the first dragon he met.

Cricket was studying him curiously. "Is it a secret?" she said. "A SilkWing secret? Do you guys have lots of secrets from us? Can you tell me some of them? I promise not to tell anyone! There's so much I don't know about SilkWings, but Father won't let me ask the servants anything."

"I don't really know what it is," he admitted, trying to stem the tide of questions. "My friend just told me they'd help me if I could find them. But I have no idea how to do that." He slid the flamesilk book over and studied it himself, hoping he hadn't hurt Cricket's feelings. "So . . . if flamesilk is so useful, then Queen Wasp probably isn't killing them. Right?"

"Of *course* she isn't!" Cricket said, startled. "We're not *barbarians,* Blue. The queen's a little scary, but she's not a murderer."

Blue would have said the same thing himself this morning. But something about watching those guards surround Luna and then hiding from white-eyed, mind-controlled dragons was making him a little less certain about the queen's trustworthiness.

"Do you think I should turn myself in?" he asked hesitantly. That sounded like the right thing to do, except that it *felt* very very wrong. Io's warning that he couldn't trust any HiveWings rang in his ears.

And here I am, of course, doing exactly that.

Cricket thought for a moment, tapping her claws on the book. "No," she said finally, slowly. "They won't kill you, but if you are a flamesilk, they'll — well, you'll end up with the other flamesilks, I guess."

"Where is that?" he said with a sudden rush of hope. *That's where Luna will be.*

"Oh, I'm sorry I made you look so excited," Cricket said anxiously. "Nobody knows where the flamesilks are kept."

"Are you sure?" Blue asked. "Someone *must* know."

"You're right," she said, leaping to her feet. "Let's think. Flamesilk orders go out all the time, because each thread only burns for about one cycle of the smallest moon before it fades. Which means *someone* has to get the flamesilk from the dragons producing it, to fill the orders. So whose job is it? And someone must keep them fed and taken care of —"

"And guarded," Blue put in.

She flinched. "Yes . . . probably that, too." She started pacing up and down between the library tables. "And of course Queen Wasp knows. So there must be a way to trace the flamesilk back to wherever the dragons are. This is definitely a solvable mystery."

Cricket hurried over to the librarian's desk and opened one of the bottom drawers. "All right, forms, where are you? She's always complaining about how many there are to fill out. Order forms . . . replacing library supplies . . . you would think a librarian would be all about alphabetizing her folders, wouldn't you? Do you think she'd notice if I alphabetized them for her? . . . Oh, light globes! Here!" She pulled out a sheaf of papers and narrowed her eyes at them.

Blue glanced at one of the lamps. It was weird to think

that there was a tiny thread of silk in there, glowing and burning. It was even weirder to think that the thread had come from a dragon very much like him, or Luna. A dragon trapped somewhere, spilling flame from her arms for HiveWings to gather and snip into little useful bits that could be packaged and sold across the continent. A dragon whose whole life would be about producing flamesilk for HiveWings and nothing else.

Maybe it came from my father.

The thought dazed him for a moment. His father was a flamesilk, kept under guard wherever other flamesilks were kept. That's why Blue had never met him. He'd only been brought out for a moment to father more dragons . . . in the hopes of creating more flamesilks, Blue guessed.

Which meant Queen Wasp knew exactly what Luna and Blue might become. She'd created them on purpose, for that purpose.

"Hmmm," Cricket said. "It looks like the order forms get sent to a department in Wasp Hive. So maybe the flamesilks are there, or maybe that department forwards it on."

"If we can figure out where they are," Blue said, "maybe I could go see what it's like. Maybe it's not so terrible. Maybe that would help me decide whether I should turn myself in."

Cricket tipped her head up at him. "And if it is terrible?" she asked. "Would you want to rescue your sister?"

"I . . . yes," he admitted. Of course that was what he was really thinking, and of course Cricket had figured that out. "But I'm not exactly the right dragon for that job."

"Why not?"

"Well . . . I mean . . ." He waved vaguely at himself. "I'm not very . . . I don't like . . . making trouble." *Troublemakers.* "I need Swordtail," he blurted. "He's the one who should rescue her."

"All right," Cricket said, whisking the forms back into the drawer. She smiled brightly at Blue. "Then let's go get him."

CHAPTER 9

"It's not that simple," Blue argued, following Cricket into the dim hallway beyond the library. "Swordtail attacked a bunch of HiveWing guards. He's either on Misbehaver's Way or somewhere worse by now. And I can't exactly stroll around the Hive with everyone looking for me."

"I bet I can solve that problem," Cricket said. "Let's think. Both problems, maybe? Will you let me try?"

"Um . . . sure," Blue said, distracted by the school around him. Rows of cubbyholes lined the corridor, many of them overflowing with crumpled papers, books, sticky bags of half-eaten nectar snacks, seed packets, and little buckets of dirt. Every few steps there was a glass terrarium embedded in the wall with something growing in it: tidy clusters of blue forget-me-nots in one, long white carrots in another, prickly cactus balls bristling in an orderly row from a third.

"Whoa," Blue said. "It's so plant-y in here."

"We're an agriculture-track school — do SilkWings have those?" Cricket said. They passed one glass case that was full of water, crowded with dark flaps of purple seaweed. Blue squinted at it and realized that it was lit by a small light globe on the roof of the terrarium — they all were. Tiny flamesilk suns kept these plants alive.

"Maybe," Blue said. "But I think they usually figure out which job to assign us after we finish school. Our lessons are things like the history of the LeafWing War, silk weaving, reading, web structure, and following directions. Lots of following directions."

"I *wish* I could go to your school for a day," Cricket said, her wings twitching as though she might fly out one of the skylights at any moment. "I'd *love* to hear what other dragons are learning, wouldn't you? Are your teachers interesting? How big is your library? Do you have music classes? I wish we did; I don't understand music at all and I really want to. But our curriculum is very focused so we can all become farmers and gardeners. That's what this is all about." She waved her claws at the corridor walls. "Every student is assigned a terrarium for practice."

"Oh," Blue said. "You . . . don't seem like a farmer to me."

"I'd be an awesome farmer if I wanted to be," she said, "which I don't. I want to be a librarian or a scientist or an inventor. But I'm a terrible farming student. Apparently there's only one way to do things and that's how it's always been done and there's no point in trying to 'innovate,' Cricket, it's a waste of seeds and oh dear why can't you just grow potatoes like a useful dragon." She paused at one of the terrariums and tapped it lightly with her claw. "This is mine."

Blue was pretty sure he could have guessed that on his own. Unlike the other, orderly terrariums, this box was a riot of leaves and color, as though a host of sunflowers had thrown a gala and some marauding butterflies had crashed it. Velvety orange petals jostled for space with elegant trailing spider plants; sapphire-blue bulbs peeked out from behind heart-shaped leaves with pink edges.

"It's like your brain as a garden," Blue said wonderingly.

Cricket laughed. "And equally popular with my teachers," she said. "Cricket, what a *disaster*. *Why* didn't you use *one* type of seed like all the other students? Why *must* everything you touch be such a mess?"

Blue stepped closer and peered through the tangle of foliage. Deep in the heart of her terrarium, well hidden by the other plants, there was a tiny tree. It was no taller than the length of two claws, but it had a trunk and miniature branches and little perfect tufts of forest-green needles all over it. It was beautiful.

"That's —" he breathed. "That's a real — How did you —?"

"I found the seed on one of our gathering field trips. I had no idea what it was until it started to grow." She smiled at it wistfully. "I had a feeling you'd see it. Most dragons don't. They think my terrarium is too messy to look at for very long; it offends their eyes or something. But my botany teacher finally spotted it last week. He wants me to uproot it and throw it away." She sighed. "Poor little innocent tree."

She turned and kept walking and Blue followed her, although he wished he could stay and stare at the tree a bit longer. He couldn't believe it was real. Surely Cricket loved it. It looked like a loved little tree.

"That's so sad," he said. "What an awful thing to ask you to do. You brought it to life."

"I'm not going to let my tree die," she said firmly. "But where can I hide it? Somewhere with light, where I can visit, but no one will find it. I'll figure something out."

She pushed open a door at the end of the hall, revealing a room with long desks covered in glass beakers and small pots of soil. A metal cabinet at the back of the room was lit by a tiny globe inside, and the shelves were lined with neatly labeled bottles of liquid, organized by color. The top shelf ranged from a bright ruby red to a pale pink; the two middle shelves were shades of lemon and emerald and lime; and the bottom shelf held a few milky-white bottles and several with nearly colorless liquids in them. Blue crouched to look at one of them and realized it was slightly aquamarine when the light hit it in a certain way. He didn't understand any of the labels printed on the bottles — there were letters and numbers and some obscure squiggle symbols in between, but none of them formed recognizable words.

"This is our chemistry lab," Cricket said. "We use some of these to help plants grow; others will kill certain weeds, if you apply them the right way. But a lot of these have other non-botanical uses, too. How many do you think I can take without Professor Earthworm noticing?"

"Take?" Blue said, startled. "You can't steal from your school!"

She paused with a vial the color of chamomile tea in her claws. "But . . . Blue, these will help us. Don't you want to get your friend?"

"Yes, but — but stealing is wrong —" he stammered. He imagined the chemistry teacher coming in tomorrow morning and finding bottles missing. Wouldn't she be upset? Wouldn't she feel guilty and worried about who had taken them and what might be done with them? She might blame her students; someone might get in trouble unfairly.

"You really are good at following the rules, aren't you?" Cricket said, intrigued. "Like, you really *believe* in them."

"Don't you?" he said. "Doesn't everyone?"

She thought about that for a moment. He liked the way she stopped and thought carefully about the things he said. Most dragons already had their ideas settled in their heads; if they paused to think before responding, it was only about how to explain to you that you were wrong. But Cricket seemed to take in information and questions and hold them up against the things she thought she knew, to see if there was anything new she'd missed.

"Weird," she said finally. "I usually think of rules as things that get in the way of all the stuff I really want to know. I mean, how can *don't ask questions* ever be a good rule? Or *only borrow one book at a time from the library*. That's just ludicrous. No one ever explains rules like that in a sensible way. But *don't hurt other dragons* — that's a rule I think everyone believes in, right? So . . . I guess I believe in some rules, and I think rules in general can be useful, but I also think it's all right to stop and question some of the rules sometimes, if they feel wrong to you. Doesn't that make sense?"

"But *don't steal* is a rule everyone agrees on, too, isn't it?" he asked.

"I think that *help dragons who need help* might be more important than *don't steal*," Cricket said. "I mean, *turn over fugitives to Queen Wasp when she's looking for them* is *probably* a rule, too, you know? But I don't think you're dangerous. And I want to know more about flamesilks and SilkWings. And I think I can help you. I'd — I'd like to help you."

Blue looked back at the citrus-colored vials. He didn't want to drag her into more danger than he'd already put her in, but he did need help. And more important, Swordtail and Luna needed help.

This isn't the first rule I'm breaking, he thought. *The first rule I broke was running even after the guards told me to stop.* He still felt shaken all the way through his scales at the memory of disobeying HiveWing orders.

But if I'm going to rescue Luna . . . or, at least, get Swordtail to rescue Luna . . . then this won't be the last rule I break either.

"You're right," he said.

"Oh my goodness," she said, looking genuinely startled. "No one has *ever* said that to me!"

"Then the dragons you know haven't been listening to you very well," he said. "I bet you're right about almost everything."

"Oooo, the perfect title for my memoir," she said, grinning. "*Right about Almost Everything,* by Cricket."

He laughed, letting her smile chase away his nerves. She carefully selected six vials from the back rows, rolled them in a thick black cloth, and tucked them into a bag she tied sideways across her chest.

"One more stop," she said. They hurried through the school again. Blue unfurled his antennae at each corner, but he couldn't sense any other dragons anywhere in the building. The hunt for him had moved on . . . or maybe paused for the night, he hoped without much optimism.

The next room Cricket took him into was huge and abutted the side of the Hive, because there was an enormous glass window all along one side of it. Outside it was very dark, with only fragments of the savanna grass shifting silver in bits of moonlight; the three moons and most of the stars were hidden by thick clouds.

After a few moments of blinking around, Blue realized this was the art room he had glimpsed briefly through the cracks in the tunnels. Here was the easel with its perfectly perpendicular lines of blue and black; in fact, there was an entire row of easels with exactly the same painting on each one. Blue wasn't sure it was a painting; it seemed more like a plan for a gardening plot. In another corner of the room, a long table was lined with large sheets of paper, each one with a nearly exact replica of an orange painted in the center. The orange that had merited all this attention was still posed nonchalantly on a stool in front of the table.

Blue looked around, but none of the artwork looked like Cricket's glorious terrarium. "Where's yours?" he asked.

"Oh, I'm not allowed to take art classes anymore," Cricket said with a kind of carelessness he was pretty sure she was faking. "You can proooooobably guess why."

"Good *heavens*, Cricket," he said, putting on the voice she'd used several times already. "No one has *ever* used that many colors on one piece of paper before. Look at this *mess*. Why can't you just draw a normal blue blueberry like every other dragon?"

She laughed so much he had to catch her before she fell into one of the easels.

"Were you *there*?" she gasped, wiping tears from her eyes. "That's *exactly* what Principal Lubber sounded like!"

"I bet your art was beautiful," he said.

"A beautiful pile of shredded scraps when she was done with it," she said with a half shrug. "I had dreams for a while that bee eaters and weaver birds found the pieces and tucked them into their nests all across the grasslands." She wrestled another cabinet open, this time revealing rows of color-coded paint pots and drawers of the cleanest paintbrushes Blue had ever seen, most of them as thin as his antennae.

"Um," he said as she started selecting brushes and paint. "Do I want to know what's happening?"

"We're going to disguise you!" she said with delight. "What color have you always wanted to be? I mean, I think your scales are perfect, but like you said, you can't wander the Hive looking like yourself, can you? That's a purple anyone would spot from the next Hive over. For a moment I thought it would be *so* cool to disguise you as a HiveWing, but then I was like, silly Cricket, that won't work, there are no wingless HiveWings. So what do you think — orange? Our cook is mostly orange."

"You're going to *paint* me?" Blue said.

"Or you could paint yourself, but I think I'd better do it, unless you're good at it — are you?"

"I have no idea," he said. "I've never painted a dragon before."

"Me neither," she confessed, "but I think it'll work if we use the right paint. Do you mind? Can I try?"

"You think," he echoed nervously.

"Maybe a darker color, to be sure it'll cover yours," she said. "Are there any sort of darkish SilkWings?"

"Swordtail has mostly dark blue scales," Blue said. "I've seen dark greens and reds and all shades of brown . . . "

Cricket pulled out a range of chocolate, maroon, and navy paints. "All right," she said, herding him onto a drop cloth that covered part of the floor. "Stay really still."

Blue closed his eyes and froze. *I'm putting myself in her talons,* he thought. *I really, really hope she knows what she's doing.*

Because if she doesn't, and someone recognizes me, and we get caught . . . we're both going to be in worse trouble than I can imagine.

CHAPTER 10

"I don't see how this could work," Blue protested as Cricket dipped a brush into paint the color of the sea during a storm. "Won't I just look like a SilkWing with paint all over me?"

"Not unless they look closely, and no one looks closely at SilkWings." She started dabbing paint lightly across the purple scales on his back. It felt like salamanders prowling over him, tiny wet toes sliding along each individual scale. It felt like purrs and whispers and ferns full of dewdrops trailing along his nerves.

Cricket switched to a sponge to smooth out the paint, then to another brush for a different color. She hesitated, lightly touching his shoulder. "I'm going to paint around your wingbuds, but I won't touch them, all right?"

He nodded. It was hypnotizing, the gentle brushing touch sweeping over him. He felt half-bewitched, as though the toxin from his wristband might still be running through his veins.

"Cricket, why are you helping me?" he asked.

Her talons stilled for a moment, then kept going. "I don't know . . . maybe because I know what it's like to hide while everyone is mind-controlled. And because I've never met a flamesilk and I'd love to know more about you. And because you're . . ." She paused, struggling for a word.

"Pathetic?" he offered. "Desperate? A tragic story?"

"No!" she said. "Not that at all. You're . . . " She trailed off again.

"Aha," he said. "Devastatingly handsome."

She laughed and poked his neck with the other end of the paintbrush. "Stop it! You mustn't make me laugh while I'm wielding paint at you." He smelled cinnamon as she leaned in to paint around his ears. After a moment, she said, "I mean, you're not *not* . . . but what I was trying to say is interesting. You're interesting, and I usually spend all day with dragons like Bombardier and Earthworm, who are definitely *not* interesting."

"Huh," he said. *She wants to study me,* he caught himself thinking. *I'm one of the forbidden library books come to life, that's all. A chance for her to learn more about my tribe and flamesilk. It's not really about me.*

Which is better. Safer. For both of us.

He sighed and closed his eyes. He imagined a thousand moths weaving a web of silk around him, shrouding him in a second skin. The paint felt like tiny beetle shells as it dried, glossy and thin and hard.

After a while, Cricket said, "Hmmm. What do you think?"

Blue half expected to see something like her terrarium when he opened his eyes. He was a little afraid he'd look like a rose garden on fire. But the dragon looking back at him from the cabinet mirror was a nondescript SilkWing in dark blues and the browns of dead leaves, with touches of deep red barely visible along his spine and snout. There were a few blobby spots around his claws, and his brighter blue peeked through here and there, but for the most part the paint was even. He looked like a dragon no one would glance at twice.

He blinked. "Wow. Thank you, Cricket."

"It's not perfect, but hopefully it'll at least get you out of the Hive," she said apologetically. "Especially if everyone is still looking for you."

Out of the Hive, he thought with a shiver. He'd never gone any farther than the webs around Cicada Hive. Unlike Luna, he'd never even wanted to.

"I guess I'm ready to go find Swordtail," he said uncertainly. He'd never walked the streets of the Hive alone at night before. He always went home to the webs before dark. Burnet and Silverspot must be so worried about him.

Which made him think . . . "Cricket, don't you have to go home?"

She glanced out at the dark savanna and the twinkling lights of other Hives in the distance. "I doubt my father will notice one way or another. Katydid will, but . . . she knows I sometimes hide for a while after Queen Wasp takes over everyone. I get nervous that it'll happen again right away. And it's . . . hard to be around dragons, even Katydid, after seeing that." She started cleaning away the paints and brushes. Blue moved to help her, but she stopped him. "No, stay still until you're completely dry. Anyway, she's the only one who cares where I am, and she'll cover for me."

For how long? he wondered. How far would Cricket's curiosity take her before she decided to leave him to his fate? All the way to Wasp Hive? To Luna? Did he dare hope for that much?

"Where do you think Swordtail is?" Cricket asked, tucking the last pot of blue paint into place. Blue noticed that she'd put two of the pots in the wrong order — one was darker than the other, so it should come later in the line — and reached past her to switch them.

"My only guess is Misbehaver's Way," Blue said. "He doesn't like being told what to do, so he's been there before. But I'm afraid — I mean, he's never actually attacked a HiveWing like he did today." He felt a fizzing twist of anxiety in his stomach. What would the HiveWings do with Swordtail if they decided he was really dangerous?

"It's still the first stop, even if he'll be moved to prison after that," Cricket said. "So that's probably where he is. I've never been to Misbehaver's Way." She leaned forward and lightly tested the paint on his snout. "Although Father is always saying that's what my teachers should do with me.

Like, *we all know it's inevitable, just stick her there now.* That kind of thing."

"You've never — haven't you at least walked along it?" he asked. He was flummoxed when she shook her head. "But — really? It's only a couple levels up from here. My school has two field trips there every year."

"*Field trips?*" Cricket echoed, fluttering her wings back. "What for? What can they possibly teach you there? Isn't it kind of scary for little dragonets?" She glanced around, making sure all traces of their activity were gone, and started for the door.

"Yes," he said fervently. "I found it terrifying every time." *I still do.* "That's, um, kind of the point, I think." His scales felt crackly and strange as he walked behind her, but kind of cool, too, like wearing a mask fitted exactly to his face.

"Oh," she said. "So it's to teach you to follow the rules? Poor little SilkWing dragonets. Do all your schools do that?"

"I think so."

"Do they spend a lot of time scaring you?" she asked. "Like, on purpose?"

He shrugged. It was hard for him to concentrate on their conversation because they had reached the front door of the school. Through the narrow windows on either side, he could see slivers of the prehistoric shapes of the playground structures outside — the ones that he'd last seen swarming with dragons trying to attack him. Now it looked deserted, like the bones of a whale graveyard at the bottom of the sea.

Cricket stopped and peered out, pressing her face to the window so she could see as far in each direction as possible.

"I don't see anyone," she whispered. She hesitated, her tail flicking back and forth uncertainly as she stared out at the playground.

Blue's heart was beating like a trapped insect throwing itself at the glass walls of its prison. But he had a sudden bolt of understanding: She felt the same way. Cricket had never gone outside while the mind control was happening. She was as scared as he was.

"I'll go first," he whispered.

"Really?" She glanced at him, her eyes darting worriedly over his painted scales. "But —"

"Don't worry. I have my awesome disguise, remember?" he said. "If the HiveWings are still under Queen Wasp's control, they'll notice that you're not right away — but with luck they won't notice a random SilkWing wandering the park. I'll signal once I know if it's safe for you to come out or not."

She hesitated again before nodding. He took a deep breath, pushed open the heavy door, and slipped down the stairs.

CHAPTER 11

Blue walked cautiously through the park, glancing around for dragons but seeing no one. He made his way to the ledge and looked out at the cloud-covered moons and rustling savanna.

What had happened to Io? Did she get away?

But there were no signs, no clues. Nothing in the quiet around him indicated that a massive dragon hunt had started here earlier that evening.

He ducked his head and started back toward the school. Halfway there, he saw a dragon hurrying out of a side street. Half in shadows, the stranger picked up a toy that had been left on one of the structures and paused, squinting at Blue.

"You'd better get back where you belong," he called in a sharp voice. "The hunting parties will be leaving at dawn tomorrow."

"Yes, sir," Blue said, trying to walk like he had a destination and study the dragon at the same time. The stranger grumbled something and left, and in the glow of the streetlights Blue caught a glimpse of black stripes across his back.

A HiveWing. One with his own eyes and his own mind. The queen had released her tribe, for now.

Blue waited until the HiveWing was out of sight, then beckoned to Cricket. She slipped out of the school and together they hurried down one of the deserted streets toward the outer spiral. Inside a few of the houses, Blue saw lights glowing or moving around. He wondered how long ago the queen had let them go. He wondered how long it had taken all the families to reunite and how they were all feeling. Were any of them resentful of the queen? Or did they blame him for disrupting their evening instead? Or perhaps they all felt as if they'd been useful and important helpers in the search for a dangerous criminal.

Me, a dangerous criminal. When all I've ever wanted is to stay out of trouble.

Wait . . .

"That HiveWing," Blue said softly. "He said something about hunting parties leaving at dawn."

"To look for you?" Cricket asked. "Uh-oh. That means we need to move fast if we want to get a head start on them."

There were guards slumped at the entrance to the spiral, but their eyes glanced over Blue's muted colors, noted the haughty tilt to Cricket's snout, and slanted away, uninterested. Cricket went first, and Blue followed, keeping his head low, acting the part of a humble servant following his mistress's midnight whim for a stroll.

She paused a few levels up and glanced back at him.

He nodded. "Through there." This was one of the only levels with a gate, although it wasn't locked. There was no risk of anyone escaping, after all. Blue suspected the gate was there so HiveWings wouldn't have to accidentally see the prisoners on their way between levels.

Cricket pushed open the gate and they emerged onto a path that was roughly cobbled with chunks of sharp stones. She winced as one stabbed her feet, then looked up at the columns that lined the walkway.

Normally, Blue came here in a crowd of other dragons, young SilkWings all wide-eyed and hushed with terror. He always tried to stay near the back so he wouldn't have to look at the prisoners too closely. But they were impossible to miss, mounted on stone pedestals for all the world to stare at, looming over the heads of the visiting students.

The stony path wound all around the level, in and out and over roughly shaped hills until it connected back with itself at the beginning again. In between the prisoner pedestals were engraved tablets listing the rules of the Hives, the consequences for breaking them, odes to the greatness of Queen Wasp, and quotes from historical figures about obedience, safety, and community. Some of the quotes were from Clearsight herself. Blue had always liked that she sounded like she cared about the rules as much as he did.

Above each prisoner hung a small spotlight, and on each pedestal there was always a list posted of that prisoner's crimes, described in dramatic detail.

Tonight, the first few pedestals on Misbehaver's Way were empty, but as they walked the path, they saw figures on the ones up ahead. Cricket gave a start, jumping back to crash into Blue, when she noticed the first one a few paces away.

"Sorry," she whispered. "Is that — is it real? A real dragon, I mean? Or is it a statue? But I can hear it breathing . . . can't I?"

"That's a dragon," Blue confirmed. "A SilkWing, but not Swordtail." The colors were all wrong, mostly white and brown with flecks of green.

She watched the immobile prisoner for a long, wary moment. "It's not moving at all."

"She can't," Blue pointed out. "None of them can move." They drew closer to the occupied pedestals and looked up at the trapped criminals.

Misbehaver's Way had no need for cages or chains. Instead, Queen Wasp used an elite unit of HiveWing soldiers, all recruited to the job because they had a nerve poison in their claws or tail stinger. Once the criminal — or "misbehaver" — was stabbed, that dragon wouldn't be able to move for an entire day.

"I read about this," Cricket said, shifting her wings uncomfortably, "but . . . it's not what I pictured."

Blue kept walking. He could see the colors of the prisoners with a glance, but it was hard to avoid getting caught by their expressions. So many of their faces were frozen in a rictus of rage or fear. Most of them had been paralyzed while trying to run or fight, so they were contorted in odd positions, stuck there until the toxin wore off.

They passed a pale pink SilkWing with long rose-petal wings, his talons outstretched as though he'd been pleading for mercy, his snout still wet with tears. They passed a snarling scarlet HiveWing in a defensive crouch, teeth bared. Another SilkWing in shades of turquoise and tan looked as though she'd been trying to leap into flight when she was caught. Her neck strained hopelessly toward the ceiling; her wings were in an awkward, half-open position that would probably feel awfully sore when they could move again.

"I thought they'd be asleep," Cricket said in a small voice. "I thought the toxin knocked them out, like putting them in a temporary coma." She glanced up at the next frozen dragon and flinched away. "But these dragons — are they awake in there? So they can see everyone watching them? Do you think it hurts?"

"It does," Blue said. "Swordtail says getting stabbed feels like fire burning every nerve in your body. Eventually the pain fades, but you're still paralyzed, so all you want to do is run or fly or even blink, but you can't move a single muscle until the toxin wears off." Everything about Misbehaver's Way featured in his recurring nightmares.

"I didn't know," she said. "I can't believe this was right here and I had no idea. I'm a terrible dragon."

"I don't think so," Blue said. He inhaled sharply as they rounded a bend in the path. "There! That's Swordtail!" He darted forward, skidding to a stop at the base of Swordtail's column.

Swordtail's paralyzed wings were spread wide, his tail frozen as it lashed back and forth. One of his front talons was outstretched, the claws curved as though he was about to slash someone's face. It was a little scary, honestly, seeing his friend on the attack like that. Swordtail's expression was determined and desperate, as though this was his very last chance to save the world.

"Hey," Blue said softly up at him. Swordtail couldn't react, but Blue knew he could still hear. "It's me, Blue. This is Cricket. We're going to — what are we going to do?" he asked Cricket. "Pick him up and carry him out of here?"

She wrinkled her snout at him, a glimmer of her cheerful side sneaking through for the first time since they'd stepped onto Misbehaver's Way. "I'm sure that would be *very* inconspicuous." She crouched on the cobblestones, took off her bag, and unrolled the pouch of vials. They gleamed like raindrops on flower petals in the light shining from above.

"I don't know if this will work," she said, pushing her glasses higher on her snout. "I thought we needed to wake him up . . . but maybe this one would be better . . . " Cricket selected a liquid the color of grass and gave Blue a wry, nervous look. "At least, we use this to save plants that have been poisoned."

"On plants?" he said. "Is it safe for dragons?"

"I think so?" she said. "Have I ever tried it on a dragon? Not exactly. But it shouldn't make things worse, anyway."

This was not the most comforting answer. Blue looked up at Swordtail, wishing his friend could give him some sort of sign. Was Swordtail willing to risk a mysterious, unproven possible antidote from a strange HiveWing? Or would he rather be left alone?

Who am I kidding? Swordtail would risk anything to save Luna. I'm the one who would find it too scary.

"Do you want me to try it on him?" Cricket said. "I understand if you don't."

"I do," Blue said. "I think we have to." He glanced back along the deserted path. He had a feeling that everyone in the Hive was at home recovering from the queen's mind control earlier, and that was why they'd seen so few dragons out. But he was also afraid that Wasp might seize control of them again at any moment. He couldn't imagine trying to fight his way out of the Hive alongside Cricket — but with Swordtail, they might stand a chance.

And Swordtail would be able to rescue Luna. He was strong and brave and not afraid of HiveWing soldiers.

"All right," Cricket said. "How am I going to do this? Let's think." She poked through the vials and drew out the tweezers she'd used on the flamesilk in the library. Blue hadn't even noticed that she'd brought them along. "Find me a big rock," she said to Blue.

That wasn't too hard here. Blue found a loose cobblestone and kicked it until he could wobble it free. He brought it to Cricket and she beat her wings once, twice, three times, just enough to lift her up to the light over Swordtail's head. Here she hesitated, glancing down.

"Can you cover his eyes for me?" she asked Blue. "And keep yours closed, too."

Blue climbed up to balance awkwardly on the corner of the pedestal, where he could lean sideways and put his talons over Swordtail's eyes. Obediently, he closed his own as well.

There was a smashing sound from above him, and tiny bits of glass pattered down all over him and Swordtail. He shook his head and squinted open his eyes into the new brightness.

"Sorry about that," Cricket said. "Are you all right?"

He nodded. She was using the tweezers to work the flamesilk thread out. He couldn't look straight at her or the thread without getting a headache.

A moment later, she had it free. He hopped down to the ground and she took his place on the pedestal. With a few careful strokes, she burned through Swordtail's wrist cuff in the same way she'd burned off Blue's. Blue met Swordtail's eyes as the heavy band clunked to the ground. He didn't think he was imagining the spark of jubilation in them.

"All right, moment of truth," Cricket said. "Would you mind passing me the vial? Very very carefully?"

He uncorked it and held it high, keeping his claws as steady as he could while she reached down for it.

"Now you might want to hold your breath," she said. "Clearsight only knows what this could do to us. Eep, this is such a cool experiment! I feel like a real scientist, don't you?" She took a deep breath herself and dropped the flamesilk into the vial.

The liquid started bubbling furiously. Cricket clamped the tweezers around the vial and held it out under Swordtail's snout. Green smoke boiled up from the top of it, enveloping Swordtail's face in a thick emerald cloud.

Blue stared up at them, his heart pounding.

CHAPTER 12

Please work, Blue prayed. *Please, please be all right, Swordtail. Clearsight, if you're listening, please set him free.*

They waited several long, agonizing moments, all three dragons frozen in place.

And then Swordtail twitched suddenly, violently, knocking Cricket off the pedestal with one flailing wing. Blue jumped to break her fall. The vial shattered on the stone path, spilling what was left of the hissing green chemical. Cricket scrambled over to pick up the flamesilk in her tweezers again, tucking the thread into a small stone jar with a tight lid that she'd also had hidden in her bag.

Swordtail let out a gasp. His jaw clenched. His eyelids closed. And slowly, he lowered his reaching talon, shaking it hard as though it had been asleep.

"Swordtail?" Blue said.

"Blue," Swordtail croaked. He opened his eyes and gingerly inched his head around to look down at them. The poison seemed to be wearing off gradually, from his face through his wings and back and at last to his tail.

"Do you feel all right?" Cricket asked him. "Anything weird? How's your nose? Did that hurt? I hope it didn't hurt, but it might have, I don't know, the plants can't exactly tell us if it does. Are you dizzy? How are your lungs?"

Swordtail raised one talon to feel the trickle of dried blood on his neck. "All right," he said thickly.

"Cricket," Blue whispered. "Are his eyes supposed to be turning green?"

The whites of Swordtail's eyes, around his normally dark blue irises, were turning a shade of emerald green only slightly paler than the liquid from the vial.

"Oh, *fascinating,*" Cricket said. "Why would *that* happen? Is it affecting your vision? Can you see all right?" she asked Swordtail.

He blinked a few times. "Bit greenish," he offered. "No, wait. Uh-oh. Definitely bad. Blue is all the wrong colors."

"Oh, no," Blue said. "That's just paint, don't worry."

"Huh," Swordtail said. "Sure. Sounds normal."

Swordtail crouched, then arched his back into a stretch like a jungle cat. He flared his wings and leaped down from the pedestal, landing in a wobbly sprawl.

"Ooop," he said. "Legs. Disagreeing with me." He sat down heavily and frowned at his feet. "Whoa. Very demanding legs."

"Cricket, you're a genius!" Blue said. "I can't believe that worked!"

"Neither can I," she said. "I should write a paper about this! No, a book! I mean, it's a real scientific breakthrough, right? We could —" She stopped, realizing what she was saying. "Oh . . . no, I guess I can't do that."

"The queen probably wouldn't appreciate it," Blue agreed.

Swordtail looked at them, a gleam in his newly green eyes. "But I know some dragons who would be *very* interested," he said. His voice was only a little bit slurred now. "Very very very ever so very interested."

Does he mean the Chrysalis? Blue wondered. He glanced back along the path, at the other frozen figures. *Would they set all these prisoners free, if they knew how Cricket did it?*

And if they did . . . what would happen then? He imagined all the prisoners staggering off their pedestals, green-eyed like Swordtail, all of them angry and free at the same time. Would they attack HiveWing soldiers? Or would they all run away? *What does the Chrysalis want, exactly?*

Swordtail shook his wings out again. "Blue! Wow. I can't believe it's you! I mean, it's amazing that it's you. You here, all kinds of amazing." He opened and closed his mouth a few times as if trying to make all his muscles work again. "That is, I mean, of all the dragons I might have expected to come rescue me," he said, "you and a strange little HiveWing are probably the last on the list. But thank you. Did I say thank you? I've been thinking thank you very loudly, probably should say it a few times." He touched Blue's shoulder with one of his talons, then let go and gave an odd hop sideways. Swordtail's whole body seemed to be vibrating just a little bit.

"Io tried to get me away," Blue said, "but we had to split up. Cricket saved me."

"Are you all right?" Cricket asked Swordtail. "What are you feeling right now?"

"What happened to Luna?" Swordtail asked, all his manic energy suddenly focused on the question.

Blue shook his head. "I'm not sure — but we think they've taken her to where the queen keeps all her flamesilks. We think it might be in or near Wasp Hive."

"So that's where we're going next," Cricket interjected.

Blue blinked at her. *That sure sounds like she's coming, too.* He didn't want to ask; he was afraid to jinx it. But he smiled at her when she looked his way, and she smiled back.

"I should get help," Swordtail said. His tail had started lashing back and forth, like a whip, but he didn't seem to notice. His claws extended and closed; his ears flicked up and down. Even his antennae were fully unfurled and waving around. "Help is a useful thing! There are dragons I can reach out to —"

"The Chrysalis?" Cricket asked. "How will you find them? What can they do?"

He narrowed his eyes at her. "How do *you* know about the Chrysalis?"

"She doesn't," Blue said quickly. "She knows as much as I do, which is pretty much nothing."

"Then it should stay that way," Swordtail growled. His shoulders twitched, making his wings flutter up and back. "Let's see. It would take a while. Leave a message, wait for a response. We'd have to find a safe place to hide."

"Blue doesn't have time to wait for other dragons," Cricket said. "He needs to get as far away from this Hive as possible before dawn. That's when the queen is going to take over everyone again and send them out looking for him."

"You can stay and contact the Chrysalis if you want," Blue said.

"But we're leaving right now," Cricket finished.

We are, Blue thought with a little glow of happiness. *Cricket and me.*

"To find Luna?" Swordtail asked.

Blue nodded.

"Then I'm coming with you," he said. "Yes. To save her! That is the most me thing to do. I am most definitely coming with you." He flexed his claws and bounced in place for a moment. And then Swordtail suddenly ran at the stone pedestal and smashed his shoulder into it.

"Swordtail!" Blue yelped.

Swordtail looked at him, grinning. Large cracks had appeared all along the stone. "Look what I did!" he said. "I feel like I could knock over everything! All the columns! Any building! The whole Hive!"

"Shhh," Blue said with alarm. "Cricket? Is this normal?"

"I have no idea," she said, wide-eyed. "What I gave him is sort of a stimulant — and it does make the plants grow bigger and faster."

"I *feel* bigger!" Swordtail declared at a horrifying volume. "I feel FASTER!" He turned and sprinted away down the path.

"Uh-oh," Cricket said. "Um. Any chance he's always like this?"

"No!" Blue cried. "This is definitely weird!"

"Hmmm," she said. "How long do you think it'll last?"

"How would *I* know?!"

CRASH! went something up ahead of them. *THUD! SMASH!*

"Ha HA!" Swordtail shouted.

Blue bolted after his friend, Cricket close behind him.

They found Swordtail merrily lifting enormous rocks and throwing them at the wall of the Hive. Even paralyzed, the two nearest prisoners somehow managed to look alarmed.

"What are you doing?" Blue yelped, catching Swordtail's arm.

"Making us a door!" Swordtail answered. "I'm in construction, you know! This is totally my job!" He lifted another boulder, which looked much heavier than anything Blue could have picked up, and hurled it at the wall. The treestuff was already splintered and cracked, with several small holes in it. "Hey, GRASSHOPPER!" Swordtail shouted, making Blue jump. "Look how hard I'm working! Are you happy NOW?"

"Swordtail, please be quiet," Blue begged.

"It's probably too late for that," Cricket said, glancing back along Misbehaver's Way.

"Take THAT!" Swordtail yelled. He heaved an entire stone tablet out of the ground and threw it as hard as he could. It smashed right through the side of the Hive and plummeted out of sight.

Blue stared at the gaping hole that was left. Fragments of treestuff feathered out on all sides of it and wood-smelling dust hazed the air. *This is vandalism!* he thought. *And destruction of Hive property! There are definitely rules about this! Possibly on that tablet Swordtail just hurled through the wall!*

On the other side of the hole he could see clouds rimmed with moonlight and the far-off lights of another Hive. *Where other dragons are having a perfectly normal evening that doesn't involve getting painted, hiding from soldiers, or watching their friends lose their minds.*

"Let's go!" Swordtail cried, charging toward the opening.

"I can't," Blue said. "We're too high. I don't have wings, remember?"

"I'll carry you," Swordtail said enthusiastically. "I can do it! I'm as strong as ten dragons! I can carry BOTH of you! At the same time!"

"Absolutely not, thank you," Cricket said. "My own two wings work perfectly fine." She turned toward Blue. "I think we have to go out this way, don't you? We can't go back. There must be guards coming to investigate the noise."

"Are you sure you want to come?" Blue said. "You could go home now. You could be safe and stay out of this whole mess."

"And never find out what happens?" She adjusted her glasses and smiled at him. "Are you kidding me?"

Swordtail flapped his wings at Blue. "Time to fly, short stuff!" he shouted.

"By all the Hive, Swordtail, what is happening to you?" Blue asked.

Instead of answering, Swordtail shot a long strand of silk at him and snared Blue's shoulders. He tugged Blue closer and wove several more strands into a quick harness to bind them together. Blue noticed that Swordtail's silk had also turned a strange new shade of pale green.

"I'm not sure this is a good idea," Blue said nervously as Swordtail clasped his front talons around Blue's chest. This close to the hole, he could see the rippling grass far, far below him. "I'm not that light and it's a long way dow —"

"TO THE MOONS!" Swordtail hollered, leaping out into the air. Blue felt a terrifying plummeting feeling in his stomach as they lurched awkwardly for a moment, down and down again toward the savanna, and then suddenly up, sideways, and up, and finally away, beating forward at a steady pace.

The wind whipped in Blue's face. It was cold out here in the dark, after the close warmth of the Hive. He peeked backward and saw Cricket soaring alongside them.

"Get it?" Swordtail said conversationally. "Because *Luna* is like *lunar*, which means *moons*, so 'to the moons' is like 'to Luna' but in code, so, awesome. I thought that was clever." He kept chattering as he flew, as though he couldn't stop the flow of words coming out of him.

Blue looked back again, this time at the vast shape of Cicada Hive and the silvery tangles of the webs far overhead. He thought of Burnet and Silverspot, sleeping alone in their cell for the first time since Luna had hatched. Could they sleep? Or were they lying awake, wishing they'd been wrong about Admiral, worrying about Luna and Blue?

Will I ever see them again?

His home was disappearing behind him. He didn't know what was ahead.

He only knew he couldn't turn back, and so he looked out toward the dark savanna and let his friends carry him forward into the night.

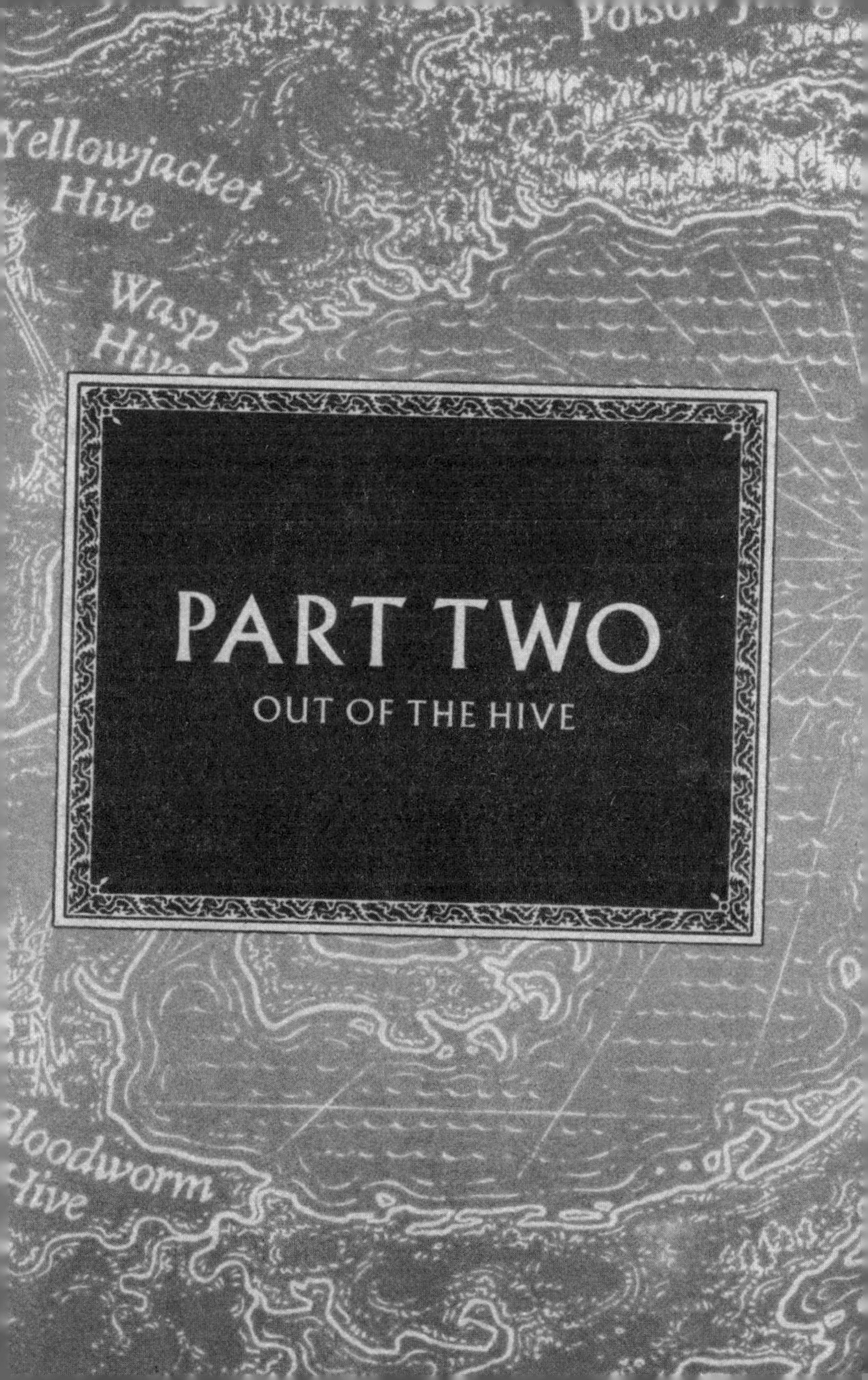

PART TWO

OUT OF THE HIVE

CHAPTER 13

They flew all the rest of that night, swooping low to the savanna whenever the moons breached the clouds, just in case anyone was watching for them.

Swordtail charted a course straight across the circle toward Wasp Hive, which made sense, but quickly brought them to a part of the savanna where dragons rarely ventured. The grass was long and wild, and shapes prowled below them. Growls and shrieks and curling hoots rose from the darkness, slicing through the constant hum of the insects.

Once he got over his fear, Blue found the rhythm of Swordtail's wings lulling him into a kind of doze. His friend seemed tireless, soaring on and on without stopping. Blue hoped Cricket was all right. He tried to call to her a few times, but the wind whipped his voice away.

After a long time, Blue noticed that he could see the outlines of shrubs below him, gray and ghostly. He glanced up and saw an expanding band of pale yellow light along the edge of the sky.

"It's almost morning," he called up to Swordtail.

"We should hide for the day, that's what I think," Swordtail answered. "It's still half a day's journey to Wasp Hive, and they'll be out looking for us in force today, and it would be better to get there at night anyway. Night! An excellent time of day for heroics!"

"Cricket?" Blue called, trying to twist around to see her.

"Hide," she panted behind them. She looked exhausted, but her wings beat valiantly. "Yes. Good. Where?"

Where . . . Blue studied the savanna as far as he could see in each direction. The yellow grass rippled, broken only by gnarled little shrubs, patches of barren dirt, or the winding path of dry riverbeds. The rainy season was coming soon, so the ground below them was dry. There was nothing large enough to hide in or under or behind. Hunting parties of HiveWings would spot them from the air with no trouble at all.

"Disguise ourselves as grass?" Swordtail suggested. "Disguise ourselves as shrubs! DISGUISE OURSELVES AS ELEPHANTS THAT'S IT LET'S DO IT."

"That stuff *still* hasn't worn off," Blue called to Cricket.

"Or I can build us a web!" Swordtail said. "A giant web! And we hide underneath it and they'll think there must be some massively enormous spiders colonizing the savanna! THIS WILL TOTALLY WORK."

"Let's fly . . . a bit . . . farther," Cricket said between breaths. "Try to find somewhere."

Blue barely blinked, he was staring so intently at the ground. Off to his left, he saw a herd of teeny tiny deer with enormous ears bounding through the grass, which was shorter and scrubbier here. A tall, long-necked gray-and-white bird stalked slowly along one of the sunbaked riverbeds, ignoring the smaller birds that perched on its back or flew down to poke the barren soil.

There was nowhere to hide. Blue's heart sank as they flew on and the sky grew brighter. This was a mistake. The savanna was the worst place they could have gone.

And then, as the sun peeked over the horizon, he saw the vast looming shape of a Hive in the distance.

Wasp Hive.

His heart kicked hard in his chest.

The home of Queen Wasp. The grandest and wealthiest of all the Hives. The location of the temple, where the Book of Clearsight was worshipped and protected by generation after generation of Librarians. A Hive full of power and soldiers and secrets.

Where the queen might be hiding his sister . . . and his father, and other flamesilks.

Are we really doing this? he thought with sudden crashing anxiety. *WHAT are we doing? Do we think we can sneak into WASP HIVE, of all places, and find something the queen wants to stay hidden?*

Swordtail banked around, making Blue's stomach drop, and swooped back to Cricket. "We shouldn't get any closer," he said. "She might send out hunters from her own Hive to search for us, too, if she's paranoid, which she is, which she should be, because —" He cut himself off abruptly and nodded a few times. "Because REASONS."

"But where?" Cricket spiraled in the air. "There's *nothing* out here. I didn't know it would be like this." She looked tired and worried, and Blue felt a surge of guilt for dragging her into his mess. He tried to imagine what it must be like for her: far from home, helping two runaway SilkWings, knowing how much trouble she'd be in if she was caught with them.

"Is that something over there?" Blue asked, pointing.

There was a dark slash in the unending sea of cracked earth and yellow grass.

"Let's find out, let's find out," Swordtail said. He beat his wings and soared toward it.

It's a hole, Blue thought as they drew closer. *A really big hole*. It looked as though the earth had suddenly dropped away here, a long time ago, leaving a cavernous shaft lined with moss-covered rocks and long, green plants trying to clamber out into the sunshine. It was impossible to see the bottom, even when they landed on the rim and tried to peer down into it. Outcroppings of rock blocked most of their view, and where they could see past those, all they saw was more darkness, disappearing down and down.

Swordtail used his claws to cut away the silk connecting him and Blue. Blue took a few wobbly steps, shaking out his legs and trying to get the feeling back into them.

"Are you all right?" he asked Cricket, who was crouching on the edge of the sinkhole, holding her glasses on with one talon while she peered down.

"Absolutely," she said. "What *is* this? How deep do you think it goes? What's at the bottom? How did it get this way? Have you ever seen anything like this?"

"I haven't been out on the savanna much either," he admitted. "I didn't know it had sinkholes."

"Are we going down it?" she asked, turning to Swordtail. "Can we?" Her eyes were shining, as though her tiredness had evaporated in the excitement of a new discovery.

"I don't know," he said, hopping from one foot to another with restless energy. "This seems like the most obvious place to hide, so I assume they'll check here, and then we'll be trapped at the bottom of a hole with no way to escape. I still think my elephant plan is the best! Elephants are great! I can look like an elephant, no problem!" He struck an odd, dramatic pose, which Blue guessed was supposed to look elephantesque.

"What do you think?" Cricket asked Blue.

Swordtail had a point. But where else could they hide? He turned to look over his shoulder at the distant shape of Wasp Hive.

For a moment, he thought his vision had gone blurry; then he thought, fleetingly, that a swarm of insects had surrounded the Hive. But finally, with a chill of terror, he realized that the buzzing motion around the city came from the wings of dragons, pouring out of every window and door and shaking the webs with the wind they raised.

Dawn was here. The hunt had begun.

"We go down," he said. "Quickly, right now!"

Cricket didn't hesitate; she dove over the edge and vanished. Swordtail hooked his front talons under Blue's arms again and leaped off as well.

They dropped down and down, pushing off from the craggy, lichen-covered walls when they got too close and maneuvering around bulbous outcroppings. The air got cooler and more damp as they descended. The shaft was narrow, leaving barely enough room in places for Swordtail to keep his wings spread.

What if there is no bottom to this hole? Blue worried. *Or what if the HiveWings get here before we find the bottom?*

Did they know about this sinkhole? How long before they came to search it?

Finally, below his claws, Blue saw the rocks converge onto a kind of ground, although it was really just more rock. But at least he could stand on it, and it seemed to be the bottom of the hole. Swordtail let him down gently and hopped onto a ledge to stretch his wings. Blue glanced up at the tiny strip of sunlight far overhead, then around for Cricket.

The rock under his feet slanted down and away from the shaft into a dark tunnel. It was the only way Cricket could have gone, so he followed uneasily. After a few steps, the tunnel widened into a cave, although by now the light was so dim that he couldn't tell how big it was. He heard the faint *drip-drop* of water somewhere up ahead.

"Cricket?" he whispered.

"Right here." She materialized out of the dark and brushed his shoulder with her wing. "This cave is enormous! And watch your step, because there's a lake that starts a little ways down this slope. A lake, Blue! Under the savanna! Would you have guessed? Isn't that wild? And there's something else strange, come see, or I guess, feel; seeing isn't really an option down here!" She nudged him through the dark until he felt water lapping at his claws, and then, a few steps later, something bumped against his leg.

He jumped back, thinking it was alive — but Cricket reached for it and guided it into his talons, so he could feel that it was a large object floating on the surface of the lake. And there was a rope tied to one end of it, which led to a stalagmite that jutted from the rocky floor.

A *rope*. Which meant someone had been here before them.

"What do you think it is?" she whispered to him.

"I have no idea," he whispered back.

"Someone must have left it like this," she said. "Maybe to carry things across the lake? But why not just fly across with whatever they had to carry? This is so mysterious!"

Blue heard the rustle of wings as Swordtail ducked into the cave with them. "I think I heard voices up above," he whispered. "Can we go deeper?"

"Let's see," Cricket whispered back, barely a breath on the air.

They felt their way deeper into the cave, staying close to the wall and skirting the edge of the lake. Soon that became impossible, as they ran out of shoreline, and they had to wade into the cold, still silk of the water. It was terrifying, wading into the dark and ever-deepening water, but not as terrifying as the thought of the HiveWings behind them.

Blue shivered as the water climbed up his legs, lapped at his underbelly, and soon covered his wingbuds. He'd seen the ocean in the distance from the top of the webs, but he'd never been submerged in water and he certainly had no idea how to swim. If the water got any deeper, he wasn't sure he'd be able to go on.

"There's a passage here," Cricket whispered, "or an alcove or something, I think."

Ripples flickered around Blue as Cricket ducked away, then came back to tug on his arm. He held out his tail for Swordtail to catch, then let Cricket guide him under a dip in the roof.

Now he could feel walls on either side of him, and to his surprise, here and there he saw what looked like sticky trails of light webbing across the roof above, or sliding down the walls. Cricket paused and brought her nose closer to one of these, studying it curiously for a moment before moving on.

They waded forward for what felt like an eternity. And then the passage curved — and ahead of them, reflecting off the slick wet walls, was the glow of firelight.

Blue froze, touching Cricket's wing. She stopped, too, with a little gasp.

Fire.

Is this it? Did we find where Queen Wasp is hiding the flamesilks?

Or . . . what are we about to walk into?

CHAPTER 14

Blue glanced back toward Swordtail, whose face was dimly visible in the phosphorescent glow from the walls. Swordtail edged past them to take the lead, and they all inched forward, step by careful step.

There was a cavern ahead. Stalactites bubbled down from a high ceiling. Streaks of orange and white marbled the stone walls, shot through with veins of glittering black-and-gold ore. The water lapped against the shore here before continuing into another, wider tunnel. Rock formations twisted up in shapes like dragon tails, making the cavern look like a weird forest of petrified trunks.

The firelight wasn't coming from any flamesilk dragons. It flickered from a small pile of burning sticks, not far from the water.

And next to the fire, sitting with its back against one of the stalagmites, was a creature Blue had never seen in any animal studies in school.

It looked a little bit like a monkey, but bigger and not

quite so hairy, apart from a patch of floppy brown fur on top of its head. It had nimble little paws, which were holding something that it was gazing at intently. Parts of it were wrapped in something like a cocoon made of jaguar fur and deep red silk.

At first, it didn't notice the three dragons emerging from the tunnel; it was too immersed in whatever it was looking at. Blue and Cricket exchanged wondering glances. She looked as bewildered as he felt, but also enchanted.

Then Blue stepped on a rock that turned under his talons, and he lurched forward with a small splash.

The creature's head popped up and its eyes, as brown and big in its face as Cricket's, went wide. It jumped to its feet, revealing that it stood on two paws instead of four, dropped whatever it had been looking at, and drew a long knife from its cocoon.

Blue and his friends stopped and stared at it. It stared at them.

What is it thinking? Blue wondered. *Can it think? What does it know about dragons? Is it just scared, or is it having other emotions? What a sweet little face it has. Like a marmoset — but I've never seen a monkey with a knife before.*

Sometimes a monkey wandered up into the webs by accident, long black spidery limbs racing up the Hive vines and out onto the silvery bridges. Blue remembered one that Io had played with for an entire day. She'd wanted to keep it, but her parents made her take it back to the savanna and release it. They told her that if the HiveWings found it, they might eat it, and that would be much more upsetting. It was hard to argue with that.

This monkey's limbs seemed the wrong shape for climbing vines or swinging from trees. And its coiled energy was more like a panther's, poised to spring at them.

"Do you think it's really going to try stabbing us with that thing?" Cricket whispered.

Her voice broke the spell. The creature spun around and fled between the stalagmites, disappearing through a crack in the wall behind it.

"Oh no!" Cricket cried. "Wait, come back!" She floundered through the water up onto the shore and scrambled after the little animal. But the crack was too small for a dragon to fit through. She crouched beside the opening, trying to peek inside. "I promise we won't hurt you, little monkey. What are you? Please come back!"

"That was really cute," Blue said. He waded onto the shore, carefully skirting the fire so he wouldn't accidentally put it out. After the darkness of the previous caves, it was nice to be able to see — and much warmer near the fire than in the lake.

"I thought it was freaky," Swordtail said. "Weird little thing. Did you see how it was looking at us? It was — I don't —" He interrupted himself with an absolutely enormous yawn.

"I really want to know what it was," Cricket said,

stamping one foot with frustration. "I thought I'd studied all the flora and fauna around here, even the prehistoric stuff. I don't remember any pictures that looked like that." She tipped her head up, staring into space as though she was flipping through pages in her mind. "Not a gorilla. Not an orangutan. Not a chimpanzee. What in the Hive . . . ?"

Blue picked up the object the creature had been looking at. "Oh wow. Cricket, check this out."

She wound her way back through the stalagmites toward him. He turned the thing over in his claws. The outside was flexible leather, the inside was many layers of smooth beaten paper, and there were little marks all over each page.

"*What?*" Cricket said, astonished. She took it from him and flipped through it gently. "Is this a *book*? It can't be! Monkeys can't write books! Or read them!"

"It's not a dragon book. It didn't come from a Hive," Blue pointed out. "Look how tiny it is."

"A dollhouse book?" Cricket tried. "Which the monkey found somewhere?" She shook her head. "No, you're right. This is the monkey's book. When we came in, I thought its expression looked familiar — and that's because it was reading." She hugged the book to her chest. "Mystery animals in a cave under the savanna — who can READ! Blue, this is the biggest scientific discovery of our lifetime! I wouldn't have to be a gardener if I told the queen about this. I'm sure she'd let me change disciplines so I could study them. Don't you think?"

"I'm a little worried she'd have them all rounded up and eaten," Blue admitted.

Cricket looked horrified. "No way! Is that really what you think of HiveWings? That because we eat meat, we're heartless monsters? Do all SilkWings think that?"

"Um," Blue said, "I mean . . . I wouldn't have said 'heartless.' But eating animals does seem kind of unnecessary."

Cricket frowned and rubbed her head, as though she'd never spent any time thinking about whether eating animals was "necessary." "We don't eat *everything,*" she said after a while. "We don't eat lizards or snakes, since they're probably related to us. And I'm sure nobody would eat a species that can read and write and might be as smart as we are."

A loud rumbling sound broke into their conversation before Blue could answer. They both spun around in a fright — and discovered that it was the sound of Swordtail snoring.

The handsome SilkWing was passed out by the fire, wings flopped across the stone as though he'd staggered out of the water and collapsed in the first dry place he found.

"Well, that makes sense," Blue said. "He did carry me halfway across the savanna. He probably needs to sleep for a week to recover."

He caught himself. It was only a joke, but who knew what would happen to Swordtail as the stimulant wore off? They couldn't afford to have Swordtail sleep for a week — they needed to get to Luna as soon as possible, before she emerged from her cocoon all alone.

"Do you want to sleep, too?" Cricket asked. "I can keep an eye out, in case any HiveWings come all the way down into the cave, find the passage, and follow it through to here . . . which I don't *think* they will . . . "

"No, you should sleep, and I'll take first watch," Blue said. "You were flying all night, too." He could easily imagine how tired her wings must be. If he were in her scales, he knew he'd be feeling very anxious and emotional as well — given the stress of running away from her own tribe and upending her safe HiveWing life. Surely even the excitement of discovering a new intelligent species couldn't outweigh the danger she'd put herself in.

Which she did for me. To help me.

"All right," Cricket said with a yawn. "If you're really sure, I wouldn't mind sleeping a little bit."

"Of course." He watched her stretch her wings and curl up on the rock, close enough for him to touch her talons, if he needed to wake her. Her orange-gold scales rose and fell, slower and slower as she drifted off to sleep. The firelight flickered little shadows across her back, as though the inkblot splatter patterns were spreading and shrinking and dancing.

Maybe she's not as scared as I would be, he thought. *Maybe for her, finding out new things is enough to drive out her fear. Maybe this feels like an adventure to her.*

But that was hard for him to imagine, especially when he pictured the army of mind-controlled HiveWings far above them, combing the grasslands stalk by stalk. Who *wouldn't* be afraid of that?

Maybe Swordtail. His best and bravest friend. He was a dragon who'd face that entire army to save Luna or Blue. His courage had always seemed foolish and dangerous and impulsive to Blue — but now he wished he had even a tenth of it himself.

He lay down with his chin on his front talons and thought about everyone who'd become entangled in this web. Io, who could be anywhere right now. Burnet and Silverspot, alone and worrying about their children. Katydid, wondering where her sister was. All the HiveWings who were being forced to hunt for him, whether they understood why or not.

And somewhere in the center of that web, Queen Wasp, stealing the flamesilks and using her subjects like puppets. Was she angry right now? Or coldly certain that she'd find him soon?

At least Luna was unaware of all of this. Somewhere deep in her cocoon, she was asleep, growing her wings in peace. She had no idea what kind of chaos her Metamorphosis had set off . . . or what strange new prison she was going to wake up in.

I'm coming, Luna, he thought fiercely. *Swordtail and I will find you. You're not going to wake up alone. I promise.*

CHAPTER 15

Blue stood at the bottom of the sinkhole, looking up. He could just barely see the glow of moonlight reflecting off some of the rocks far overhead. His tail flicked a damp patch of moss on one of the rocks and he shivered.

"Do you think it's safe to go up?" Cricket asked.

"HiveWings prefer to hunt by day," Swordtail pointed out. "Their night vision is poor and they're lazy and arrogant, so I'm sure they're at home asleep, confident they'll catch us tomorrow."

Cricket blinked at him, looking slightly hurt. "*I'm* not at home asleep," she observed.

"Right," Blue said. "That's not fair, Swordtail. They're not all lazy and arrogant. They're dragons, just like you and me and everyone we know, some bad and some good."

"Dragons who've stolen your sister and spent the last day hunting you so they can throw you in their secret prison, too," Swordtail said sharply.

"That's Queen Wasp making them do that," Blue said. "They're not all like her."

"So what? They let her be like that and never complain or speak up, because it means they get to be comfortable," Swordtail said. "Sorry, Blue, I'm not in the mood to feel sorry for the bad guys right now." He spread his wings and launched himself up the shaft. "I'll go check if the coast is clear."

Blue sighed as Swordtail flew away. The strange frenetic energy of the stimulant had worn off, and after sleeping almost the entire day, Swordtail had woken up pretty much his normal self again. Which was great, except for how his normal self could sometimes be a big honking rhinoceros trampling over everyone else's feelings.

"I'm sorry," he said to Cricket.

"*Don't* be," she said. "He's right. I never worried about how we treat SilkWings or what happens to flamesilks before."

"Neither did I, really," Blue admitted. "But you're helping us now. You're not like the others."

"If Queen Wasp could control my mind, I probably would be," she said. "It's just luck or some kind of mystery science that it doesn't work on me."

Swordtail swooped back down toward them. "All quiet, as far as I can see and hear," he said. "If we fly now, we should make it to Wasp Hive before morning."

"And then what?" Cricket asked.

"Then we figure something else out," he said.

That sounds like a Swordtail kind of plan, Blue thought, but he didn't have anything better to offer, so he kept quiet.

Swordtail spun a harness around Blue again and braced his forearms around Blue's chest. "All right!" he said. "Off we —" He vaulted into the air and immediately lost his balance, smacking into the side of the canyon and thudding to the ground again. Blue's claws barked painfully against the stone and he yelped.

"Ooof," Swordtail grunted. "Sorry. Let me just —" He braced his legs and shoved himself aloft again, clutching Blue even more tightly.

No luck. Blue could feel himself slipping, even with the harness, and Swordtail's muscles were clearly straining to hold him. His wings beat as hard as he could, but a moment later he had to drop back down.

"Uh-oh," Cricket said, hovering above them.

Blue glanced up at the far, far distant top of the hole again. Uh-oh was a bit of an understatement.

Swordtail sliced away the silk connecting them and crouched, gasping for breath.

"If you can't carry him anymore," Cricket said, "how are we going to get Blue out of this cave?"

"I don't understand why I can't!" Swordtail protested. "I carried him all DAY yesterday and it was no trouble at all!" He flexed his arms and winced. "I guess I do feel a little sore *now* . . . "

"It was the stimulant," Cricket said. "It made you

stronger and gave you energy, but only until it wore off. That is so *interesting.* I wonder if anyone has any idea that it has that effect on dragons, or if other scientists have only ever used it on plants." Her eyes went a little dreamy. "Maybe for the science fair next year . . ."

"Do you have any more of it?" Swordtail asked, eyeing the pouch tied around her chest.

She shook her head. "No . . . and I wouldn't suggest taking it from a normal state," she said. "Not without some dilution experiments and animal studies first. I mean, you started off completely paralyzed, and look what it did to you."

"What it — what did I say?" Swordtail asked. "Did I sound like a total idiot?"

"You were fine," Blue assured him. "It was adorable."

"Oh, good," Swordtail grumbled. "Adorable is just the look I was going for on our heroic mission."

"So what else can we do?" Cricket said, studying the rocks around them. "Blue, could you climb out?"

"Of course," Swordtail answered for him. "SilkWings are all *great* climbers."

"Well, maybe, but . . . all that way?" Blue said, his courage failing. "I mean, I don't mind the climbing part, but the maybe-falling part and the very-long-way-to-fall and the certain-death-if-I-fall parts, those I'm kind of less excited about."

"Plus there's no way he'll make it to the top before morning," Swordtail said. "And then what do we do? Climb back down? Risk the open savanna again?"

"There might be another option — hang on," Cricket said. She spread her wings and flew away, up and up till Blue could hardly see the shimmer of her sunlight-colored scales. He had a horrible moment of imagining that she might not come back . . . that she'd reach the top, realize she could just go home, and leave them and all their messy, troublesome danger behind.

"Blue," Swordtail said in a low voice.

Blue glanced at him and saw pity in his friend's dark blue eyes.

"Remember how you warned me once about falling in love with Luna?" Swordtail said, folding his wings back. "You said we might not be partnered together. You said it would be better for both of us if we could wait to fall in love until we knew who our partners would be."

Blue looked down at his claws. That felt like a very foolish thing to say now. As though a dragon could inject a nerve toxin into his feelings and leave them paralyzed until they might be usable. But he'd imagined how Luna and Swordtail would feel if Queen Wasp separated them, and it had been so awful. He'd been trying to protect them from that.

"This is much worse, Blue," Swordtail said. "She's a *HiveWing*. You can never, never be with her. You should tell her to go home now, before it's too hard to say good-bye."

"I think it already is," Blue said softly. "At least, for me."

Swordtail put one wing over Blue's back and rested his head against Blue's. "I was afraid of that," he said.

Cricket came swooping back down in a flapping of wings and landed on an outcropping a little ways above them. "There's a crevice near the top," she said. "It's not very big, but I think Blue could hide in it. If we can get him to it by morning, he could wait out the day there, and then we'd keep going to Wasp Hive tomorrow night."

Blue felt the tension ripple through Swordtail's body. He knew what he was feeling: another day's delay; a whole night wasted on one wingless dragon climbing out of a hole. When Luna was out there and needed their help *now*.

"You can go on without me, if you'd rather," he said to Swordtail.

He could see that Swordtail was tempted. After all, what use was Blue going to be in a rescue anyway? He couldn't exactly fight. And if they had to escape in a hurry, he would massively slow them down.

"No, don't do that," Cricket said. "I was hoping you'd use your silk to help Blue climb out." She pointed up. "To catch him if he falls."

"Oh," Swordtail said, light dawning in his eyes as he saw what she meant. "Of course. That's a good idea."

"Cricket is full of good ideas," Blue said. She ducked her head and smiled at him, and he felt his heart explode.

Definitely too late. I can't say good-bye to her. Even if it means it'll hurt more later, I still want to be with her for as long as I can.

"All right, let's try this," Swordtail said, again shooting

silk from his wrists, this time the thicker, stronger strands that were usually used for building web bridges. He wound it around Blue, leaving his limbs free to climb, then leaped up to the ledge above Cricket, still holding the other end of the silk. "Go ahead!" he called.

All right, this is happening, Blue thought. He sent up a silent prayer to Clearsight and started up the side of the rocky canyon.

In fact, it was easier to climb than he'd expected. There were a lot of little crevices and nooks for him to dig his talons into, and the stone overall felt much sturdier than the webs he'd grown up clambering around on. At least the rocks didn't bounce and sway in the wind.

And when he did stumble, losing his footing for a moment, he felt the strength of the webbing catch him — the strength of Swordtail, just above him, braced to save him before he fell. And Cricket was beside him the whole way, suggesting the easiest paths, pointing out places for him to rest.

Not for the first time, Blue felt very, very grateful for his friends.

Even though the climbing went well, it still seemed to take forever — it was a really deep hole, after all. Blue's whole body was aching before he was halfway up. He found himself daydreaming wistfully about honey drops and tiny sugar bees and silk hammocks.

And when at last Cricket said, "It's here, it's just above you," he looked up and saw that the sky was already pale gray and most of the stars had disappeared. Cricket was right; they were near the top, and he'd be able to climb out early the next night. If he wasn't caught by then.

With one last heave, he hauled himself onto the ledge next to Cricket, letting Swordtail help lift him with the webbing. He sprawled there, breathing hard and wondering if his legs would ever work again.

Swordtail poked his head over the rim of the sinkhole and squinted in the direction of Wasp Hive. "I don't see anyone yet," he said, flying back to them. "But you should still get hidden, to be safe."

"Back here." Cricket flicked her tail at the rippling stone of the rock wall. Blue crawled over and saw how the bend of the rock and the dangling plants hid a narrow crack, just big enough for him to squeeze through. He was amazed that Cricket had even found it in the first place.

She held the green leaves aside so he could wedge himself in, and he discovered that the crack extended into the rock, like a small cave, so he could go farther in, squishily turn around, and lie down.

Cricket poked her head in and watched him settle. "Do you want company, which would be kind of cramped, or do you want the whole space, but alone?"

"Company," Blue said. "If — if you don't mind."

"I don't mind if *you* don't mind my wings in your face," she said. She wriggled back out to tell Swordtail, and Blue heard the whoosh of his friend's wingbeats retreating back down to the safety of the lake cave.

Then Cricket was wedging herself in through the gap, making little squeaking noises as she tried to keep her wings clear of the rough stones. Blue pressed himself back as far as he could, and after a minute she managed to get all the way in and lie down facing him.

"Thank you for your delightful invitation," she said in a pretend lordly voice, adjusting her glasses. "I adore what you've done with the place. I'll be expecting tea and sliced avocados, of course."

Blue put his chin on his talons and chuckled. "Don't make me think about food."

"I can't STOP thinking about food," she said. "I'm STARVING. Those fish I caught for breakfast were so small! And super weird; did you see that they didn't have eyes? Oh, right, I showed you. Fish with no eyes! Do you think that's because there's no light down there? I guess I wouldn't rather eat something *with* eyes. But you should have tried them anyway; I could have caught more."

"That's all right," Blue said with a smile. "I can wait for something in the vegetable family."

Cricket studied him. "What will you do with Luna?" she asked. "I mean, if you can set her free. Where will you go? Queen Wasp isn't going to stop looking for you."

"I have no idea," Blue said slowly. Honestly he'd been

imagining getting Luna and going home to their mothers. A part of him still felt as though this was a big misunderstanding, and if he could only convince Queen Wasp of how harmless they were, she'd let them go back to their normal lives.

I wish we could do that. Why can't there be a way?

Although . . . would it ever feel the same, now that I know about the flamesilks and the mind control?

Would we ever feel safe again?

"Maybe you could go live in the caves with the reading monkeys," Cricket said with a dreamy smile in her voice, as though she was making a joke, but actually thought that sounded amazing.

"That one we saw did look very welcoming." Blue laughed. "In a stabby kind of way."

"But . . . I'd go farther away, if I were you," she said. "As far from Queen Wasp as you can."

"Like one of the peninsulas?" he asked. "I thought they were too dangerous for dragons."

"That's what we're told," Cricket said, nodding. "But maybe it's not true."

Blue wasn't so sure. He'd seen drawings of some of the plants in the Poison Jungle, and they certainly *looked* as if they'd be happy to eat a few dragons. Or impale some dragons. Or melt some dragons and convert their bone sludge into nutrients.

"You could go farther than that, though," Cricket said hesitantly.

"I could?" he said. "How?"

"Maybe . . . across the ocean," she said.

He stared at her with wide eyes. Her body blocked most of the dim light from outside, so he couldn't really see the expression on her face. Was she joking?

"Are you joking?" he asked. "The Distant Kingdoms aren't real."

The tilt of her head said she was puzzled. "Of course they are. That's where Clearsight came from."

"Yes, but — but Clearsight was magic." Blue had always imagined the night-black seer dragon as a mythological figure, like a star becoming a dragon and flying down to visit them. "We say she came from the Distant Kingdoms, but we might as well say she came from the moons or the sky."

"The moons and the sky are real places, too," Cricket pointed out.

"Not places we can *go*," he protested.

"But we *could* go to the Distant Kingdoms," Cricket said. "I'm sure of it. It's just another big island, somewhere out to the east, full of other dragons."

He stared at her silhouette, thinking of how different their educations had been. At Silkworm Hall, he'd learned to revere Clearsight and accept the wisdom she'd passed down in the Book without question. He'd never been taught to think of her as a regular dragon like him, from a normal kingdom like his.

"Other dragons like Clearsight?" he asked. "Is it a whole continent full of dragons who can see the future?"

"I don't know," Cricket said. "Maybe! Wouldn't it be so interesting to find out? Can you imagine being the first dragons to cross the ocean in thousands of years? I mean, what kinds of tribes live over there? Do they look like us? Do they have other powers? Do THEY have reading monkeys?"

"But if it *is* real and it's that easy to get there," Blue argued, "then Clearsight wouldn't be the only one to have done it in all that time." He shook his head. "I think it's a myth."

"*I* think it's the perfect place to hide if Queen Wasp is looking for you," Cricket said. "But you're right that it wouldn't be easy to get there. We'd have to find out how Clearsight did it."

"Magic," Blue said promptly.

Cricket leaned forward and bopped his nose with hers. "Magic is just science we don't understand yet," she said. "So maybe we can figure out her science."

"How, exactly?" he asked.

"With BOOKS," Cricket said, as though that was obvious. "There must be clues in a book somewhere!"

He unfurled his antennae, sensing danger, and put one of his talons over hers. "Shhhhhh."

There were sounds coming from outside.

CHAPTER 16

Blue and Cricket waited in tense silence.

Wingbeats. Voices. A whoosh and then a cracking sound, like an antelope's neck being broken, and munching noises as it was devoured. Blue shivered.

"Who said you could eat?" said one of the voices, deep and sharp and female.

"I didn't eat all day yesterday!" another voice answered, whiny and male. "*You* know. She never lets us, while she's in control. So I figure, as long as we're out here and in charge of our own skulls for once, we can hunt breakfast and runaway SilkWings at the same time."

The other HiveWing growled, but there was a noise of ripping meat, as though she'd taken a chunk of the prey for herself.

"This is a waste of time," she muttered, chewing. "Who cares about one stupid dragonet who might or might not have fire in his silk? He probably got eaten by a pack of lions or fell down a hole and died already."

"A hole like this one?" The voices drew nearer and Blue felt Cricket's wings trembling. "Should we check down there?"

"Ugh," said the first dragon. "My patrol went down there yesterday. It's dark and wet and haunted. I think we can skip it."

"HELLO!" the second dragon shouted down the chasm, making Blue jump. "HELLOOOOOOO, ANNOYING WINGLESS DRAAAAAAGON. ARE YOU DEAD AT THE BOTTOM OF THESE ROCKS? OR ALMOST DEAD? COULD YOU CROAK 'YEAH, I'M HERE, TOTALLY DEAD, CARRY ON' SO WE CAN ALL GO HOME AND SAY WE FOUND YOU?"

His companion actually laughed, which was the most surprising part of the conversation so far from Blue's point of view.

"Come on, finish your intestines so we can get going," she said. "There are some scrub thickets over by Tsetse Hive that I think are worth checking out."

It felt like a long time and a lot of chewing noises later when they finally flew away. Blue let out a breath and wondered how long he'd been holding it. His limbs were aching and heavy from the long night of climbing. And now that the danger had passed, he felt his eyelids drooping. It seemed safe enough to sleep. If anyone found him, he couldn't exactly escape in a hurry anyhow.

He rested his chin on the ground and closed his eyes and slept.

Blue slept for most of the day, drifting in and out when there were sounds of the hunt overhead; but each time he woke, Cricket was there, and he felt safe enough to sleep again.

At last she nudged him awake and they squeezed out of the hidden crevice onto the ledge outside. The sky was just turning purple blue and a few stars were out. Blue stretched out all his cramped muscles while Cricket flew down to get Swordtail.

After that, it took only a little more climbing before he reached the top of the sinkhole and scrambled onto safe, flat ground. It was strange how dry it felt up here, after the dampness of the deep cave. Dust billowed up between his claws as he cut off the silk harness and threw it down the hole.

Now that he wasn't flying, though, Wasp Hive looked horribly far away. Could they possibly make it there before dawn? Even if they did, would there be anywhere else to hide as safe as the sinkhole?

"I'll scout ahead," Swordtail called, soaring away. His deep blue wings were soon swallowed up by the night, and all Blue could see of him were the little flickers of white along his back, like a flurry of snow moths.

Cricket landed to walk beside Blue, between the tufts of grass and stabby little thornbushes. He glanced down at his talons and realized that a lot of the paint had flaked off, probably from wading in the lake and scraping against the rocks. His real colors were showing through all over his body, glints of aquamarine and violet shimmering like buried jewels.

They went as fast as they could, although sometimes they had to detour around particularly dense shrubs or anthills as big as they were. At one point a scorpion ran across Blue's foot and he nearly shrieked, but managed not to. The air was full of buzzing and zipping and the tall grass rustled as snakes glided out of their way.

Two of the moons were full; the other was barely a sliver behind a veil of clouds. Cricket tipped her head back to look up at them.

"Did you see the comet about half a year ago?" she asked. "The one that looked like an extra moon in the sky? It was so big. I wished so much that I had a telescope to study it with, but there's only one in Cicada Hive, and Lady Scarab won't lend it to anyone."

"You know Lady Scarab?" Blue asked.

"*You* know Lady Scarab?" she replied skeptically.

"No, we just — we ran into her, in The Sugar Dream, early on Luna's Metamorphosis Day. She was . . . I feel like *nice* is the wrong word, but she was sort of fiercely not awful to us."

"That sounds like her," Cricket said ruefully. "Fiercely not awful."

Blue sensed there was more to Cricket's connection with the old dragon, but she didn't seem to want to talk about it. He changed the subject to astronomy, and they happily discussed constellations and her theories about other planets until Blue realized they were reaching the outskirts of Wasp Hive.

They crested a small hill and studied the structures laid out below them. Wasp Hive was not quite like the other Hives — it was bigger, for one thing, and the oldest Hive on Pantala, so it was built in a heavier, more ornate style. There were carvings of cruel-eyed wasps adorning the entrances, brandishing the wealth of the Hive in their excess wood and onyx inlays. An enormous marble statue of Queen Wasp loomed over the ground-floor doors, so anyone entering that way would have to pass under her merciless gaze.

But most dragons would enter at a higher level. Blue glanced up at the moonlit webs twining overhead. He could see the dark forms of SilkWing family clusters up there, hundreds of sleeping dragons, like stones seen through water. Did any of them know about flamesilks? Did any of them help imprison and feed dragons like Luna and his father — and did they hate it every day, or was it just a normal job to them? He wondered if the Chrysalis extended across Hives, and whether any of them were in it.

All around the Hive were neatly laid-out rows of enormous greenhouses — at least thirty of them — in concentric circles surrounding the base of the Hive. Some were wild with growth, leaves rioting against the glass roofs. Others were quieter, with orderly rows of vegetables and soil boxes visible inside.

That many greenhouses . . . so much glass. *She needed fire to make that glass to build these,* Blue thought. *Fire she took from SilkWings. From my dad.* Flamesilk was necessary to everything the queen did.

She wasn't going to let them go easily.

Swordtail landed softly beside them. "The main door is barred for the night, and possibly guarded inside as well. There's no way in there." He tipped his head back to study the Hive.

"Let's think. Could we climb to one of the ledges?" Cricket asked. "Using the vines and your silk for Blue?"

Blue eyed the smooth walls of the Hive uncertainly. It looked like a much more treacherous climb than the one out of the sinkhole, and the nearest opening was a very long way up.

"Or . . ." he said slowly. "Could we hide in one of the greenhouses? At least until we know a little more?"

"That's a good point," Cricket said. "If we go into the Hive, we might get trapped in there, and it might not even be the right place to look, right? But if we find a place to hide, tomorrow I can go in and ask around about where the flamesilks might be."

Blue gave her an alarmed look. "By yourself?"

"Of course," she said. "You two are probably all over the wanted posters by now. But who cares about me? I'm just a HiveWing, doing normal HiveWing things."

"Like suddenly appearing in a Hive that's not your own?" Blue said. "Asking obvious questions about the very thing that's got the queen running dragon hunts all over the savanna?"

"They won't be OBVIOUS questions," Cricket objected. "They will be VERY SUBTLE. I am an EXCEPTIONALLY subtle dragon, sir."

"Hmm," Blue said dubiously.

"Besides, it won't be suspicious because *everyone* will be talking about flamesilks right now," she pointed out. "And someone has to know where they are."

Swordtail was shaking his head. "That's another day wasted," he said. "Luna's only going to be in her cocoon five days. We have to find her before she comes out. And before Blue starts his own Metamorphosis."

Blue twitched, startled. His own Metamorphosis! Swordtail was right. That was . . . soon. Very VERY soon.

Where am I supposed to have my Metamorphosis, if I can't go back to the Cocoon? And how can I help Luna if I'm stuck inside my own silk?

"I say we storm the Hive right now," Swordtail went on. "I fly in, start knocking over guards, force them to tell me where she is."

"I'd call that a splendid plan," Cricket said, "if it resembled a plan in *any way*."

"You'll end up on the Wasp Hive version of Misbehaver's Way before the sun is over the horizon," Blue agreed.

"And the Wasp Hive version might be more like Headless Corpses Way," Cricket added.

Swordtail stamped his feet. "I can't sit around all day again."

"We're not sitting around," Cricket said. "We're spying. And gathering information. And *thinking*. You'd be surprised what a useful step that is when it comes to plans."

She started down the hill toward the greenhouses and the two SilkWings followed her, Swordtail grumbling under his breath. Blue felt guilty for being on Cricket's side. Of course he wanted to rescue Luna just as much as Swordtail did. But he didn't want to fight any guards or demand answers or rush in all teeth-bared. He kind of wanted to do whatever would get him in the least trouble that would also help Luna.

The greenhouses were all the same size, which was remarkably large, and divided from one another by neat gravel paths. Stakes with signs and arrows printed on them pointed the way to particular types of plants, and a list was affixed to the door of each greenhouse: CARROTS, BEANS, EGGPLANTS on one; CLEMENTINES, LIMES on another; PAPYRUS, BAMBOO on a third.

They avoided the greenhouses that were too tidy, where every corner was visible, and headed for the ones that looked the most overgrown.

"These are probably tended every day," Blue realized as they walked between the towering glass walls. He was starting to feel anxious about his plan. "Gardeners will come in to water the plants and find us."

"I will BONK THEM AND CONK THEM OUT," Swordtail declared.

Poor dragons, just trying to do their jobs and take care of some plants. They don't deserve a day of being knocked unconscious plus a massive headache, Blue thought.

Well, said his brain unexpectedly, *YOU don't deserve to be chased across the savanna and treated like a mass murderer, so perhaps there's a little unfairness to go around.*

He wrinkled his forehead, thinking about that. Did their injustice toward him mean that he'd be justified in hurting them?

He wasn't the kind of dragon who ever hurt other dragons. But he could imagine what Luna would say. *You're allowed to fight back. You should, when the world is like this.*

"Look," Cricket whispered, pointing to one of the last greenhouses, in the innermost circle near the back of the Hive. The plant growth inside was dense and leafy, but what was even more interesting was the fact that the door was covered with a silk-spun web barrier.

They crossed to it and read the sign beside the door: DO NOT ENTER, BY ORDER OF QUEEN WASP. PROPERTY OF THE QUEEN. TRESPASSING PUNISHABLE BY MAIMING, DISMEMBERMENT, IMPALING, AND DEATH, IN THAT ORDER.

Blue lightly tapped the silk with one of his claws and the threads vibrated. "This is here so she'll know if anyone tries to break in."

"Can you re-create it?" Cricket asked Swordtail. "From inside? Seems like a perfect place to hide, if no one can come in here."

"Except, you know, *Queen Wasp*," Blue pointed out.

"Yeah, but . . . she probably won't?" Cricket guessed.

"This sign is really clear, though," Blue said anxiously. "No trespassing at all. Maiming and impaling and death! I mean. This sign seems to think it's a really serious rule."

"*I* think 'keep Blue safe from brainwashed HiveWings' is a *more* serious rule," Cricket said firmly.

"Yeah, I can do this," said Swordtail, who'd been studying the web. "It might not be an exact match, but it should look convincing enough from a distance."

As Blue watched nervously, Swordtail carefully dismantled the web enough for Cricket to open the door. She stepped inside and let out a small gasp.

"It's *really* hot in here," she whispered back to them. "How does she keep it this hot?"

"I have a guess," Swordtail hissed. He scowled at the silk spiraling out of his wrists as he started reweaving the door cover.

Blue squeezed in behind Cricket and felt the humidity hit him along with several flapping wet leaves. It was like walking into a storm cloud. He glanced down and wondered if the stone floor was lined with flamesilk to keep it this temperature.

"Why do you think Queen Wasp keeps everyone out of here?" Cricket whispered to him. "Do any of these plants look unusual to you? I recognize some of them, but not all of them. Huh." She brushed his shoulder with her wing and they moved farther into the tangle of greenery.

That was a good question, Blue realized — one he hadn't thought about because he was so tangled up in anxiety about breaking the rules. What was in here that Queen Wasp wanted to keep secret? Why was this place so forbidden?

Now he could see that there were beds of dirt edged with boulders, and something like a path between them, but the plants had grown so wild that they vaulted over the paths, twined their branches together, and flung down curtains of hanging moss and trailing vines to disrupt any possible order. He and Cricket had to duck and weave through the greenery, and he kept getting his claws snagged on roots and unexpected runners.

There were flowers everywhere, too: glorious purple exploding stars, delicate pale orange orchids, clusters of petals the color of bananas, and odd little globes in ruby red and sapphire blue.

"What are these?" Cricket whispered, mostly to herself, fingering a vine of bright pink tendrils. "And those? Why haven't we studied these? How did she get these two to grow next to each other? Whoa, is that a new kind of fern?" She wandered ahead, murmuring questions, while Blue stopped to watch a really surprisingly cute snail sauntering slowly up a tree trunk.

Suddenly Cricket's voice cut off with a shriek that was

quickly muffled. Blue's head jerked up. Was Queen Wasp *here?* Inside the greenhouse? Had she caught Cricket?

He ran after her, stumbling as he fought through vine tangles and got smacked in the face by eighty more large, wet leaves. He had to explain to the queen that none of this was Cricket's fault! He had to turn himself in!

He pushed through a curtain of moss and felt himself seized by strong claws. They threw him to the floor, flipped him onto his back, and tied all his talons together before he could even blink. He opened his mouth to yell for Cricket, and another vine immediately looped around his snout, snapping his jaw shut. It felt as if barely a moment had passed, but there he was, lying on the ground, completely helpless.

Blue craned his neck to look for Cricket and spotted her, tied up the same way he was and propped against a tree. Standing over her was a wiry dark green dragon.

So, not Queen Wasp, he thought. *Could that be the SilkWing who covers the door for her?*

He tried to twist around to see his own attacker and realized there were three of them altogether. All of them had scales in shades of dark green, and they were all poised and waiting to catch Swordtail, who was blundering toward the noise Blue and Cricket had made.

And then.

Blue noticed something.

Their captors . . . they had *two* wings each, not four.

Long, graceful, swooping wings shaped like leaves.

CHAPTER 17

LeafWings!

They weren't extinct. They were HERE. In Queen Wasp's greenhouse! Attacking dragons! Real actual LeafWings! The posters were right!

I should alert a HiveWing authority immediately! Blue thought, feeling a little hysterical. *But I can't because they'll arrest me!*

But LEAFWINGS! This close to Wasp Hive!

He tried to grunt loudly to warn Swordtail, but it didn't do any good. The trio of LeafWings moved with ruthless efficiency, and within a few heartbeats Swordtail was tied up next to Blue, blinking with similar bewilderment.

"Are there any more?" one of them asked.

"I'll check," said another, and he quietly melted off into the trees.

There was a long moment of silence. Blue glanced over at Cricket again. She was watching the LeafWings with the same wide-eyed expression she'd had when she saw the reading monkey in the cave.

This is not an exciting scientific discovery, Cricket! he wanted to shout. *These are VERY DANGEROUS DRAGONS!* The LeafWings had tried to wipe out both their tribes in the last war. Wasn't she deathly afraid of them?

He tried to look at the LeafWings with Cricket's eyes. Maybe he would be less scared that way. Maybe he just needed to see them as fascinating and unusual, instead of deadly and really extremely deadly.

The two that had stayed were both female, and their faces were similar enough that he wondered if they were related. The one standing by Cricket looked no older than he was — about six years old — although he had no idea if LeafWings grew differently than SilkWings. Small gold scales were speckled along the edges of her wings and talons and across her snout, crinkled up in her scowl.

The other one was a lot older and bigger, with an air of authority about her that made Blue instinctively want to hide or say he was sorry or both. Her scales were lighter green with patches of brown, and she had strange pale burn scars splattered across her talons and up her forearms. Her scowl was also pretty terrifying. Both dragons had several small pouches hung about them, woven from long grass or fashioned from leaves. Blue wondered what was inside but had a sinking feeling that he would regret finding out.

What are they thinking? he wondered. The matching scowls were a pretty good clue that whatever it was, the general sentiment was hostile. *How long have they been here? What are they here for? Are they glad they caught us, or annoyed that we stumbled into their hiding place?*

Most important, what are they going to do with us?

The leaves rustled and the male LeafWing returned. He was a green dark enough to disappear into shadows and wore a small white seashell on a cord around his neck. He shook his head at the others. "No one else."

"Good," said the older female. "Did they break the web on the door?"

"Yes," he said, "but rebuilt it."

"Useful of them," she said.

Huh, Blue thought, momentarily distracted from his panic. *How did the LeafWings get in? They can't spin silk, so they couldn't have covered the door themselves. Could . . . could Queen Wasp know they're here?*

He doubted that. Queen Wasp *hated* LeafWings for refusing to accept her rule. Why would she keep three of them stashed in a greenhouse?

Across from him, Cricket flicked her tail, trying to get the smaller LeafWing's attention, but the scowling dragonet ignored her. .

The tall female — who seemed to be the leader of the group — scanned her three captives with calculating green eyes. At last she stepped forward and yanked the rope off Blue's snout.

"Ow!" he yelped.

"Who are you," she demanded, "and what are you doing here?" She jerked her head at Cricket. "Two SilkWings with a HiveWing. Do you work for her?"

"No," Blue said. "She's my friend."

The youngest LeafWing let out a scornful laugh, but Blue's interrogator looked intrigued. "HiveWings don't befriend SilkWings," she said. "They control you. They enslave you. They order you about. But then, that's what you signed up for, isn't it?"

"I . . . um," Blue said. "I didn't sign up for anything? I think?"

"True," said the male LeafWing. "Too young."

"Don't be so literal, Hemlock," the leader scoffed. "You. Tell me your names."

"I'm Blue," he said. "And that's Cricket, and that's . . . " He trailed off as he turned to Swordtail and found him furiously shaking his head. "Uh. Someone else."

"Trying to keep secrets won't do any good at this point," the LeafWing said. "I only see two ways for this to end: with you all helping us, or dead. In the former case, it'll be much easier if we know your names. Or we could skip to the latter case right now."

Swordtail growled and the little LeafWing bared her teeth at him.

"W-What are *your* names?" Blue tried, thinking that was astonishingly brave of him.

The LeafWing smiled slightly. "I'm Belladonna, and that's Hemlock. Our daughter is Sundew."

"Why would you *tell* them that?" Sundew snapped in a burst of fury. "They can't help us! They'll turn us in the moment they get a chance! We should kill them now and leave their corpses somewhere that'll really scare those worms in the Hive." She lifted one of her wings and pulled a fiery red centipede out of a pouch. It flailed violently at the air, waving all its feet and hissing.

"Sundew," Belladonna said warningly. "Save that for later. Corpses lying around will notify the queen we're here, which would make our mission harder. Remember?"

Sundew dropped the centipede back into its pouch. Her scowl deepened.

"B-Besides," Blue said, "killing us would probably make the queen very happy. And I think m-maybe you don't want to do that?"

Belladonna narrowed her eyes at him. "The queen wants you dead? Why?"

"Well," he said, but he'd never been a good liar, and he couldn't come up with anything fast enough, and he didn't know what the right thing to say might be, so he went with the truth. "She wants me locked up in case I'm a flamesilk." He held out his wrists, which looked as ordinary as ever, other than being covered in flaking paint. "And she probably wants Swordtail dead because he attacked some guards to save my sister and then he escaped Cicada Hive. Cricket . . . she doesn't know about Cricket yet." *I hope.* "But if she did, she'd be mad because Cricket's been helping us hide from her."

"A helpful HiveWing?" Belladonna said thoughtfully. She regarded Cricket in a way that made Blue think of quicksand and crawler vines at midnight. "That does sound like a useful dragon to know."

"Sounds like a bunch of four-winged lies," Sundew spat. "If Queen Wasp wanted you locked up, you'd *be* locked up."

"Not necessarily. She wants your whole tribe dead, and apparently you're, uh . . . not all that dead," Blue pointed out. "By the way, how are you not dead? Are there a lot of you left? Where have you been living?"

"None of your business," Sundew hissed. "As if we'd tell you anything! Tree killers!"

Tree killers, Blue thought, startled. What an awful name. Was that how LeafWings saw the other two tribes? *Of course it must be. After all . . . that's what we did.* Even the SilkWings, though? The SilkWings only cut down trees under orders. Mostly they stayed out of the way as much as they could. *But if I were a LeafWing, all I would see is HiveWings destroying my home and SilkWings helping or standing by.*

"If you are trying to hide from Queen Wasp," Belladonna interjected, "what are you doing in her greenhouse?"

Blue hesitated again. Swordtail was shaking his head so hard Blue thought it might topple right off his neck. But so what if these LeafWings knew about Luna? The longer he talked, the longer they all stayed alive. And maybe if he explained, and promised not to tell anyone they'd seen the LeafWings, Belladonna would decide to let them go. After all, it had to be pretty clear that he and his friends wouldn't be talking to Queen Wasp or any HiveWing guards anytime soon.

"We're looking for my sister," he said. "She's a flamesilk, and Queen Wasp took her. We think she's keeping all the flamesilks somewhere around here."

Belladonna, Hemlock, and Sundew all glanced at one another, suddenly alert.

"That's —" Sundew started.

"Yes," Hemlock answered.

"Aha," said Belladonna.

"What?" Blue asked. "What aha?"

"It seems," Belladonna said, taking a step closer to him, "that we can be of use to one another after all."

"We . . . can?"

"You see," Belladonna went on, "we know where the flamesilks are."

Blue's jaw dropped. Cricket sat up, her ears twitching and her eyes bright. Even Swordtail looked suddenly more excited than worried.

"Where are they?" Blue asked. "Did you see a new cocoon there? Was it all right?"

"We can take you to their prison," Belladonna said. "We can even help you sneak in to rescue your sister. You just have to do *one* thing for us first."

Blue's heart sank. Whatever the LeafWings wanted, it couldn't be good. Or safe. Or smart.

"I won't hurt anyone," he said.

"You don't have to," Belladonna said with her quicksand smile. "We're not here to attack the Hive or fight any dragons, no matter what your queen's propaganda says about us. We're here for one little thing, and since we've been having quite a lot of trouble figuring out how to accomplish our goal, I think you've come along just in the nick of time. A desperate SilkWing and a helpful HiveWing are just what we need."

"For what?" Blue asked. "What do you want us to do?"

"If you want our help finding your sister," Belladonna said smoothly, "all you have to do . . . is steal the Book of Clearsight for us."

CHAPTER 18

Blue felt a reverent shiver run through him even thinking the words *Book of Clearsight*. He'd spent a hundred nights lying in his hammock, gazing up at the silk-shrouded stars and imagining what it had been like to be her. The greatest seer who ever lived. The wisest of dragons. Grandmother to an entire tribe.

The legends said Clearsight had been able to see the future — but not just one future: all the possible futures. She had used that power to keep the tribes safe during her lifetime. They had survived hurricanes, forest fires, and a malevolent princess or four, thanks to Clearsight. Her children and grandchildren and great-grandchildren were protected from every danger, growing strong and powerful and more numerous as the years went on.

Then, when Clearsight saw her peaceful death approaching, she left one last gift for her descendants: a book that foretold the future.

It warned them about everything in the years to come.

The lightning strike that sheered away part of the sea cliff. The population explosion of sharks in the bay. The possible spread of a devastating bark disease in the forest. Clearsight wrote it all down, centuries of warnings, so that she could continue to protect her beloved HiveWing children, even long after her death.

The Book of Clearsight was the HiveWings' greatest treasure. It was the reason they were the most powerful tribe in Pantala. Queen Wasp had used it to defeat the LeafWings in the war. It made her invincible.

And surely, Blue thought, cold tentacles trailing through his mind, *surely* it included warnings about any dragons stupid enough to try to steal it from her. She might even know they were here *right now.*

"I know," Belladonna said, studying his face. "I thought the same thing. But we've made it this far, and we've been hiding in her own greenhouse for four days without anyone showing up to capture us. If the Book has warned her about us, she hasn't bothered to do anything about it."

"Yet," Hemlock added impassively.

Belladonna shot him a look.

"We don't need them!" Sundew cried. "I can steal the Book of Clearsight by myself!"

"You can't even get near the front door by yourself," Belladonna observed.

"Neither can we," Blue said. "We're no use to your plan. We're wanted fugitives."

"*She* isn't," Hemlock said, flicking one claw at Cricket.

That was true. Cricket could — but Cricket was shaking her head. Blue's small flame of hope spluttered out.

Of course she would say no. He couldn't blame her. She'd never even met Luna; she wouldn't risk her tribe's entire future to save a SilkWing she didn't know.

Helping a pathetic dragon hide from hunters was one thing — an exciting adventure, complete with antiparalysis smoke and reading monkeys.

Stealing the Book of Clearsight, though . . . that was an unforgivable crime. She'd be betraying her whole tribe, not just her queen.

"No?" Belladonna growled, suddenly furious. She darted across to Cricket and seized the HiveWing's jaw in her talons. "You don't say no to me, HiveWing. You have no right, after everything your tribe has done to our homes and our dragons."

"Don't hurt her!" Blue cried. He tried to pull his talons free, but they were bound tightly. "Look, can't you understand why she'd refuse? She wants to protect her tribe, same as you. You say you're not here to hurt anyone, but then what are you planning to do with the Book once you have it?"

Belladonna hissed in Cricket's face and shoved her away. "All we want to do is level the wind currents," she spat. "Do you really think it's fair that the HiveWings have had this secret knowledge for so long? That they've abused it to dominate and destroy other tribes? Do you think that's what your precious Clearsight intended?"

Cricket looked down at her feet, blinking rapidly.

"Queen Wasp has already read the whole thing," Belladonna went on. "She probably even has a copy somewhere, unless she's an idiot. We just want to read it, too. Then we'll all know the same things; we'll have the same advance information. The LeafWings won't have anything more than what the HiveWings have had for generations. Equality. That's what we're looking for."

"Seems only fair," Hemlock agreed.

"But, um," Blue said nervously, "but then won't you use that information to attack the Hives?"

Belladonna's eyes glittered. "That depends on what the Book says."

"Stop being so nosy!" Sundew said fiercely. Her talons twitched toward one of her pouches, but whatever was in there, she stopped herself from bringing it out. "Either you help us, or you die. It's very simple!"

Blue glanced at Swordtail. He could see instantly that Swordtail was fine with this plan. He'd be happy to help even LeafWings if it meant saving Luna, and he didn't care what happened to the HiveWings afterward.

But Cricket . . . this was too much to ask.

And yet the truth was, it would be impossible to pull off without her.

Blue closed his eyes and took a deep breath. "I need to talk to my friends," he said. "Give us some time to think about it."

"To THINK about it?!" Sundew growled. She picked up a fallen branch and started snapping it into jagged splinters. "ARRRRRRRRRRGH."

"You have until midday," Belladonna said, beckoning to her daughter. "Then we start formulating our plan." She turned and disappeared into the leaves, with Sundew stomping furiously along behind her.

Hemlock untied the vine around Swordtail's snout, then stepped across and did the same for Cricket. He paused as the vine dropped away and met Cricket's eyes.

"Choose wisely," he said to her.

And then he, too, slipped away into the foliage.

Blue looked up. This section was so overgrown that he couldn't see the walls or the ceiling of the greenhouse; it was like they were in a cave made of leaves. But he could tell from the bright green color leaching into the plants that the sun was rising outside. He wondered if hunters were out already, looking for him.

Had anyone noticed Cricket was missing yet?

He rocked himself onto his side and scooted awkwardly over the rocky ground until he was next to her. She gave him a halfhearted smile and nudged his neck with her nose.

"I'm sorry," he said to her. "I'm really, really sorry I dragged you into this."

Cricket looked very surprised. "Did you?" she said. "I'm pretty sure I dragged myself into it. Or leaped into it, with all four feet and all four wings. I might have been yelling 'wheeee, adventure!' in my head, if I didn't say that out loud."

"Well, maybe," he said. "But you couldn't have expected this."

"Neither could you," she pointed out reasonably. "Being captured by LeafWings! It's kind of amazing, isn't it? I can't believe they're still alive! Where *have* they been all this time? I must say they're a little more belligerent than I would have imagined." She moved her jaw from side to side, wincing.

"Really?" Blue said. "We were taught that LeafWings would kill us on sight, so to me it seems quite friendly of them to postpone killing us until later."

Cricket gave him a rueful smile. "Is there any chance they won't kill us at all?" she asked.

"Maybe if we help them," Blue said. "Or get away from them somehow."

Blue glanced across at Swordtail, who was flailing around on the ground, trying to bite away the vines binding his talons.

"Um, Swordtail?" he said. "What do you think?"

"I think they're listening to us," Swordtail growled, "so it's no use trying to make any escape plans."

"True," Belladonna's voice called from somewhere up in the branches.

"But I think we *should* help them," Swordtail said. "They have a point. The HiveWings did destroy all their trees. Queen Wasp used the Book's knowledge to nearly wipe them out. So why shouldn't they get to see the Book? I don't care, as long as they take us to Luna. The only thing I'm not sure of is whether we can trust them to help us after we do what they want."

"You can," Belladonna's voice called again.

"Of course you can, you ungrateful beetles!" Sundew yelled from somewhere else. "We're not lying, conniving HiveWings! We're LeafWings! We're honorable!"

"If you want to be in this conversation," Blue shouted, "just come back and be in it already."

There was a moment of rustling silence.

"No, no," said Belladonna's voice. "Carry on. Pretend we're not here."

Swordtail snorted.

"Well, I'm worried," Blue said to Swordtail. "First of all, I'm sure it's impossible to steal the book. Secondly, even if we could, giving it to a tribe who tried to wipe us all out once upon a time seems like maybe a bad idea."

"THAT'S NOT WHAT WE —" Sundew bellowed.

"Shhhhhhhhhhhhhhh." Belladonna hushed her.

"We're leaving anyway, aren't we?" Swordtail said. "We can't ever go home. You and me and Luna and Io, if we can find her — and you, too, if you want to come," he said to Cricket. "We'll have to find a new place to live, far away from Wasp and the Hives and all her zombie hordes. So why should we care what happens to her or them after we're gone? We'll be safe, far away from here."

"But — what about everyone else?" Blue asked. "Burnet and Silverspot? Your parents? All the dragons we went to school with? All our teachers? Cricket's sister? Don't you care about any of them?"

Swordtail coiled his tail in close and spread his wings. "I care about Luna," he said. "That's it."

Blue couldn't imagine that was true. Blue cared about all of them: every dragon he'd ever spoken to and all the ones he'd never seen. There were dragons out there eating blueberries and dragons laughing at clumsy tiger cubs and dragons learning to dance and dragons crying as though their hearts would break over missing homework. He'd been all of them in some way, and he couldn't just toss them into the talons of these angry, vengeful dragons and fly off.

He turned back to Cricket. She'd managed to snap off a twig from the bush behind her, holding it between her teeth and passing it to her bound talons. She caught Blue's eye and tapped the dirt with the stick.

"I'm not sure we have a choice," she said out loud.

Awkwardly she wrote, *PRETEND TO AGREE. ESCAPE LATER.*

Blue tilted his head at her. Could they do that? Say yes to the LeafWings' plan . . . agree to go after the Book . . . and then run off once they were inside the Hive?

They wouldn't have the LeafWings' help to find Luna, but with luck they could find her themselves.

It felt underhanded. He didn't like lying to anyone, or breaking promises.

Of course, he didn't love stealing priceless artifacts either.

"It's like Sundew said, right?" Cricket went on. "We do what they want, or they'll kill us."

"I won't let them kill you," Blue said.

Something like a "HA!" came from the direction of Sundew's voice, followed by a "SHHH" and the sounds of a scuffle.

Cricket tapped her message again, watching him significantly. "Let's hear their plan," she said. "If stealing the Book means helping your sister — and not dying — I can do that. They're right that Queen Wasp and the Librarian already know everything that's in it anyway."

Swordtail had given up on untying his vines and lay in an undignified heap on the path, frowning at them. From his angle, Blue was pretty sure Swordtail couldn't read what Cricket had written. But it didn't matter — once they were away from the LeafWings, he'd explain, and Swordtail would understand.

"Sounds like we're all in agreement," Swordtail said.

Blue sighed and leaned forward to brush away Cricket's message. "All right," he called. "We'll steal the Book of Clearsight for you."

CHAPTER 19

Cricket's plan began to fall apart immediately. In the first place, the LeafWings were adamant that Sundew had to go with them to sneak into the temple.

"What?" Cricket said. "How? There's no way to get her through the Hive unnoticed. The first guard who spots her will kill her — in fact, any HiveWing who sees her would probably do the same."

"It's true," Blue agreed. "There are terrifying posters about you everywhere."

"We've been working on that," Belladonna said. Blue couldn't help thinking she seemed remarkably unconcerned about sending her daughter into danger. The tall LeafWing produced a pair of leaves that were similar in shape to the second, smaller pair of wings on a SilkWing. Sundew stood still, shooting daggers at Cricket with her eyes, while Belladonna and Hemlock fastened the fake wings below and behind her real ones, using a system of rigging them with vine ties under Sundew's many pouches.

"No flying," Hemlock said sternly, touching Sundew's snout.

"But as long as she keeps her wings folded, it should be convincing enough inside the Hive," Belladonna said. "Walking up to the guards outside, in sunlight, with plenty of opportunity for them to watch her coming — that was the part we were having trouble with." She smiled at Cricket, a smile that went nowhere near her eyes. "That's where you come in."

"She's still very green and leafy-looking," Cricket protested. "Even her real wings look like leaves. And she's *so* green. Blue, there aren't any SilkWings *that* green, are there?"

He spent a moment trying to remember all the green SilkWings he knew, before he realized that Cricket wanted him to say: "Oh, no, never that green."

"We can fix that, too," Sundew said spiritedly. She dumped out one of her pouches, sending a rainstorm of flower petals to the ground. Without choosing carefully, she grabbed a scarlet flower and rubbed it on her shoulder, leaving a patch of reddish green.

"Let me," Hemlock said, gently taking the flower out of her talons. He sorted the petals quickly into piles by color, then started applying rubbings of yellow, red, and blue in an even pattern.

Cricket watched skeptically, but Blue was fairly impressed. It wasn't as thorough as the paint Cricket had put on him, but it did make Sundew look much less like a LeafWing by the time Hemlock was done. Although maybe not quite a SilkWing.

She looked a little too furious to be a real SilkWing, and the combination of colors wasn't exactly beautiful. But Belladonna might be right; it was at least possible now that Sundew could pass through the corridors of Wasp Hive without getting caught.

Wait. That's bad, he remembered. *We want to leave her behind. We'll never be able to escape with her watching us.*

But there was no way to convince the LeafWings without raising their suspicions — and then it got worse.

"These two stay behind with us," Belladonna said, pointing to Blue and Swordtail.

"No way," Swordtail blurted.

Cricket folded back her wings and lifted her chin. "I'm not going without them," she said. "I won't do it. I don't trust you."

"And I don't trust *you*, HiveWing," said Belladonna. "Which is exactly why they're staying where I can keep an eye on them. You can have them back when I have the Book."

"No," Cricket said, standing her ground. "I can't do this alone."

"You'll have Sundew," Belladonna pointed out.

"Yeah!" Sundew said. "You'll have ME. That's like the *opposite* of being alone. I can do anything twenty dragons can do."

"I need my friends," Cricket said firmly.

Belladonna and Hemlock exchanged a long, thoughtful look. Finally, Hemlock said, "Just one."

"Both," said Cricket.

"One," said Belladonna. "Choose which, or we'll kill one of them and make your choice very easy."

Cricket hesitated. Blue felt awful for her. How could they all escape if one of them was stuck in the greenhouse? But there wasn't anything she could do; he could see that.

"Blue," Cricket said in a subdued voice. "I'll take Blue."

"You should take Swordtail," he said. "He's a better fighter than me, if things go bad."

"I assume that's what *she's* for," Cricket said, nodding at Sundew. "I really want you to come with me, Blue. Please?"

He realized that she was scared, maybe even more scared than he was. She had gotten into this for him, and she felt safer with him than Swordtail, who she barely knew and who had a tendency to say mean things about HiveWings. Blue was afraid he'd be more than useless to her — but if she wanted him, he'd go to the ends of Pantala, or anywhere she asked.

"Of course," he said. Maybe they'd have a chance to slip away from Sundew. Maybe they'd come up with a way to save Swordtail and get out of this . . . even if he couldn't think of any solutions right now.

Hemlock cut them loose and let Cricket use some of the flower dye to cover the spots where Blue's real colors were showing through. The result was lopsided and weird-looking, like he had some kind of scale disease where bits of him were flaking off. But maybe that would make other dragons, especially HiveWings, keep their distance from him.

The day felt endless and yet it was alarmingly soon when Belladonna said, "It's dusk. Time to go."

Blue took one of Swordtail's talons in his and squeezed. "We'll come back for you," he said.

"I know," Swordtail said. "With the Book. I know you can do it."

How do I tell him we're only pretending? Blue thought desperately. *How do I warn him he needs to escape?*

There was no way. Hemlock was standing next to him, watching them like a hawk.

"Right," Blue said. "See you soon, Swordtail."

Sundew led them through the tangled greenery to the back of the greenhouse, facing away from the Hive. Carefully she tapped on a pane of the glass wall, then wedged her claws in the cracks around the edges and levered it out.

"Oh!" Cricket said. "I wondered what you did to get in. Oh dear, isn't that going to be bad for the plants?"

"I don't care two frogs about the plants," Sundew snapped. "Go on."

Cricket ducked through the opening. As Blue crouched to follow her, he saw Belladonna poke Sundew between the shoulders so she'd stand more upright.

"Make us proud," she said to her daughter. "Do not fail. Remember this is what you were hatched to do. Remember how evil they are. Let your rage carry you."

"Yes, Belladonna," Sundew said firmly. "I will not fail."

And then Blue was outside, on one of the neat paths,

standing next to Cricket under a whale-gray sky. Low clouds blotted out the moons and most of the stars. The rainy season was definitely upon them.

Sundew emerged a moment later, sliding the glass back into place behind her. They slipped silently between the greenhouses, weaving toward the front of Wasp Hive. As they got closer, Sundew held up one talon to stop them, then darted to the next corner and peered out at the Hive entrance.

"Two guards," she whispered. "Then this should work." She dug into a pouch and carefully pulled out a wooden box, which she opened to reveal a flower the size of a stingray and the color of moonlight. "Take this," she said to Cricket. "CAREFULLY. Do NOT crush any part of it until you get close to the guards. Then make them look at it, and smash it under their noses."

"What will it do?" Cricket asked, eyeing the beautiful white bloom. "Is it poisonous? Where did it come from? I don't want to poison anyone."

"It won't poison them," Sundew said impatiently. "It'll just knock them out for a while. Don't *you* inhale it, though, or you'll be useless to us."

Cricket held the flower as far away from her as she could, took a deep breath, and stepped out of the cluster of greenhouses. She moved slowly, cautiously hobbling on three legs so she could hold the flower up in one talon with infinite gentleness.

It hit Blue suddenly that this was a dangerous turning

point for Cricket. Up until now, she hadn't been seen with the fugitives. She could have returned home at any moment, slipping back into her ordinary life with a shrug and an excuse about mind control and hunting, or something like that.

But now she was facing real HiveWing guards, who were likely to remember her. Whatever happened next, Cricket would be in trouble — probably really bad trouble.

I'm so sorry, Cricket, Blue thought mournfully. *I wish . . .* His thoughts trailed off. He couldn't say "I wish we hadn't met," because that was the furthest thing from the truth. He wished she was safe, that was all.

Both guards leaped to their feet when they saw her approaching.

"Halt!" one of the guards called. Cricket stopped where she was, halfway to the door, and the guards started whispering to each other.

Blue glanced over at Sundew, who was watching with tension humming from every bone in her body. She looked ready to sprint out there and stab the guards if they so much as sneezed funny.

"So," he said to her. "Your mother said you were hatched for this . . . what's that all about?"

Sundew looked over her shoulder at him incredulously. "Are you seriously making small talk with me right now?"

"No!" he protested. "That wasn't small talk! That was big talk. Actual talk? I actually want to know, I mean."

"It's nothing mystical," Sundew growled. "She wanted a

daughter to carry on our family's legacy. She trained me my whole life for one purpose: this."

"Stealing the Book of Clearsight?"

She narrowed her eyes and paused for a moment. "Sure."

That didn't sound like the whole story, but now the guards were calling Cricket forward again.

"Who are you?" one of them asked. "Why weren't you back by curfew?"

"And what have you got there?" asked the other.

"I found something amazing," Cricket said. "The queen will want to see it right away." It was hard to hear her from here; her voice was much quieter than the guards'. Blue strained to listen.

"Unless it's a map to that blasted flamesilk, she's going to bite your head off," said the first guard. "I'd try the Librarian first if I were you, little dragon. She likes unusual things."

"And she's a bit less murdery than the queen," agreed the second guard, smiling.

Blue felt a sharp twist of guilt. These guards were so friendly. And they were going to be in *so* much trouble if Blue and Sundew got into the Hive and Queen Wasp found out. Would they lose their jobs, or would their punishment be even worse? He worried at one of his claws. Why did it have to be such nice, friendly guards in their way?

A voice in his head that sounded like Luna whispered, *Maybe they're only friendly because they're talking to a*

HiveWing. Have you ever seen a guard be that nice to a SilkWing? Did you even know they COULD smile?

These same guards might have been out for the last three days hunting you. They might have been in the unit that came to shove me in a cage. They might spend their other shifts poking flamesilks with spears to make them burn faster.

Blue shivered, trying to shake off the voice.

"So what is it?" the first guard asked, craning his neck as Cricket approached.

"Isn't it beautiful?" she said. "And it smells like nothing I've ever smelled before." She held out the flower between the two guards, so they both leaned in to sniff it.

And then Cricket squeezed her claws shut, crushing the petals in her grip.

Blue couldn't see exactly when it hit them, but a moment later, the guards crumpled to the ground. One of them hit his head on the Hive wall as he fell and Cricket flinched, reaching toward him too late. She crouched over him, folding in his splayed wings and checking his pulse. The pearlescent flower lay where she'd dropped it on the dirt, its edges brown and wrinkled now.

Sundew sprinted toward the entrance and Blue scrambled to follow her.

"Leave them," Sundew snapped at Cricket. "I don't know how much they got or how long it'll last. If I were you, I would have shoved it right up their snouts."

"Well, I wasn't going to do that," Cricket said crossly.

"And it worked fine, didn't it? What kind of flower is that? Is it related to nightshade?"

Blue bent over the second guard, surreptitiously making sure she was alive (she was) and that she'd fallen in a comfortable position. Sundew strode on without waiting, and both Cricket and Blue had to jump up and run after her, under the malevolent gaze of the giant Queen Wasp statue.

The ground-level doors to the Hive were massive and ostentatiously made of wood, with wasps carved all over them and a profile of the queen on each side. Sundew paused in front of one for a moment, then reached up and raked her claws across the queen's elegant snout, leaving splintery furrows in the wood.

"That was unnecessary!" Cricket protested. "You ruined a really nice carving!"

"Wait until I get to her *actual* face," Sundew snarled. She yanked the door open a crack and peeked through, then shoved it a little farther and squeezed herself through the gap. Blue and Cricket went next, spilling out onto the streets of Wasp Hive's lowest level.

What they saw was a deserted street of warehouses: rows and rows of blocky buildings, each a perfect beige cube reaching from floor to ceiling with one large door. Storage, Blue guessed, although of what exactly he wasn't sure. Each door was marked with a symbol, all of which were unfamiliar to him.

He only had a moment to think about it because Sundew

had already started up the path that led to the next level. Blue ran after her and caught her shoulder.

"WHAT?" she snapped.

"Let Cricket go first," he said. "And walk like a normal SilkWing. We don't charge around with I-have-somewhere-to-be-and-someone-to-set-on-fire faces. Even if your disguise was way better than it is, walking and scowling like that will get you caught in a heartbeat."

"Fine," she said, fuming. "Show me how *you* walk."

Blue turned to Cricket. "Have you been here before?" he asked her. "Do you know where the temple is?"

"Yes," she said. "My class visited the temple last year, and my dad took me a couple of times. It's up in the center of the Hive."

He nodded and stepped back so she could lead the way. Then he ducked his head and trailed after her, looking as harmless and inconspicuous as he could.

Sundew fell into step beside him, growling and muttering under her breath.

"Tuck your chin a little more," Blue suggested softly. "Keep your eyes on the ground. Don't look directly at any HiveWings. Try not to make any noise."

She hissed at him. "You're just like I always pictured SilkWings," she spat. "Subservient worms."

He stopped midstep and frowned at her. "We are *not*," he said. "We're pacifists, yes. And we follow the rules. But it's kept us alive, hasn't it? There's a lot more SilkWings left in the world than LeafWings. I bet," he added hurriedly, since he wasn't actually sure. Up until this morning, he'd have guessed the number of LeafWings left was zero.

But he must have been right, because she spun and glared at him. "If you'd been willing to fight *with* us, we'd all still be alive!"

"Or we'd all be dead," he pointed out. "The significantly more likely scenario."

"I don't know why Willow wants to save your tribe," Sundew snapped. "You're as much of a problem as the HiveWings, with your nodding and smiling and agreeing to let them trample all over you. I'd throw you all into the sea if it were up to me."

Cricket came back around the bend in the tunnel. "Can we try to be a little more quiet?" she said. "We'll be at the residential levels soon."

Which meant more dragons around, and more HiveWings who might overhear Sundew and Blue arguing. He bit back everything he wanted to say to the LeafWing and hurried after Cricket, walking like he normally did around HiveWings, which was a perfectly fine way to walk, he thought, in that it kept you out of trouble, and it was polite, and was Sundew right? Was he confusing obedience and good behavior with letting the HiveWings trample all over him?

What else was I supposed to do, exactly? he wondered. *Stare right at HiveWings, speak up, pick fights? End up on*

Misbehaver's Way all the time like Swordtail? I don't like being yelled at. Acting the way I do has been a good way to avoid that.

Wasp Hive was constructed much like Cicada Hive, but bigger, with wider hallways and tunnels and higher ceilings on each level. The walls of the tunnels were painted with black and yellow stripes or six-sided honeycomb patterns, alternating by level. Weavings and posters of Queen Wasp glared at them around every bend.

The tunnels became busier as they ascended, and Blue drew closer to Cricket with a nervous jittering in his chest. They passed a family of HiveWings arguing over where to go for dinner; a SilkWing carrying a basket of clean blankets; a pair of HiveWings singing and teasing each other about getting the words wrong. Everyone seemed so normal. Their lives were carrying on despite days spent under the queen's mind control. A few of them nodded politely at Cricket, but nobody even glanced at Blue or Sundew.

And then Cricket slowed down, flicking her wings back as she stepped out of the tunnels and onto a polished floor made of real wood, not treestuff. Blue bit back a gasp as he followed her onto the smooth surface. It gleamed in waves of gold and amber and brown, all the way across the vast space in front of them, to the foot of the Temple of Clearsight.

CHAPTER 20

Blue had read that the Temple of Clearsight was the most beautiful structure in the world. He knew that it had been built by Clearsight's grandchildren, then partially destroyed hundreds of years later during the war with the LeafWings, and then moved to be reconstructed here, in the heart of Wasp Hive, where it could be kept safe.

Books had told him that it was made of sixty different kinds of wood, all polished and painstakingly fitted together so it looked like a perfect miracle.

But books couldn't describe the feeling of peace that hit him when he saw it.

The Temple wasn't an enormous towering structure, as he'd always imagined. It was no bigger than the Cocoon, but built with elegant balance and graceful proportions. The columns that lined the front of it were of a wood so dark it was almost black, embedded with tiny flecks of quartz that looked like distant stars. The roof swept into dragon-tail points at each corner, and a central dome was covered in curved golden wood tiles that looked like scales.

It sat quietly in the center of the vast wooden courtyard, surrounded by reflecting pools and little nooks lined with bookshelves. Even at this hour, Blue saw a few dragons curled here and there — on a bench, beside a pool, on a bamboo mat between shelves — all of them reading. Tiny flamesilk lanterns glowed beside them; a few floated on the water of the pools, and others hung from the rafters of the temple.

Another light glowed on the dome, and when Blue looked up, he realized there was a skylight overhead that pierced all the levels, all the way up to the top of the Hive. In the distance, he could see the stars, and the corner of one of the moons shining down on the temple. It must be covered with glass, to keep the rains out, but it was kept so clean it looked like a direct hole to the sky.

The effect was somewhere between magic library and peace garden, and Blue found himself consumed with sadness that he'd never been here before . . . and most likely would never be able to come here again. He wished he could live like these HiveWings, with this place at his claw tips every day. He wished he could work for the Librarian, taking care of the temple and all these books, sweeping the floors and feeding the koi and keeping it beautiful, and never getting yelled at by angry LeafWings or chased by angry queen-zombies.

Instead he was here to destroy this peaceful place, by stealing the one thing it was built around.

They walked toward the temple as quietly as they could. A long carpet of dark blue silk stretched toward the temple door and muffled their talonsteps. Golden dragonflies and green lizards were woven in a subtle pattern through the carpet. It was more beautiful than even Blue's favorite Cocoon weavings, and it felt impossibly ancient.

He glanced sideways at Sundew, to see if the aura of the temple had calmed her down at all. She caught him looking and hurried a scowl back onto her face.

"Don't you think it's amazing?" he whispered.

"No," she whispered back ferociously. She waved her tail at the carvings around them. "How many trees had to die to make this place?"

He didn't answer. He felt in his bones that the temple was worth everything it took to make it — but he could also imagine how hard it was for Sundew, mourning the vast forests of trees that used to cover Pantala. Queen Wasp and the HiveWings had destroyed all of that. Not just the LeafWings' homes, but the spirits of the trees they'd clearly loved, too.

Two HiveWing guards stood on either side of the arched temple door, holding long spears. Blue felt panic stirring in his chest. He tapped Cricket's wing and she paused, turning back to him.

"Sundew and I don't have wristbands," he said softly. "These guards — I think they'll notice."

Cricket nodded as though he'd drawn her attention to an interesting fish. She strolled off the carpet path and over to one of the pools, sitting down beside it and beckoning for Blue and Sundew to do the same.

"Those aren't the only guards," she murmured when they were beside her. She crouched closer to the water. "There's another pair guarding the inner door, and in the room with the Book itself, there's always either two more guards or the Librarian. The Book is in a wooden case, which is locked, and only the Librarian has the key."

"Where is the Librarian if she's not with the Book?" Sundew whispered.

"She lives in a back room of the temple, so she can be near the Book at all times. Once a Librarian is chosen, she never leaves the temple again."

Blue hadn't known that. Yikes. What would it be like to be a dragon who was never allowed to fly or see the sky? Even though the temple was perfect, he couldn't imagine anyone who'd be happy to be trapped in it forever.

"So possibly six guards, plus the Librarian," Sundew muttered. "You know, it would have been quite helpful if you'd mentioned any of this earlier today, during the planning stages."

"I forgot until I saw the temple," Cricket said innocently. "Sorry. I haven't been here in a while."

Sundew growled softly and started poking through her

pouches. Cricket caught Blue's eye and gave him a small, nervous smile.

Blue was sure Cricket had remembered the details of the guards all along, but she was still trying to find a way to get out of stealing the Book. He wished he could do something to help her. He wished he could think of a way to rescue Luna, protect the tribes from an invasion of LeafWings, save the Book of Clearsight, and escape with his friends. Ideally with a minimum of danger, violence, or dragons yelling at him.

His heart stopped suddenly.

Maybe there *was* one possible way out of this. The problem was, it was risky and insane . . . but then, so was stealing the Book of Clearsight.

We could tell the guards, he thought. *We could turn in Sundew and expose her disguise. We give her to Queen Wasp. We tell them where Belladonna and Hemlock are hiding, so the soldiers can swoop in and save Swordtail and catch them.*

We'd be heroes.

Wouldn't we?

Surely capturing three LeafWings and exposing a plot to steal the Book of Clearsight would be the greatest gift they could ever give Queen Wasp. She would HAVE to forgive them for everything else.

Wouldn't she?

He tried to follow that thought. Would she forgive Swordtail for attacking her soldiers? What about Io; could she be forgiven, too? Would Queen Wasp let Blue and Luna go back to their safe, ordinary lives with their mothers? (Maybe if they promised to give all their flamesilk to her?) Would she let Swordtail and Luna be partnered together?

What about his father — would she set him free, too? (If he was even still alive?)

What about all the other flamesilks, if there were others? Would she think three LeafWings were a fair trade for however many SilkWings she had trapped in her flamesilk factory?

If not, could he accept his own freedom and Luna's, knowing he'd left others behind?

Or what if Queen Wasp took the information, destroyed the LeafWings, and then gave them nothing in return?

He might betray Sundew and break his promises, only to end up in a thousand times as much trouble as before. He'd be walking straight into the queen's clutches with no leverage.

And how would we explain Cricket? he realized. *What if telling the queen about the LeafWings . . . and how we found them, and where we've been for the last three days . . . means she figures out that Cricket can't be mind-controlled?*

He needed to keep her out of this, if he did it. He had no idea how. He needed to ask Cricket for advice. He needed to think, but he didn't have time.

Sundew slipped something out of one of her pouches and palmed it. She nodded to Cricket. "Walk straight inside. Don't look guilty."

"What are you going to do?" Cricket whispered.

"Something effective," Sundew hissed. "Let's go!"

Cricket led the way back to the silk path and headed toward the front door of the temple. One of the guards was watching them intently, while the other had his gaze focused on his spear. Blue found it harder and harder to breathe. Should he do it now? He could run forward and throw himself on the guards' mercy. If he was going to betray Sundew, he had to do it *before* they were caught, in order to earn Queen Wasp's gratitude.

But Cricket . . . is this what she would want?

He heard whisking sounds from behind him, like two tiny puffs of air. He glanced back at Sundew. She jerked her chin at him: Keep walking.

Cricket had reached the steps of the temple. This was it. The guards would step forward and demand to see their wristbands. They'd arrest him and Sundew on the spot, and it would only be a moment before they realized Sundew's second pair of wings was fake.

Turn her in. Turn her in now.

Blue took a deep breath and focused on the guard who'd been watching them.

Which is when he realized . . . the guard wasn't moving. His eyes were still fixed on the carpet where they'd been, several steps back. His black wings, spotted with large yellow and red splotches, were halfway raised and his mouth was slightly open as though he'd been about to speak.

But he was as still as the statue of Queen Wasp outside.

As still as the prisoners on Misbehaver's Way.

Blue whipped his head around to the other guard. She was paralyzed the same way, frozen with her spear in her talons and a slight frown on her face.

How did Sundew do that? Only HiveWings had that kind of nerve toxin, and only a few of them. And as far as Blue knew, they could only wield it from up close by stabbing little stingers into their victims.

But Sundew had done it from a distance somehow, and so quietly that none of the dragons in the temple grounds had even looked up from their books. Unless someone looked carefully at the guards, it was possible no one would notice they were paralyzed at all for most of the night.

"Keep moving," Sundew whispered. "You're both staring."

Cricket shook herself and stepped through the archway. Blue wished he could pull her aside and talk. She must be terrified. At least, *he* was terrified.

The room they stepped into was as tranquil as the grounds outside. To their left, a painting of Clearsight took up almost the entire wall, with small lanterns flickering on either side of it. She looked kind and wise, like Blue had always imagined. Offerings were piled below the painting: bundles of wilting marigolds, tiny silver sugar cakes, little weavings of poems.

To their right, the wall was divided into hundreds of small cubbyholes in a honeycomb pattern. Most of the holes held scraps of paper — wishes written by dragon claws, dreams for what they hoped the future would hold, folded and tucked inside. A desk stood in the corner with more paper for anyone who wanted to write one of their own.

Blue imagined all the dragons who had come through here, all their shaking talons asking Clearsight for hope, for luck, for love. HiveWings and SilkWings alike visited the temple and believed in Clearsight. She helped them believe in a better future.

Will they lose that faith without the Book? If we steal it, does this all fall apart? Will anyone come here anymore?

He knew what he wished he could write on one of those scraps of paper. *Please keep my friends safe. Please tell me what to do.*

Cricket didn't pause in the antechamber. She kept walking, toward the inner sanctum. Blue, who had slowed down to look around, was able to watch Sundew as she went past him. He saw her lift something to her mouth and swiftly blow into it. Once. Slight tilt to the right. Twice.

She had uncanny aim. He saw the moment each guard froze — spears slightly lifted, mouths ajar as though they'd sensed a threat and were about to order them to halt.

Whatever she was shooting, the guards were no use to him now. He couldn't hand over Sundew to a pair of statues.

How are we going to get out of this?

There had to be more than just guards between them and

the Book. Maybe the case would be impossible to get into. He really hoped it was.

Cricket stepped between the two guards, casting them each a nervous glance. Neither of them so much as twitched. With a deep breath, she opened the double doors and stepped into the final room.

This one was small and shadowy and perfectly square, like standing inside a wooden box. Blue squinted at the glimmering ceiling and realized that it was inlaid with moonstone stars. The only light in the room was a lantern that hung over the case that held the Book.

Blue caught his breath. He knew it wasn't the Book itself, but the case was carved to look like a book, too . . . a book with dragons sweeping across the cover and clambering around the spine, tails twining into vines, wings spilling into clouds, eyes like suns. The podium holding up the case was shaped like a leafless tree, branches spreading to support the book. For a moment he couldn't understand why Queen Wasp had allowed that here, when trees were forbidden in all other art. Then he realized that the podium was probably as old as the temple, from a time long before Queen Wasp's decrees . . . a time before the forests were destroyed.

He stepped to Cricket's side, and she reached to brush his shoulder with her wing. He knew she felt it, too . . . the sacredness of this place. The magic of the Book of Clearsight.

But if Sundew felt it, she didn't let it slow her down. She shoved past them, darted to the podium, and grabbed the case.

It didn't move.

For a moment she wrestled with it furiously, trying to pick it up, but the case was inextricably joined to the podium — and when she tried to pick *that* up, she discovered it was as firmly rooted to the floor as though it had grown from the wooden planks.

With a growl of frustration, Sundew seized the lock and tried to yank it off. Blue realized that that, too, would fail, and then her next step was going to be smashing the ancient case.

He stepped toward her, trying to raise the nerve to argue with her. And then a voice spoke from the darkest patch of shadows at the back of the room.

"Stop. The Book of Clearsight is not for you."

The Librarian stepped into the light: a tall, bony dragon whose scales were the pale orange of unripe apricots, marked with a zigzagging triangle pattern of black along her spine and tail. She wore a dark silk veil that shrouded her face.

"Little dragons," she hissed. "I've been expecting you."

CHAPTER 21

She knows. She knows everything. The Book told her we would try to steal it, just like I knew it would.

Blue's heart hammered loudly against his ribs. They were trapped.

If I talk fast, maybe I could still turn Sundew in. Maybe they don't know where Belladonna and Hemlock are. The queen might still have mercy on us, if we go quietly and tell her everything.

If I don't fight. If I follow orders. If I keep my head down and say I'm sorry.

But staring into the Librarian's hooded face — he knew he couldn't do any of that.

He couldn't hand the LeafWings over to the queen's cruelty. He couldn't bow his head and go back to being obedient, now that he knew about flamesilks and the mind control and the Chrysalis. After seeing the guards closing in on Luna, he knew he'd never trust the queen again.

The Librarian took another step forward and tilted her head toward Sundew. A hiss escaped from under the veil.

"You're a *LeafWing,*" she snarled.

"You seem surprised," Sundew said mockingly. "I thought you were 'expecting' us. Didn't your precious Book tell you I'd be a LeafWing?"

"A LeafWing, a SilkWing . . . and a HiveWing," the Librarian mused, looking at each of them in turn. She seemed to stare at Cricket the longest, and then suddenly she reached up and ripped off her veil.

Her eyes were blank and white as pearls.

Cricket gasped, flinching backward.

"What strange treason is this?" the Librarian roared. "Why can't I get inside your mind, worm?"

Blue jumped in front of her, not even really knowing what he was doing, only that he needed to be between Cricket and the queen who could see everything.

"I'm the one you're looking for!" he cried. "Blue — Luna's brother. The maybe-flamesilk." He rubbed at his arm so the paint flaked off a bit more and his true colors shone through. "See? I'll turn myself in. Please just let them go."

"Never," the queen snarled in the Librarian's voice. She reached for them with long stingers sliding out from under her claws.

And then Sundew cannoned into the Librarian's side and slammed her into the wall. The Librarian turned with a shriek and slashed at Sundew's face, but Sundew ducked and spun in the same movement, smashing her tail into the Librarian's chest.

The Librarian was bigger and stronger, but the LeafWing fought like a cornered tiger. They wrestled furiously around the tiny space, hissing and clawing and kicking at each other, until Sundew suddenly seized the Librarian's head and threw her to the floor. She caught one of the HiveWing's wrists as the stinging claws came for her again and snapped the arm bone with a brutal crack.

The Librarian screamed again and stabbed her back claws into Sundew's underbelly. They rolled into the wall, leaving a smear of blood along the floor.

What would Clearsight think of us? Blue thought with despair. *Fighting over her legacy like this. What did she see in this vision, and what did she think of it? Was she proud of the Librarian for defending the Book? Did she hate us for trying to steal it?*

He looked up, as though her spirit might be in the moonstones above them, watching the scene unfold.

I'm sorry, Clearsight, he thought. *I never meant to cause trouble like this. I didn't ask for it. I tried to be good.*

Something sparked in the stones, a bright reflection that dazzled his eyes for a moment. He looked down and saw where it had come from — an object on the floor that had caught the light of the lantern.

A key.

The key.

It had been torn from the Librarian's neck in the struggle with Sundew.

He glanced at Cricket, but she was crouched by the door with her talons over her face, and he felt a wave of enormous guilt crash over him. The queen knew Cricket's secret now, and it was all his fault. Her whole life was going to change, even if they did somehow manage to escape this room. She could never go home. The queen would want to find her and figure out why she couldn't control her.

Queen Wasp had taken Luna's life and Blue's life and Cricket's life; she'd taken the free will of her entire tribe; she'd taken the lives of thousands of LeafWings and their beloved trees.

It was time someone took something from her.

Blue snatched up the key and leaped toward the case. With trembling claws, he fit the key in the lock and turned it.

Please forgive me, Clearsight.

He felt the weight of all the rules he'd never broken settling over his scales and sinking into his heart as he opened the lid of the case.

There it was. The real Book of Clearsight. It was much, much smaller than he'd expected, and it wasn't bound in gold either. The leather cover was dyed blue but had no other decoration; it was soft and worn, as though it had been read a million times. The pages inside were ancient, flaking around the edges and yellowed with age. It smelled like books and a far-off hint of pine forest.

He lifted it gently into his talons.

"Wait," Cricket said, and he turned quickly to her, but she wasn't speaking to him. She was talking to Sundew, who had the Librarian pinned against the wall.

"Don't kill her," Cricket said.

"Why *not*?" Sundew demanded. Her stomach was bleeding and her fake wings had been torn off, along with a few of her pouches. She was breathing heavily, raggedly, as was the Librarian.

"Because she's not the one fighting you," Cricket said. She took a step closer and peered into the Librarian's eyes. "The queen is. Does the queen control you . . . all the time? Is that why you always wear the veil?"

The answering glare was as blank and white as ever.

"It would make sense," Cricket said softly. "That's the one way to be sure the Librarian never reveals the Book's secrets. The tribe thinks two dragons share the Book's knowledge — but really, only the queen does, because the Librarian isn't herself anymore."

Blue shuddered. He'd thought being trapped in the temple for her whole life was bad enough — but it was even worse. The Librarian was trapped in her own mind, unable to get out or make any of her own decisions ever again.

Sundew studied the dragon with sharp eyes. "I heard rumors that the HiveWing queen could control her subjects. But I thought they were just stories the old ones made up to frighten us."

The queen in the Librarian barked a laugh. "No," she said, "it's all true. I can control all of them. That's why every dragon in the Hive is on their way to surround the temple right now. I can't move the guards you paralyzed, but I can reach everyone else. The moment you step outside this temple, they will kill you all."

"But you're not sending them inside," Cricket murmured, "because you don't want them to know you control the Librarian this way."

"Let's try something," Sundew said. "HiveWing."

"It's Cricket," Cricket corrected her.

"Cricket," Sundew amended, and something about using her name made the young LeafWing sound like a real dragon for a moment, not just a swiftly moving ball of fury. "Find my pouch with a large *A* marked on the outside."

Cricket searched the pouches on the floor, then edged close enough to Sundew to poke through the pouches still clasped around her.

"Found it," she said.

"Open it *very carefully,*" Sundew instructed, "and take out the jar inside, but *don't open that* until I say so."

"Any chance you could be a little more ominous about

this?" Cricket asked wryly. She drew out the jar and held it between her front talons.

"Now," Sundew said, "I want you to open it and shake it out on her tail, then get as far away as you can."

Cricket upended the jar over the Librarian and jumped back to Blue's side. Two small black ants fell out, landed on the Librarian's tail, and clung to it with their small wriggling legs. Their antennae searched her scales as though puzzled.

"What are you doing?" the queen demanded.

"When you're inside a dragon," Sundew said, "you can feel everything they can, can't you? Or else you wouldn't have screamed when I broke your arm."

"Yes," Cricket answered for her. "I know she leaves dragons when they're hurt or dying."

"Oh, I see your game," the queen scoffed. "I can take a lot more pain than a broken arm, though. I'm not afraid of anything you can do to this body."

"That may be," said Sundew, "but I'm guessing that's because you've never been bitten by a bullet ant before."

Blue had never even heard of a bullet ant, and from her silence, he guessed the queen hadn't either. They all watched the tiny ants circle for a moment and then start climbing, up and up the Librarian's tail and along her spine. The Librarian didn't move and didn't move and didn't move — and then, as one of them ran toward her neck, she flicked her wing instinctively to knock it off her.

Instead it latched on to the wingtip and bit down with little pincer jaws.

The scream that came out of the Librarian was like nothing Blue had ever heard before. She collapsed as though her bones had melted, and Sundew dropped her to the floor, where the dragon lay shaking all over and screaming that terrible scream.

Sundew stepped over the patches of blood on the floor, took the jar from Cricket, and neatly scooped up the two ants without letting them touch her. She screwed the lid back on very tightly and packed it away again in her pouch.

Then she crouched by the Librarian's head and peeled open one of her eyelids.

"Had enough?" she asked the white eyeball beneath. "This pain is going to last half a day, just so you know. It's not stopping anytime soon."

"I'll *kill you* for this," the queen hissed, and then, abruptly, the eye rolled back and became a normal eye. Dark orange irises and dilated pupils stared up at Sundew.

The Librarian stopped screaming.

"You — you did it," she said in a strained voice. "Ow. Ow. *Owwww* I know it's worth it but *oowwww* it's hard to really know that right now. I tried once before to hurt myself badly enough that she'd set me free, but it didn't work. This is so much worse, though." She sat up, holding her wing out at an awkward angle and moaning softly.

"Is she really gone?" Sundew asked.

The Librarian nodded. "Yes. For the first time in years." She inhaled and exhaled slowly, then glanced at her wing and winced again.

"If she's really gone, then here," Sundew said, digging out a pair of dark green leaves from another pouch. "Chew this and spit it on the spot where the ant bit you. It'll deaden the nerve and should dull the pain for a while, at least."

"*Thank* you," the Librarian said. She put the leaves in her mouth and started chewing.

"It'll also make your tongue feel very weird," Sundew added. "Just to warn you."

"Hrmgrah," the Librarian agreed, making a face.

"Has the queen been controlling you all this time?" Cricket asked.

The Librarian nodded, talking awkwardly around the leaves in her mouth. "Ever since the initiation ceremony. I woke up from the ritual with her inside my head. When she sleeps, she makes me sleep. She's always in there." She shuddered. "I was so proud to be chosen. I never knew what it would mean — I had no idea she did this."

"That's horrible," Blue said softly. The Book felt fragile and warm in his talons. He wanted to protect it with all his heart, and he was sure anyone who wanted to be the Librarian must feel the same way. They didn't need to be brainwashed into it. Queen Wasp didn't even give them a chance to show their loyalty; she forced it upon them instead.

"She'll be back in your head as soon as she thinks it's safe," Cricket pointed out.

"I know," the Librarian said, nodding. "But even a moment to be myself is more than I ever thought I'd have again." She spread the leaf paste over the edge of her wing, and the pain lines around her eyes relaxed. "Oh, thank Clearsight."

Sundew glanced across at Blue. "So," she said. "We have the Book, which is great. But we're surrounded by Hive zombies who would really like to kill us. Which is less great."

"Can you throw bullet ants at them?" he asked. "Or blow-dart them?"

"I don't have many more blow darts," she said. "Or enough bullet ants for everyone in the whole Hive, although that would be my kind of revenge." She started collecting the pouches she'd lost during the fight, checking their contents, and resettling them around her. She kicked the pair of fake wings into the corner.

"I'll help you," the Librarian said quietly.

"You will?" Blue said, surprised. "But we're stealing the Book. Your whole purpose in life is to keep it safe."

The Librarian looked at the Book in his talons, and her eyes were sadder than any dragon's he'd ever seen before.

"I think it's time someone else knew the Book's secrets," she said. "And if the queen kills me for it, I'll still be better off than I was this morning."

"How can you help us?" Sundew asked practically. "Is there another way out of here?"

"Not exactly," she answered. "But I can get you up to the dome, at least."

The Librarian got to her feet, wincing from the other wounds Sundew had given her, and limped to the back corner where she'd first appeared. She couldn't put any weight on her broken arm, and Blue wondered if Sundew felt anywhere near as terrible as he did about that.

A secret panel in the wooden wall slid aside at her touch, and they all followed her through into the Librarian's quarters. Compared to the other rooms of the temple, this one felt cold and empty. A bamboo mat in the corner and a small bookshelf were the only two items in the room.

It looks like a prison cell, Blue thought. The position of Librarian was supposed to be the tribe's greatest honor. But instead it was a trick, a snare set to trap one of the brightest minds of the HiveWings and keep her useless forever.

Another panel slid aside to reveal a spiral staircase going up. They climbed after the Librarian, rounding the last curve to find themselves in an attic that smelled of wood chips and boiled silk. The underside of the dome curved over their heads, and Blue saw a door on one side that led to a small balcony.

"What was this for?" Cricket asked, blinking around at the dust and abandoned boxes. She picked up an odd-looking tool that looked a bit like a curved dragon tongue.

"I think Librarians used to make books up here," the Librarian said wistfully.

"Oh," Cricket said. She ran one claw along the top of a dusty table. "That's what I thought they did, too."

"Not anymore. Not in a long time." The Librarian led the way to the balcony door and peeked out through the glass. "Oh dear."

Sundew edged in beside her and looked out as well. "Hrmph," she snorted. "I can take them."

"Every HiveWing in Wasp Hive?" Cricket said. "You are terrifying, but I still find that a little hard to believe."

"Unless you have something else alarming in one of those pouches?" Blue said hopefully.

Sundew tapped the floor thoughtfully with one claw. "Maybe," she said. "But I'd need fire to make it work."

"I have fire!" Cricket said. She scrambled to pull out the little stone jar with the flamesilk thread inside and tipped it to show Sundew. "Would this work?"

The LeafWing's eyes gleamed. "I think so."

"Be careful," the Librarian pleaded as Sundew took the jar in her claws. "Don't set the temple on fire. You can have the Book, but please leave the temple."

Sundew hesitated, as though she would have loved to set the whole Hive on fire. But after a moment, she nodded. "Stand back."

She took a branch covered with long, waxy-looking, red-brown leaves out of another pouch. With careful, slow movements, she dipped the point of each one into the jar until it touched the flamesilk and caught fire. A bright flame flared for a moment on each leaf, then vanished into curls of reddish smoke. Sundew handed the jar back to Cricket and opened the door to the balcony, holding the burning branch out away from her.

Now Blue could see the temple grounds — and the HiveWings who covered every inch of space between the temple and the door. Orange, yellow, red, and black scales rippled like a vast sea of poisonous snakes. As Sundew stepped onto the balcony of the dome, every head snapped toward her in unison, blank eyes latching on to her.

One branch of burning leaves seemed very small in the face of all those talons and teeth and claws. Blue shivered, and he felt Cricket put one wing over his back and lean against him.

I should be comforting her, he thought. *I'm the one who's ruined her life.* But if she was still willing to be close to him, perhaps she forgave him — perhaps she still liked him anyway.

Sundew hissed at the crowd of HiveWings. Smoke was rolling off the leaves now, growing thicker and thicker and redder and darker. She glanced at it one more time, checking that it was all smoke and no flames, and then she threw it with all her might directly into the middle of the watching dragons.

It hit a yellow-black dragon, who shook it off and hopped

away with a yelp. The dragons closest to him began coughing. They sank to the ground, one by one, hacking and wheezing, as the smoke billowed up and out, swallowing the dragons around it.

But it wasn't enough. For each HiveWing incapacitated by the smoke, there were five more still grimly standing between them and the only way out.

"**Capture the flamesilk,**" they intoned. "**Kill the other two.**"

The buzz of their wings filled the chamber as dragon after dragon rose into the air and surged toward the dome.

Blue's heartbeat surged with panic.

Wait . . . that's not the only way out.

He looked up. There was the skylight, and the stars far above them. The hole was barely large enough for a dragon to fit through, but he and Cricket and Sundew were all fairly small. If they could break the glass at the top, they could at least get outside the Hive.

"Up!" he shouted, grabbing Cricket's arm and pointing. "We can go out the skylight!"

She followed his gaze, then looked back at him. "What about you?" she asked. "How do we get you up there?"

Oh. He twisted to look back at his wingbuds, as though perhaps they'd have magically turned into wings in the last several heartbeats.

"We'll carry him." Sundew threw open her wings and

leaped up off the balcony. "Let's go — and *hold on to that book.*" She started smashing HiveWings aside with her tail and talons.

He clutched the Book to his chest. Cricket whirled around in a panic and grabbed a long, twisted silk rope from one of the tables. She and the Librarian threw it around Blue's shoulders and chest and tied it fast. They each took an end and ran to the balcony.

I wish I had wings, Blue thought, closing his eyes. *I wish I were more than a dead weight for my friends to drag around.*

The rope jerked tight under his arms and he was dragged smack into the balcony railing, nearly tumbling over it, before the rope steadied and he felt himself lifted up, up into the air. He tilted sideways almost immediately as the Librarian's bigger wings soared ahead and Cricket faltered under his weight. Then Sundew swept up beside her and took the rope as well, tugging him upright.

All he could do was dangle helplessly, holding on to the Book for dear life. Right below his talons, the smoke still billowed and the seething mass of HiveWings snapped and churned. Three of them surged toward his feet and he kicked at them frantically.

"Ack! Help!" he shouted.

A cascade of little red centipedes poured down from above him. Each dragon they struck let out a shriek of alarm or pain and dropped away, clawing at his face.

The dome was shrinking below him. Blue looked up and saw Sundew, then Cricket duck into the skylight hole. The Librarian was hovering beside it, taking up the slack in his rope, waiting to let them go first.

And then suddenly she looked down at him, and her eyes were white again.

"Nice try," she said.

"Cricket!" Blue screamed. The Librarian's claws slashed through the rope connecting him to his friends. He tumbled sideways, jerking to a stop at the end of the severed rope, but feeling the knots start to slip loose around his chest.

Cricket shot back down the shaft and flew at the Librarian's face. The Librarian ducked away, gave her an evil grin, and let Blue's rope fall from her hands.

His stomach flipped as he started to plummet, then jerked to a stop again as Cricket caught the end of the rope. But she wasn't strong enough to lift him alone. Even with her wings beating as hard as she could, they were both sinking down toward the HiveWings.

"Cricket!" he yelled. "You have to go without me! They won't kill me, but they're under orders to kill you. Take the Book and go!"

"I'm not —" she started to shout back, but he was already tossing the Book up toward her.

She had to drop the rope to catch it. She did it instinctively, as he'd known she would; she was as well trained to love the Book as he was. All their lives, they'd known it was the most precious object in their world. She'd reach for it without thinking, even if her conscious mind would have chosen to save Blue instead.

As he fell, as a thousand claws reached up to seize him, he saw Cricket clutch the Book to her chest and shout his name. He saw Sundew pummel the Librarian hard enough to knock the HiveWing out of the air. He saw Sundew grab Cricket's arm and pull her away, and he saw Cricket's last look back, and he saw their tails disappearing away up the skylight.

And then all he could see was orange and yellow and black and red, as the talons closed around him, and the queen had him in her grasp at last.

PART THREE

METAMORPHOSIS

CHAPTER 22

Blue was dragged roughly through the Hive tunnels. The queen had dispatched five dragons to take him away, which was four too many for a dragon as harmless as Blue. They kept stepping on one another's toes and growling and bumping wings and all trying to hold on to his elbows at once, which he definitely did not have enough elbows for them to do.

Their eyes were their own again, so the queen had apparently decided she didn't need to be concerned about Blue anymore. Which meant all the rest of her brainwashed subjects were off hunting for Cricket and Sundew.

Did they get away? Are they all right?

He worried and worried about this as he was shoved between blustering HiveWings. They were descending through the levels, but to where, Blue had no idea. He kept expecting the queen herself to appear. He jumped each time they turned onto a level with black and yellow stripes.

They reached the bottom level with no sign of her, though. The guards pushed him out into the streets of warehouses he'd seen on the way in. One flicked her wings at him and he realized the tips were sharp little stingers, probably venomous. Another kept baring his fangs, so those could probably kill him with just a scratch, too.

Where are they taking me? Blue wondered, staring at the blank walls as they marched past. *How am I going to be punished?* He remembered the tortured faces on Misbehaver's Way and shivered.

This feeling — of being in trouble, of having done something wrong, of knowing so many dragons were angry at you — this was everything he'd tried to avoid his whole life. He *hated* it. He wanted to go back to his desk and get all the answers right on the quiz and have the teacher smile and say, "Nice work, Blue." He wanted to dig out his Good Citizenship award and show it to these HiveWings to prove he wasn't as bad a dragon as they thought he was.

But . . .

I'm not. *I mean, I've done all the things they think I have. But that doesn't make me bad.*

He clung to that thought like it was a harness and someone was lifting him through the sky. *Yes, I broke HiveWing rules. But I had good reasons to. I'm not trying to hurt anyone — I just wanted to find my sister and set her free. Queen Wasp didn't have to be so secretive and menacing and terrifying in the first place.*

The HiveWings stopped suddenly in front of a blocky building that looked exactly the same as all the others. The only difference was a carving on the gray door, this time of a small lantern, little sparks coming off it to indicate it was glowing.

Blue suddenly had a guess about where he was going.

One of the HiveWings pounded on the door in a series of knocks: three quick, four slow, two quick. After a moment, it was flung open, revealing a wizened, mostly orange dragon with black patches here and there. He gestured for them to come inside and slammed the door behind them.

Shapes loomed around them in the dim interior — giant crates, as far as Blue could tell, stacked up to the ceiling. They maneuvered between these: left, right, right, left again, until Blue lost track. But he thought they were about in the center of the warehouse when they reached a wide open, well-lit space surrounded by a circle of watchful HiveWing guards.

At first, Blue thought they were staring into empty space, or perhaps at one another across the way. It wasn't until he got closer that he realized they were looking down . . . down through an enormous sheet of glass at a stone cavern below the floor. That was also where all the light was coming from.

The dragon from the door shoved him past the guards before Blue could take a close look. But he caught a glimpse of cauldrons that seemed to be full of molten gold and dragons moving between them.

Shortly beyond the circle of guards, the old dragon shoved aside a crate and heaved open a trapdoor underneath, revealing a set of stairs descending into the earth. He started down and Blue's guards nudged him into following.

Lamps punctuated the turns of the stairwell, but they seemed unnecessary; the glow from the light at the bottom of the stairs could have illuminated a stairwell three times as long. Blue had to shield his eyes and blink hard for a moment when they reached the bottom. His head ached as though he'd walked right up to the sun.

"What's this?" a gruff voice demanded while Blue's eyes were still adjusting.

"The flamesilk everyone's been looking for," came the answer.

"Can't be." Someone poked his shoulder. "Wrong color. Aaaack! Did his scales just fall off?!"

"It's . . . paint or something?" said another dragon. She started scraping at his scales with her claws. "Eeeeeyeesh, look, it comes off. Fetch a scrubber."

"Wait, *this* little scrap is the dragon we've been hunting across the savanna?" someone else chimed in. "He's not a flamesilk! He hasn't even got wings *or* silk yet."

"We knew that, idiot," said the first voice. "He's just *probably* a flamesilk. We have to keep an eye on him in case he is."

"Oh, boring. When's his Metamorphosis?"

"Dunno. Soon, I reckon."

Blue's heart gave a nervous jump. It *was* soon — really, really soon. He kept forgetting to worry about it. His was supposed to start right after Luna's ended. Would he have to spin his cocoon here? Far away from his mother, his Hive, and the Cocoon where he'd always expected to transform?

He felt his wrists gingerly. They seemed normal . . . no pain, no burning feelings. What if he went through his Metamorphosis and *wasn't* a flamesilk? What would the queen do with him then?

Sending him back home to Burnet and Silverspot didn't seem like the most likely option, somehow.

Someone arrived with scrubbing brushes and briskly scoured the paint off his scales. He stood still and didn't struggle. There wasn't much point in being a different color now, after all.

Besides, his eyes were finally adjusting to the light, and he was transfixed by his new surroundings. They were standing on a ledge at the bottom of the stairs, looking out over the cave he'd glimpsed from above. If he looked up, he could see the green-yellow-orange glow of the eyes watching through the glass ceiling.

More HiveWing guards were stationed down here, peering into the cauldrons and occasionally poking the working SilkWings with their tails or spears. Several of those SilkWings were ordinary dragons, doing ordinary work:

transporting cargo, carrying food and water, cleaning, putting out fires.

But the rest . . .

The rest were flamesilks.

Blue counted nine at first glance. They were scattered across the cavern, each on his or her own rocky perch. Four of them were asleep; two were eating. The other three had their wrists extended, fiery silk threads spilling out into the massive stone cauldrons set below them.

He stared at them, trying to guess which one was his father. The large, bored one who looked like he might fall asleep and topple into his own silk fire? The lime-striped one who was nibbling a persimmon as though it had greatly offended him, but he'd decided to eat it anyway? The one with pale pink wings whose talons twitched constantly in his sleep?

And then, at last, he saw what he most wanted to see: an incandescent gold cocoon, tucked in its own hollow on the far side of the cave.

Luna.

He took a step toward her, hesitated, and looked back at the guards. The scrubbing brushes had been carted away. His original escorts had gone back up the stairs, leaving the one guard from the door and the three who'd come to investigate his arrival. These four were all leaning on their spears or chewing on strips of dried gazelle, chatting to one another.

One of them noticed his glance. She grinned at him with all her teeth.

"Go ahead," she said. "Get used to the place. I gather you're going to be here for a while."

The others chuckled, although Blue didn't think it was really the most clever menacing comment she could have come up with.

He took another few steps away, but they all went back to their conversation and ignored him.

I guess I really can walk around. He'd expected a cage, or a paralyzing nerve toxin, or some kind of beating, perhaps. But maybe this was the queen's way of letting him know how unimportant he was. Or how trapped . . . he could wander as far as he liked, because there was nowhere to go and no way out.

Blue clambered down from the ledge, hopping from rocky foothold to craggy stalagmite until he reached the same level of the cavern as Luna's cocoon. Behind him, he heard the HiveWing guards laughing, and he wondered if they were mocking his winglessness.

Well, I won't be wingless much longer. His biggest fear — his Metamorphosis — was only days away. It didn't seem fair that he'd have to deal with that, too, in the middle of everything else terrifying.

His route to the cocoon led him past the bored-looking flamesilk, who glanced up with a spark of interest in his eyes.

"Hey," said the flamesilk in a lazy but commanding voice. "Who are you?"

Blue hesitated. He didn't want to alienate anyone who might be a friend down here — and for all he knew, this could be Admiral.

"I'm Blue," he said. "My sister's in that cocoon over there."

"Ohhhhh," said the other dragon. He shook one of his wrists vigorously, watched the silk spool for a moment, then turned his gaze back to Blue. "Right. The new blood."

"Did you know we were coming?" Blue asked.

"Some of us hoped," he answered. "Ad's been counting the days." He nodded over at Luna's cocoon, and Blue finally noticed that there was a dragon sitting next to it.

Ad . . . Admiral.

Blue moved forward, studying his father. Admiral was a shimmering blue green, somewhere between Blue's bright morpho butterfly blue and Luna's elegant caterpillar color. He had darker purple streaks along his wings and matching spots of white on each one. His eyes were brown with a faint gold tinge to them, and he traced one claw around and around in an infinity loop on the ground as he watched Luna's cocoon.

For a long moment, he didn't look up, even when Blue stopped right across the cocoon from him. But at last Admiral raised his head and saw his son.

His eyes lit up.

"You're the other one!" he said. "You're early!"

"Oh . . . yes," Blue said. He gestured vaguely at the guards on the entrance ledge. "I was, uh . . . " *Well, captured, I guess.*

"I'm so glad you're here," Admiral said warmly. "I'm your father. I'm Admiral."

"I know," Blue said. "My name's Blue. Wait — you're *glad* we're here?" *Glad that Luna and I are trapped down here, just like you?*

"We have such an important job," Admiral said, rubbing his wrists. "So important! When do you think she'll wake up?"

Blue calculated backward. "Not tomorrow night, the night after that," he said. "That would be five days from when she went in."

Admiral nodded. "I can't believe one of mine is a flamesilk," he said. "And maybe both! Clubtail was taken out to have eggs a year before me, but neither of his had any flame whatsoever." His chest swelled with pride.

"But . . . " Blue looked around at the cavern again. "Isn't it . . . sorry, but isn't it kind of terrible? Being a flamesilk?"

"Terrible! Gosh, no," said Admiral. "I mean. I'd make some changes. I'm working on that."

"Working on what?" Blue asked. Was his father also part of a secret resistance?

Admiral waved at a rocky nest nearby, where piles of papers were neatly stacked along the stone shelves around it, each stack tied with a pale gold thread. "Changing the system!" he said. "Solving problems!"

"With . . . papers?" Blue squinted at them.

"They're letters," Admiral said patiently. "My copies of them, obviously. I write one to the queen every seven days, outlining the current problems I see and offering proposals for fixing them."

"Oh," Blue said, impressed. That was a lot of letters. "So she writes back? Or she comes to visit you?"

"Well, neither," said Admiral. "But she's very busy. Lots of Hives to run. Two tribes to manage. LeafWings to guard against. The dip in flamesilk production is just one of her many problems. Which I'm going to help solve!"

"There's a flamesilk shortage?" Blue said.

"No!" said Admiral unconvincingly. "And it's not a problem, because we're solving it. With her help," he added, nodding at Luna's cocoon, "and hopefully yours!"

Blue stared at him in alarm. "Was this your idea?" he asked. "Fathering potential flamesilks so more dragons could be trapped in this cave?"

"Well, no," his father admitted. "The queen came up with that. Very clever. And works out well for me because (a) better company and (b) more signatures for my petitions!"

"Petitions," Blue echoed.

"*My* suggestion was longer rest cycles between production and more citrus in our diet. Which we got! The citrus, I mean. Tangerines for everyone with every meal. Every.

Meal. Really makes you wish for a lemon or a banana now and then. Good for us, though! She vetoed the longer rest cycles. That's all right."

"So . . . what else have you changed?" Blue asked.

"Oh, lots of things," Admiral said with a modest shrug. "I started almost as soon as I got here, once I realized there was a system and a way to accomplish real change within that system."

"Yeah?" Blue was intrigued. Doing things inside the rules . . . that sounded like something he could handle a bit better than Swordtail and Luna's revolution. Maybe his father could teach him how to do it. Maybe there was a way to be a good dragon, stay out of trouble, and still make things better.

Although. Tangerines were not quite the epic change Blue wanted to see in the world.

"Can I read some of your letters?" Blue asked.

"Of course!" Admiral leaped excitedly to his feet and bounded over to his alcove. He came back with an armful of papers and laid them out in front of Blue.

"Wait . . . is this flamesilk?" Blue asked, touching the thread that tied one stack together. He squinted at it, puzzled. "Why isn't it setting the letters on fire?"

Admiral laughed. "This is great!" he said. "I feel like such a dad! I get to teach you so much! There are different kinds of flamesilk, buddy. It wouldn't be much good to us if it *only* burned everything in sight. We need the kind for building webs, too. Something we can sleep on. Stickier silk for climbing with. We can choose which kind we produce." He tipped his wrists up, flexed his claws, and glanced at the nearest guard, who wasn't paying any attention to them. "Um . . . I'll show you later. Not a good idea to waste any silk, you know."

Blue flipped through the letters, thinking about this new information. It was quite a relief to hear that he wouldn't accidentally set the world on fire every time he used his silk. Maybe going through Metamorphosis with his flamesilk parent nearby actually was a good idea.

Maybe the queen was trying to help me and Luna by bringing us here.

And yet . . . he glanced around at the cavern. The flamesilk dragons looked fine. They didn't seem miserable. But if they were so important and the queen was willing to listen to them — why were they kept imprisoned in this cavern? Why were they such a big secret — at least, from most other SilkWings?

Why weren't they allowed to choose this life — or something else?

"Father," Blue said. "Do any flamesilks ever leave this place?"

"Sure," Admiral said unexpectedly. "I mean, *I* left, didn't I? Long enough to have you!"

"Right, but — how long was that for?" Blue asked. "Did

you get to decide when and where you went? Or who you were with?"

"Well, no," Admiral said. "But it was a lovely visit. Cicada Hive is so pretty. That Mosaic Garden, wow."

"Have you gone anywhere else?" Blue asked. "How often do you leave?"

"Ummmm." Admiral scrunched up his snout as though he was counting in his head. Blue leaned forward hopefully. "Right. That was it, actually. That . . . one time."

"In your whole life?" Blue asked, dismayed. "You've spent your whole life in this one cave?"

"Oh, no," said Admiral. "I grew up in Hornet Hive. Didn't move here until my Metamorphosis. Went into my cocoon there, woke up here! Quite a surprise. Really delightful, once I realized how important we are and what an honor this is."

Blue regarded him skeptically. "Haven't you ever asked the queen if you could leave?"

"Sure," Admiral said. "That stack on the end is vacation time requests and field trip proposals and some of my theories on how more flying might improve our silk production. Afraid I don't have any good evidence for that, though! More of a wishful-thinking kind of hypothesis. I realize that. Completely reasonable that she always says no."

Blue picked up another letter. His father's handwriting was neat and very legible. His spelling was perfect, his sentences concise and convincing. This one was a politely worded outline of a proposal for a skylight or anything like a window, suggesting that a little sun on their scales might also be beneficial for their silk output.

There were several letters below it along the same lines, with modifications to the proposal to make it as cost-effective or easy to accomplish as possible. One even included a drawing of a sequence of mirrors that could bring the sunshine to them via a long path of reflections.

Blue could clearly see, from looking at the cavern, that every one of these letters had been ignored.

"Who's the midget?" one of the other flamesilks — the one with green stripes — shouted at Admiral. "Is that your offspring? He's scrawny like you! Is he a vacuous earthworm, too?"

"Mind your own business!" Admiral roared. "He doesn't need to hear your toad-sucking voice!"

"Better than your millipedian claw-waving folderol!" the dragon yelled. "Are you poisoning his ears with your stupid ideas already? Did you tell him the queen chews up all your letters and spits them out? Because they're the dumbest things she's ever read?"

"That's not true! And it would help if CERTAIN DRAGONS weren't such TROLLS about everything!" Admiral yelled back. "As IF anyone would EVER believe that LESS citrus might be helpful! I swear," he said to Blue, "I think he sneaks over and reads my letters just so he can write ones arguing for the exact opposite of anything I propose."

"Who *is* that?" Blue asked, wide-eyed. "Why is he so mean?"

"That's Fritillary," Admiral growled. "He just wants everyone to hate the world as much as he does. Don't talk to him." He made an effort to smile at Blue. "See, this is why I'm glad you're here. It'll be nice to have someone new to talk to! Someone with a little perspective. Someone who knows how to look on the bright side. You do know how to look on the bright side, don't you?"

"I guess I do," Blue said. Wasn't that what he'd spent his whole life doing? Finding a silver lining to any cloud? Convincing himself that there was nothing wrong with how SilkWings were treated. Ignoring Luna's complaints. Assuming that their safety was worth sacrificing a few freedoms.

He looked down at the letters in his talons again.

After all these years of trying to work with Queen Wasp's rules, in Queen Wasp's hive, under Queen Wasp's control, had his father accomplished no more than a handful of tangerines?

Had he accepted the loss of all his freedom because he thought he could find a way to make it work?

Didn't he want more out of his life? Didn't he want to fight back?

Do I?

It was like Cricket said — some rules were unjust. And some things were more important than following the rules.

He put down the letters and rested his front talons on Luna's warm golden cocoon. It was very hot, but it didn't burn him.

This is not going to be our life, Luna, he promised silently. *I won't spend the next hundred years writing fruitless letters. Father's way, obeying the system, hasn't worked.*

So we'll find another.

Or we'll burn it all down.

CHAPTER 23

Admiral found a place for Blue close to his own nest: a hollow in the rock large enough for a dragon to settle into, with several crannies in the wall where he could keep things, if he ever had any things. (Apparently there was a request process involving a number of forms.)

At first the hollow seemed a little too big to Blue . . . and then he felt a shiver across his wings as he realized his father was thinking of Blue's future, and how much bigger he might grow. Admiral had chosen a nest where Blue could spend the entire rest of his life.

But I'm not going to. That's not going to happen.

He tried to believe it as he lay down to sleep, but his dreams were restless and unhappy. He dreamed of getting his talons stuck in a crevice and trying to pull them out. He dreamed of letters piling up around his claws. He dreamed of Clearsight, sitting on the steps of her temple, looking down at him with enormous disappointment.

When he woke up, his wrists were itching.

Am I going to be a flamesilk?

The cavern was quiet. Most of the regular SilkWings were gone, and seven of the flamesilks were asleep. Blue climbed down to Luna's cocoon and leaned against it. He wished he could talk to his sister. Or Cricket.

Is Cricket all right? Did she escape?

Or . . .

His mind shied away from the alternative. He couldn't imagine the world without Cricket in it. He couldn't imagine his own life without Cricket in it.

A HiveWing guard came stomping over and Blue sat up hopefully. Maybe this dragon could tell him something about what had happened.

But the guard went right past him and jabbed Admiral in the side with one of her sharp claws. Admiral woke up with a snort, blinking rapidly.

"Time to spin," the guard snarled. "You're late."

"So sorry," Admiral said, rubbing his eyes. "You're quite right. I've been a little discombobulated by the arrival of my children, of course. Otherwise I'm always on time, aren't I? Very punctual dragon, that's me. Very little reminding required. Don't you agree?"

"Quit your yapping and excusin'," the guard grumbled. "Silk. Now." She dragged a cauldron out from under Admiral's nest and thunked it into place right below Admiral.

"Of course." Admiral held out his arms and closed his eyes. A long, dragging moment passed, and then a thread of flame emerged from one wrist. It spiraled down into the cauldron, pouring slowly, like cold honey. It was another long moment before a second thread appeared from the other wrist, and this one seemed dimmer than the first.

The guard scowled at the slow-moving silk, and Blue wondered what she was feeling. Was she worried about what would happen to the Hives if there was a flamesilk shortage? Or did the guards get punished if the flamesilks didn't meet a certain quota? Or was there any chance she was actually concerned about the dragons under her charge?

What a weird life this would be, he thought. *Every morning you wake up and go through a secret warehouse staircase into an underground cavern. You spend the day poking other dragons to make them work and standing guard so they can't leave.*

Isn't it boring? It must *be boring. Especially for the ones sitting in a circle in the dark warehouse, staring through the glass all day.*

The HiveWing turned to leave and Admiral's eyes popped open.

"Sandfly," he said quickly, "have you met my son? This is Blue. He says my daughter's name is Luna. And she'll be coming out tomorrow night. With her wings! And silk to add to the quota. Isn't that wonderful?"

Sandfly looked down at Blue and the gold cocoon. She didn't say anything for a few heartbeats. Her scales were pale yellow and speckled everywhere with tiny black spots, like a swarm of flies in the desert; it was easy to see how her parents had chosen her name.

"They're very young," she said at length.

Blue couldn't tell if she was feeling sorry for them, with a life of imprisonment lying ahead, or if she was pleased at the idea of how much silk they'd be able to produce over the length of that life.

"Excuse me," he said. "I'm sorry to bother you, but I was wondering . . . do you know what happened to the dragons who stole the Book of Clearsight yesterday?"

Sandfly leaped backward as though he'd jabbed her with an electric eel. "WHAT?" she roared. Half of the sleeping heads in the cavern popped up and turned their way. "That didn't happen! No one would dare!"

"Oh . . ." Blue trailed off. It hadn't occurred to him that the queen would lie to everyone about this — and make the Librarian lie, too — but now that he thought about it, he wasn't surprised. Losing the Book of Clearsight would be pretty terrible for morale. She could easily just close up the case and pretend it was still in there. That is, if Cricket and Sundew did escape with the Book.

"What a HORRIBLE thing to say!" Sandfly barked. Behind her, Admiral gave Blue a pained "fix this" expression.

"I'm sorry!" Blue said. "I'm so sorry. I meant, the dragons who *tried* to steal the Book of Clearsight. Of course the

Librarian stopped them. Of course it's safe. Um. Those dragons, though? Do you know if they got away?"

Sandfly was shaking out her wings as though they were crawling with caterpillars. "Ugh," she said. "I'm going to have nightmares for days. What kind of traitor would steal the Book of Clearsight? That's so obviously wrong."

So obviously wrong. Blue stared down at his talons — the talons that had unlocked the case and lifted out the precious book. *It was me. I'm the traitor.* But the Librarian had wanted them to have it, when she was herself. She'd said it was time for other dragons to know the Book's secrets.

He decided not to mention that, in case Sandfly had another heart attack. He was also carefully avoiding the fact that one of the criminal dragons was a LeafWing, in case that wasn't public knowledge and might set off a riot.

"Right," he said, trying one more time. "So the queen really wanted to catch them . . . but did she?"

"I have no idea," Sandfly said. She settled her wings again. "I was down here until midnight last night. No one at home mentioned any public executions yesterday, but maybe they'll be held today or tomorrow."

Blue managed not to gasp. Or burst into tears.

She assumes they were caught because she's a HiveWing. But she doesn't actually know. They might be safe.

Or they might be in another prison somewhere, waiting to be executed.

If only he could escape and go look for them. But he didn't have Cricket's clever ideas or Swordtail's impulsive courage or Sundew's helpful pouches of weapons. He was just a little wingless dragon stuck in a cavern of flame.

Still. He could at least *try*.

Blue spent the rest of the day exploring every corner of the flamesilk cave. He walked the entire perimeter, clambering up and down the rocks wherever he needed to. The guards by the staircase gave him weird looks as he went by, but they didn't stop him. Nobody stopped him, although he got the distinct feeling that all the flamesilks were watching him whenever they thought he wasn't looking.

There were three female flamesilks and seven males, most of them quite a lot older than Blue. He guessed that Admiral might be the youngest one the queen had. A couple of them seemed to stay in their nests all the time, cycling between sleeping, eating, and producing silk, without ever moving from their spots. He saw a few others get up and fly around, although they couldn't go far. There was enough room to spread their wings, but they couldn't soar, and there wasn't any wind to ride.

If this is my future, will I never get to fly in the clouds? How will I even learn to fly properly, without any wind currents down here?

The guards and the flamesilks seemed to have a very precise schedule in their heads. They rotated production cycles and rest intervals in careful synchronization, so there were always at least three flamesilks working, even in the middle of the night.

Blue had covered almost the entire cave by the time his father's turn at the cauldron was done. There were a few ledges and corners that he hadn't figured out how to climb up to yet, but he had walked between all the stalagmites and surreptitiously poked his nose in every large gap in the rocks. So far he hadn't found any secret passages, though.

From across the cave, he saw Sandfly drop a bucket of food beside Admiral and roll the cauldron away. He started back, his head full of questions.

"Hello, dear," one of the flamesilks said, popping her head over the edge of her nest just as he was about to pass her. He jumped, and she giggled. "I'm Danaid. My, aren't you a shiny one. We haven't had any visitors in so long — and now we'll have two new flamesilks! How delightful." She sighed happily. Her scales were so orange she almost looked like a HiveWing, but there was no black among them; instead, flecks of white dotted her spine and long streaks of white striped her wings. She looked old enough to be Blue's great-grandmother.

"I might not be a flamesilk," Blue said, checking his wrists again.

"Not to worry," she said. "I'm sure you'll still be delightful company. Better than all these grousing old dragons anyhow. Some of them can't keep a secret." She shot an irritated look at the pale pink flamesilk. "And SOME of them think VERY highly of themselves."

"I can HEAR you," Fritillary shouted from his nest.

"We all can!" called another.

"I KNOW," Danaid shouted back. "We're in a CAVE! But I'm having a PRIVATE CONVERSATION, so stick your snouts somewhere else!"

"I *told* you, I thought you *wanted* me to tell Fritillary that you liked his stripes," the pink SilkWing said in a wounded voice. "Aren't you *ever* going to forgive me?"

"Well, I don't like them anymore!" Danaid snapped. "I think they make him look skinny and arrogant and potato-brained!"

"You WISH you were as smart as a potato!" Fritillary bellowed.

"Go suck a lime!" Danaid shouted. "I hope your face gets eaten by dung beetles!"

"Now, now, settle down," said one of the HiveWing guards in a bored voice.

"Anyway, where were we?" Danaid said to Blue, her voice suddenly all sweetness again.

"And it wasn't *my* fault that Festoon overheard me telling Heliconian that you thought he was stealing all the radishes," the pink dragon went on querulously. "You should be mad at *him* for eavesdropping, not *meeeeeee*."

"I was," Danaid snapped, "but he died five years ago, you half-wit."

"Oh, right." The pink dragon flopped sideways in his nest.

"Ignore them, sweetheart," Danaid said to Blue.

"Is it always like this?" Blue asked. He waved his hands at the flamesilks.

"Like what?" Danaid asked cheerfully.

"The . . . arguing?" he tried. He'd seen at least three other shouting matches erupt that morning, while he'd been searching the cave.

"Who's arguing?" Danaid said. "Was it old Fritillary? He's the worst. Don't talk to him. Xenica is terrible, too, always gossiping and bad-mouthing everyone. You already know you can't trust Pierid over here." The pink flamesilk let out a grumbling sigh and turned his head away from them. "Clubtail is perfectly nice, but by all the Hives, he never stops talking. Heliconian ruins everything." She flipped her tail over the side of the nest and smiled at Blue. "Really, I'm the only one worth knowing."

"Danaid, stop poisoning my son's mind," Admiral said, appearing at Blue's side suddenly. "He's on *my* side, not yours."

"There are sides?" Blue said, confused.

"No," Admiral said, "but Danaid is definitely on the wrong one. Let me introduce you to the dragons you *should* be friends with."

Danaid hissed at him. "You can't keep the new friends all to yourself," she cried. "New friends are for sharing! Let him decide for himself who he wants to talk to!"

"Eat bugs, Danaid," Admiral said sharply. He led Blue away, his snout in the air. "Isn't she dreadful?" he said, loud enough for the orange SilkWing to overhear.

"She seemed all right to me," Blue said.

"No," Admiral said. "She's dreadful."

"What is going on?" Blue asked, bewildered.

"With what?" Admiral paused to toss Blue a tangerine, smiling.

"It's just . . . you guys seems to spend a lot of time fighting with each other," Blue pointed out.

"Do we?" Admiral looked surprised. "No more than most dragons, I'm sure."

"*Way* more than the dragons I know," Blue said.

Admiral flipped one of his wings dismissively. "Well, I suppose we've all been stuck together for so long. There's bound to be a little tension here and there. Come meet Xenica, though. She's very sweet and always has clever things to say about the others."

Xenica shared her kale and kumquats with them and spent their entire conversation glancing around the cave to make sure everyone else saw that she was officially getting to meet the new SilkWing first. She also made a point of warning Blue away from Danaid and a few other flamesilks.

This went on with each dragon Blue met, and by the time he wound up back in his nest, he was exhausted. He couldn't keep track of who hated who, except they all seemed to hate

Fritillary, which was mutual. The cavern was seething with petty rivalries, long-held grudges, and easily provoked tempers.

He flopped down next to Luna's cocoon and rested his head against it. He couldn't wait for his sensible, funny, normal sister to come out.

No wonder they're starved for new company. Being trapped in here for so long has turned them all super weird.

"Almost my turn again," Admiral said, shaking his wrists out. He tapped the insides of his arms with his claws, as though hoping it would wake up his silk glands.

"Father," Blue said, "why do you all fight with each other? Aren't there more important enemies?"

"Like who?" Admiral asked.

"The queen. The HiveWings. The guards who imprison you here," Blue said, lowering his voice.

"Oh, tosh," said Admiral. "The queen is our employer. The guards keep us fed and safe and on schedule."

Blue shook his head. How could his father not understand that this was a prison? *Maybe after you've been here for a while, you have to convince yourself you chose this so it all feels less awful.*

He'd met two dragons among the flamesilks who he suspected weren't as resigned or falsely content as Admiral. Heliconian was restless and fidgety and glanced at the exits a lot; she also asked the only questions about the outside world and what was happening beyond the cavern. And Pierid seemed desperately unhappy, although he wouldn't say anything bad about the HiveWings.

Also Fritillary, with his everlasting bad temper — surely he wanted to escape.

"I just think it's silly to be so mad at each other," Blue said, "when there are far worse things going on and dragons who are treating you far more terribly than Danaid. If you all could stop fighting and stand together, maybe you could actually change things."

"No, no," Admiral said firmly. "I would never work with Danaid or Clubtail or Whitespeck. They are selfish ignoramuses and wrong about everything. I can get things done through the queen."

Blue sighed. He could see these dragons had baked their opinions of one another in a furnace and were determined to stick to their factions.

He slept poorly again that night, troubled by dreams of searching for Cricket through the dark halls of her school. No matter how many corners he turned or how many doors he opened, he never found the library. But he ran into Danaid and Fritillary and Pierid over and over again, all of them yelling over his head at someone else across the room. Then, just before he woke up, he found a room with Luna's cocoon in it — but the threads were cut open, and no one was inside.

He scrambled out of his nest before he was fully awake, stumbling over his claws as he hurried to her cocoon. It was still there, still safe, still warm. The silk walls seemed thinner than before, so he thought he could see the shadow of Luna on the other side. He leaned against it again and whispered, "Luna. I miss you."

The silk moved against his scales, a slight push and give, as though the dragon inside was rolling over or nudging him back.

"She's coming out tonight," Blue said, grinning, when Admiral came over to check on him. Even in this peculiar place, he couldn't help feeling excited for Luna. She'd finally have wings, like she always wanted.

But would she ever get to really use them? His smile dimmed as the cocoon rocked again. Even though this was the last place he wanted to be, he was glad he'd be here for Luna when she came out. He was glad he'd be the one to explain everything, instead of a bunch of squabbling strangers.

"Dad," Blue said, "what do you think will happen to me if I end up not being a flamesilk?"

"You'll get one of the regular SilkWing jobs down here," his father said breezily. "Moving cauldrons or chopping food or cleaning, that sort of thing."

"But what if I want to go home?" Blue asked, wishing he could stop his voice from trembling. "Would I really have to stay here?"

Admiral drummed his claws on the rocks below him. "Well," he said, "the queen doesn't exactly like to have

SilkWings wandering around who know where this cavern is." Blue's shoulders slumped, and Admiral hurried on quickly. "But tell you what, I'll write her a letter! Or lots of letters! If you're not a flamesilk, I'll think of some very good reasons why you should get to go home. I'll convince her. Don't worry. It might take a while. But then, maybe you'll decide you want to stay? It's quite nice here. And this is where I am," he finished with a wistful note in his voice.

"I know," Blue said. "I'll think about it," he added, to make his dad feel better.

That day passed much like the one before. Blue prowled all the corners again, looking for loose stones or a breath of air from outside. He tried to avoid getting dragged into the fights between the flamesilks, but it was almost impossible. Every time he walked across the cave, someone would call him over, and then someone else would start shouting about how he shouldn't associate with worm-eating lowlifes like that, and soon they'd all be arguing over an offensive remark one of them had made ten years ago, and finally Admiral would have to come hustle Blue away to safety.

But he did find a spot — just one — that gave him a spark of hope. It was in the wall under the ledge where the HiveWings guarded the staircase. Here the rock slanted back a ways into a craggy corner, and when Blue ran his talons over the stone, he found a hole.

It wasn't a very big hole. It was just large enough for him to fit one of his arms through it, but when he did, he felt open space on the other side. Open space and a touch of chilliness, as though there was another big cave back there, or maybe even a passage. The rocks he could feel on the back of the wall seemed damp. He tried peering through, but he couldn't see anything but darkness.

He returned to his nest, trying to think like Cricket. How would she get through the wall, if she were stuck in here?

It was early evening when Luna's cocoon started squirming. He crouched beside it, touching the silk gently with his talons whenever it seemed as if it might rock too far away. Their father was there, too, watching with shining eyes.

A crack appeared at one end of the golden cocoon. Blue held his breath as it widened, slicing off the tip. Claws appeared in the gap, pushing away the top of the cocoon, and then he could see Luna's head shoving her way out as well.

"Luna," he called. "I'm here. You're doing great. You're almost done!"

She couldn't answer yet, but he saw her antennae unfurl and wave at him. Luna wriggled and heaved and slowly dragged her whole body out, until finally she left the empty husk of the cocoon behind her.

"Whoosh," she said, collapsing on her stomach on the warm rocks. Her wings unfolded gracefully from her back and spread out to dry, like cascading petals of green sunlight. They were beautiful.

"You did it!" Blue cheered. He lay down beside her and nudged her snout with his. "Your wings are amazing! So amazing, Luna!" His throat closed over everything else he wanted to say.

She smiled sleepily at him. "Then why are you crying, little brother?" she asked. "Overwhelmed by my gloriousness?"

"Pretty much," he said with a sniffly laugh. "I missed you so much."

"Awww," she said, covering one of his talons with hers. "It was only five days, silly."

"Yeah, but . . . they were really stressful days," he said.

She blinked at him for a long moment, and then her gaze slowly shifted to the cave walls behind him, and the glow of the light from all the flamesilk cauldrons, and the stranger watching them eagerly from extremely close by.

She rolled her wrists in and stared at them, then sat up abruptly.

"Hi!" said Admiral. "Oh wow! I can't believe this is happening! I'm so happy to meet you!"

Luna stared at him, then at Blue with an "explain this" face.

"This is Admiral," Blue said. "Our dad." He felt a twinge of pain in his own wrists and glanced down. Uh-oh. Were those pinpricks of gold lava under his scales?

"This is the greatest day of my life!" Admiral declared with the most enormous grin on his face.

"Enough smiling. Time to spin," Sandfly said, stomping up and poking him in the shoulder.

"I give them three days until they figure out that you're the most annoying dragon in here!" Fritillary shouted from across the cavern.

Luna glanced around frantically, her wings fluttering. She leaned forward and seized Blue's talons between hers.

"Blue," she said. "*Where are we?*"

CHAPTER 24

"So Swordtail . . . "

"Might be nearby," Blue said. "Or might have been captured."

"This is somehow too much information and absolutely not enough information at the same time," Luna said, rubbing her forehead.

"Tangerine?" Admiral offered.

"Thanks," she said, taking it and peeling it quickly. She'd been eating nonstop while Blue told her the whole story. Admiral, it turned out, had a stash of food tucked away in his nest, and he was surprisingly adept at tossing fruit while spinning flamesilk at the same time.

"But the queen hasn't come down to yell at you or anything?" Luna asked.

"No," Blue said. "I really thought she would. Or that I'd get dragged into her throne room and punished. But this seems to be it. She just . . . had me thrown in here."

"Like a lost *thing* that she found and put back in its place,"

Luna said grumpily. "I mean, I'm glad you weren't punished, Blue. But the queen uses punishment mostly to send a message to the rest of her subjects. So I'm guessing she didn't want to draw attention to the fact that she has flamesilks — or that a little wingless SilkWing was able to hide from her for so long."

"That was only because I met Cricket," Blue said. "She's the one who figured out how to hide me."

Luna rolled her eyes at him affectionately. "Trust you to find the *one* good HiveWing in the entire tribe. Now I'll never be able to convince you that they're all evil."

"Because they're not!" he protested. "There must be others as nice as Cricket. Maybe not as smart or pretty or funny or kind. But probably a few that are nice."

Luna shook her head. "I doubt it — but even if they are, they never get a chance to be, because of the queen's brainwashing." She shuddered from antennae to tail. "That mind-control thing sounds *so* creepy."

"It is," Blue said.

"I hope Io's all right."

"Me too. I hope she found the Chrysalis. Luna, did you know about the Chrysalis?"

"A little bit." Luna stood up, shaking out her wings and testing different positions she could hold them in. "I knew Swordtail and Io had just met them. I was hoping to join once I had my wings. I didn't quite figure on waking up in here."

Blue winced and she gave him a sharp look. "Is your silk coming in? Does it feel hot?" She took his talons and turned them over to study his wrists. It was hard to see if they were glowing, with all the light from the other flamesilk in the cave.

"I'm supposed to spin my cocoon tomorrow night," Blue said. "I wish I didn't have to do it in here." He'd been nervous enough about his Metamorphosis when he knew it would happen in the tranquil, peaceful safety of the Cocoon. But it was much more unnerving to imagine spinning his silk here, in this too-bright place with its shouting dragons and stomping guards all staring at him.

"There must be a way out," Luna said. She looked up at the guards by the stairwell. "How many guards do you think there are?"

"Luna," Blue said, "there's no way we can fight them. Just you and me? That's crazy."

"But now I can do this!" she said. She held out one arm and a flaming silk thread burst from her wrist. It hit one of Admiral's piles of letters and instantly set it ablaze.

"Ack!" Admiral cried. He leaped over and knocked the burning pile away from the others, then stamped it out with his talons. When it was a pile of ashes on the rocks, he picked up the fiery strand of silk and brandished it at Luna. "This is not a toy! Look what you did! Now how will I remember what I've already written? The queen doesn't like repetition! This is terrible. You need to learn to be careful with your flamesilk, young lady."

"Sorry," Luna said innocently.

Blue blinked at Admiral. "Dad, you're — you're holding the flamesilk! In your talons! Why isn't it burning you?"

Admiral climbed back into his nest and dropped Luna's flamesilk into his own cauldron. It glowed a much brighter orange gold than what was already in there. "Flamesilk dragons can't be burned by flamesilk," he said. "That would be absurd."

"Wow," Blue said. "Wait, so if some already burned me . . . ?"

"No, it will still burn you until you've gone through Metamorphosis, whether you're going to be a flamesilk or not," Admiral said. "Luna, come here and let me show you the different kinds you can make. Flamesilk is a big responsibility."

Luna rolled her eyes at Blue, but she went over to their father and gave him her full attention.

Blue sighed, rubbing his wrists. His wingbuds were tingling, too, in a way that was both exciting and uncomfortable. He wished he could go run through the savanna, under the stars, just breathing air that wasn't thick and hot and overly stuffed with oranges.

He scrambled down to the central floor of the cavern and made his way to the spot under the staircase ledge, where he'd found the hole earlier that day. He guessed it was close to the middle of the night. Only two guards were on the stairs and the regular SilkWing workers were gone, to a cramped apartment home in one of the warehouses, according to Admiral. Most of the flamesilks were asleep. Danaid, Admiral, and Fritillary were the only ones awake, pouring silk into their cauldrons.

Blue could feel Danaid's eyes on him as he poked through the rocks. He was out of sight of the staircase guards here, but the ones up above the glass could still see him. He glanced up to confirm this, and the glow of at least six pairs of eyes stared back.

So even if he could chisel through the wall, he'd never get a chance to. There was no way to do anything surreptitious in here.

He found the hole again and slipped his claws through, reaching for that feeling of freedom. The dark open space on the other side that might lead anywhere . . . to the outside world . . . to the sky and all its stars . . .

On the other side of the wall, unseen, something slipped gently between his claws and squeezed.

Blue came *this close* to screaming his head off. But at the same moment, he heard someone whisper, "Shhhhhhh." He bit down hard on his tongue and froze.

"Blue," the voice whispered.

He tilted his head closer to the wall. "Cricket?"

"Shhh. Yes. It's me."

"And me!" someone else whispered fiercely.

"Is Luna all right?" whispered a third voice — Swordtail.

"She's amazing," Blue said softly. "I can't believe you're all —"

"Blue, don't talk," Cricket interrupted. "They're watching you very closely. It's suspicious enough that you're over here with your arm in a hole; if you keep talking to the wall, someone's going to investigate." She squeezed his claws again and let go.

Reluctantly he pulled his talon back, although it felt emptier than ever now, as though it had found its missing half and now it had to be alone again. He wanted to reach for her once more, to be sure she was real and really there and really alive. But he could see how that might look a bit strange. Danaid was pretending to look at her wrists, but she was leaning so far toward him that she was in danger of toppling out of her nest. The eyes up above stared and stared. He wasn't sure they ever blinked. Was that a HiveWing power some guards had? No need for eyelids?

He sat down and started building a small pyramid of pebbles, trying to look harmless. That was something he was usually pretty good at.

"The LeafWings were trying to build a tunnel," Cricket said softly. "To get into the Hive from below. That's how they found this place, by accident, as they were digging underneath. Did you find your father? Sorry, I know you can't answer. But Luna came out of her cocoon? Are there a lot of flamesilks down here? Oh, you can't answer that either. I can't believe how big this cave is."

Not big enough, if you're trapped in it for your entire life, Blue thought. He thought he should be more horrified by the idea of LeafWings tunneling into the Hives. Six days ago, the image of LeafWings suddenly bursting out of the ground inside his city would have been the most terrifying thing he could possibly imagine.

But he'd met a few other more terrifying things since then.

"Listen," Sundew hissed. "Cricket wants to get you out of there."

"I do, too!" Swordtail chimed in.

"Right, but I don't care what he thinks," Sundew clarified. "Cricket nearly died with me, though, so I kind of feel like I owe you guys one. My parents have more important things to do . . . but I might be able to come up with a plan. Can you be ready tomorrow night?"

Blue's heart sank. He shook his head and shifted himself around the rock pyramid, pretending to reach for another stone, but really angling so whoever was peering through the hole could see his wingbuds.

He heard Cricket let out a soft gasp. "He's about to go into Metamorphosis," she whispered to Sundew. "We have to get him out now. Tonight."

"Oh, rotten bark beetles," Sundew grumbled. "Fine. I'll do it the messy way. Blue, can you see a crack in the wall, near the bottom, that arches around in a half circle?"

Blue glanced casually at the wall. He spotted what she meant immediately — it looked like a sun setting.

"Can you and Luna fit through there, if I can knock out the chunk of rock underneath the crack?"

He thought so, although he hadn't spent enough time with Luna's wings yet to be sure how big they were. He was a little more worried about how to fit Admiral through, but his father was quite skinny. He'd just have to squish.

Blue gave a very slight nod, scattering his pebbles as though he'd gotten frustrated with his construction.

"Great. Go get her, and everyone be ready to run."

"Good luck, Blue," Cricket whispered.

"Tell Luna I'm here!" Swordtail interjected. "Very heroically!"

"You sat around in a greenhouse and then followed me into a tunnel," Sundew observed. "I'm not sure you qualify for a statue in your honor just yet."

"Shhh." Cricket scolded both of them.

Blue picked up a pebble and pretended to peer at it closely, then set it down and headed back over to Luna.

"Everything all right?" Danaid asked as he went by. She leaned her elbows on the edge of her nest, watching him with wide-eyed interest.

"Oh, yes," Blue said. "Just some pretty rocks I think my sister would like."

"You will introduce her to me, won't you?" Danaid said, and her voice was an odd mixture of pushy and wistful. "No matter what your dad says?"

"Of course," Blue said, feeling guilty. He couldn't stay here just to keep these lonely flamesilks company, but he was sorry that escaping with Luna meant abandoning them to their endless quarrels.

Is there any way to bring them along? Could they come with us?

He didn't know how to alert the other flamesilks without attracting the attention of the guards. And given what he knew about them so far, he was afraid even the idea of an escape plan would somehow trigger a screaming match that would give everything away.

He hurried back to Luna, worrying over the problem in his head. Rescuing her was everything; it was the whole reason he'd broken so many rules and gotten in so much trouble. It was the most important thing, getting her out of here.

But he wished there was a way to rescue all of them.

Luna sat up as he approached, and her eyes gleamed when she saw the expression on his face. She'd always been able to read him, ever since they first hatched.

"You've found a way out," she whispered excitedly.

"Our friends are here," he whispered back.

"Then let's go!" She jumped to her feet and looked up at Admiral.

"Hmm?" he said, blinking down at them. "I was just composing another letter in my head. To thank the queen for bringing you here, of course. My letters can't all be complaints, you know! Ho, no, that wouldn't do. I must also show my gratitude when she is so generous with us. My thank-you letter in regards to the tangerines was a work of art." He shot a regretful look at the pile of ashes, as though wondering how many more masterpieces had been lost to Luna's flamesilk.

"Father," Blue said softly, "we have a way out of here. But we have to go right now."

"Go?" Admiral echoed. "What do you mean?"

"We're going to escape," Luna said. "All three of us. Come on, quick, while the guards are looking sleepy."

"But I'm in the middle of my spinning rotation," Admiral said. "And I haven't made nearly enough for the quota. You're going to have to make it up with all your bright lovely silk. They'll probably give you a turn in the morning, once you've rested a bit."

"No," Luna said firmly. "I'm not giving anyone my 'bright lovely silk.' It's mine. And I'm escaping with Blue right now."

Admiral twitched, as though the word *escape* was finally crawling into his ears. "No, no," he said. "The Hives need our silk. We're providing a great service. We're very important — you're very important. You can't . . . you can't *leave*. What are you even talking about? We're not allowed to leave. That rule is pretty clear."

"Come with us, please," Blue begged. "This is no way to live, Father. We could be together *and* free, out there."

"Out where?" Admiral scoffed. "There's nowhere the queen doesn't control. No, no, we mustn't anger her with ungrateful stunts like escape attempts. Oh dear, oh dear. You'll get us *all* in trouble. It'll make everything worse!"

"How could it be worse than this?" Luna asked.

"In the beginning there were chains!" Admiral said. "On our ankles! I was the one who got rid of those! It only took me about four years and two hundred or so letters, but I finally convinced her we could be trusted without them. And now you want to break that trust!"

"This is not a mutual relationship," Luna said. "The queen is using you. She's giving you next to nothing, and you're letting her walk all over you instead of fighting back. We're not going to be part of that." She turned to Blue. "I don't think this is going to work. We have to go without him."

"Oh, *no,*" Admiral cried. "You can't! You'll undo all the progress I've made with the queen! We have rules for a reason, you know. And she'll be so disappointed."

"So escape with us!" Blue couldn't give up. He couldn't just leave his father here. "Father, you don't have to follow rules that are unjust, and you don't have to do everything the queen says. Don't you feel like there are rules in your heart that are more important? About helping other dragons, and standing up for anyone who's being treated badly, and loving whoever you want, and choosing to live your life in your own kind, peaceful way?"

He glanced over and saw Luna staring at him in surprise. She reached out with one wing and pulled him into a hug.

"Wow," she said. "It really was a long five days, wasn't it?"

"Well . . . I just understood it finally," he said. "That there are dragons who aren't safe, and dragons I could help, and being a good little SilkWing who follows the rules was making my life easy, but also helping to keep a bad system in place. I didn't know before how bad it was for so many dragons. Like you, Father. Like all the flamesilks in here. This isn't right."

"And you shouldn't want it for your children," Luna said. "If you want to stay, that's fine. But we're going." She turned Blue toward the center of the cave.

"No," Admiral said. "No, no! It's wrong. I can't let you do this. GUARDS!"

Blue inhaled sharply. The HiveWings by the staircase whipped their heads toward them.

His father was sabotaging their escape — turning them in to keep them trapped here!

They had to run . . . but their escape route looked a whole continent away, and it wasn't even open yet.

"GUARDS!" Admiral bellowed. "Listen!"

"Stop annoying the guards!" Danaid shouted at Admiral, interrupting him. "They don't want to hear your thoughts on potassium at this hour! Or ever!"

"It's not that!" Admiral yelled back. "Although my thoughts on potassium are very well researched and relevant! But hey, guards! Guards! My dragonets —"

"Your brains are a pile of bananas!" Fritillary hollered from his perch, never one to miss out on a fight. "Your dragonets are boring!"

"They are NOT!" Danaid and Admiral roared in unison.

"I think they're charming!" Danaid yelled.

"You don't even know them!" Admiral shouted. "They're MY dragonets and they're FASCINATING! But they're —"

"Well, then they're the opposite of YOU!" Danaid bellowed.

"What is *happening*?" Luna said to Blue, covering her ears.

There was something about the sparkle in Danaid's eyes . . . Blue wasn't sure if it was her usual spirited fury, or if maybe . . .

"I think Danaid might be trying to help us," he said quietly. He glanced up at the guards. They were sitting down again, rolling their eyes at one another as though they'd heard fights like this a million times. "Follow me. Walk, don't run. Act casual."

He climbed down through the stalagmites, trying to quiet his thudding heart.

"GUAAAAAAARDS!" Admiral yelled again. But as Blue had hoped, Admiral didn't jump up and chase them. He would have to stop his silk spinning to do so, and that was yet another rule he'd never break.

"Shut UP!" Pierid whined, sitting up and rubbing his eyes. "Why are you making SO MUCH NOISE? It's the middle of the night!"

"Yeah, some of us were SLEEEEEEEPING!" Whitespeck shouted.

"You're not helping matters with YOUR bellowing!" Heliconian chimed in from the nest closest to him.

Now all ten of them were awake and shouting. It was perfect cover. The HiveWing guards looked like the last thing they wanted to do was come down and get involved in this. And no matter how much Admiral roared, they couldn't hear his accusations over the noise of everyone else.

Blue paused at Danaid's nest. "Thank you," he said, holding one talon up to her.

She took it and squeezed it with a wink. "Whatever I'm doing, it's great fun."

"This is Luna," he said. "Luna, this is Danaid. Who is definitely a dragon worth knowing."

Danaid beamed over the edge of her nest at Luna. "Nice to meet you," she said. "Now scoot! I can see something exciting is about to happen!" She nodded over at the wall, and Blue realized that the crack looked wider than before . . . and something seemed to be coming through it.

"You could come with us," he said.

"I'm not sure my old heart could stand running for my life," she said. "But if you find a more sedate way to get us out of here, come back for me."

He nodded. "I will try. I promise."

She went back to shouting at the other flamesilks as he and Luna moved away. It was funny to think of Danaid wanting anything sedate, when she seemed so delighted in the middle of chaos.

The stone gave a low *crack* as they crouched beside it, and Blue realized that it was being pushed out of the wall. By . . .

were those roots? He gingerly touched one of the thick brown fingers that were shoving their way through the crack. It felt like branches, woody and knobbly under his claws.

Sundew was growing something, somehow, faster than anything should be able to grow. And it was shoving the rocks apart, breaking through the crack.

Creating an opening.

He dug his talons in around the boulder and yanked. Luna did the same, and with a lot of grunting and muscle-pulling, they felt it slowly give way, until it tumbled out at their feet.

The hole in the wall yawned at them, and on the other side, beyond the roots, he saw three faces crowding in to peer through.

Swordtail reached toward Luna. "You're safe!" he whispered.

"And I have wings!" she answered giddily. She shoved Blue in front of her. "Go on, quick!"

Suddenly there was a furious pounding overhead, *SMASH, SMASH, SMASH* against the glass. They'd been spotted. That meant the guards were coming — *all* the guards.

Blue dove into the hole and wiggled through into the dark, navigating a small thicket of leafy branches. He felt the warmth of Cricket's talons lifting him up and saw light glinting off her glasses.

"I'm so glad you're alive," he said breathlessly. "I had a

feeling you'd rescue me. Except I thought maybe I had to come rescue you. But I didn't know how."

"You did rescue me, just by being you," she said. "Oh, gosh, that wasn't corny at all."

Luna popped through and Swordtail swept his wings around her. "My love!" he cried.

"By the forest, all of you stop being sickening and run!" Sundew cried. She took off in a whirl of green scales, disappearing rapidly into the dark.

Luna produced a small wisp of flame that lit up the tunnel just enough for them to see, and they ran.

But before she did, for that moment in the dark, Blue had glanced down at his wrists.

And saw tiny globes of fire under his scales.

CHAPTER 25

They ran and climbed and ducked and slid down loose pebbly dirt slopes, following the flicker of Luna's silk and the flash of Sundew's tail up ahead. Their escape route smelled like earthworms and cut grass. Twice they had to squeeze through gaps so narrow, Blue was worried Swordtail wouldn't fit. Most of the time the ceiling was low enough to scrape their heads, and sometimes the dirt turned to damp mud, clogging up their talons.

But after a while they slowed down to listen, and they couldn't hear anyone behind them.

"Maybe they couldn't get through the hole from the cavern," Blue said. Maybe Sundew's fast-growing roots had blocked the way.

"Or they got stuck at the bottleneck gaps," Swordtail said, rubbing his shoulder.

"They'll be out searching for the other end of the tunnel," Sundew said. "Good thing it's quite a long way from the Hive."

She turned to keep going and they followed, moving at a steadier pace now.

Soon the dirt tunnel shifted up and released them into a stone cave, similar in size to the flamesilk cavern, but cold and dark and empty. From there on, they climbed through natural passages in the rocks. At one point, they hopped up the side of a trickling waterfall that sprayed their scales with mist. Blue thought he heard a river rushing somewhere close by.

He also heard odd whispering, chittering sounds inside the echoes, as though the caves were haunted by musical squirrels.

Or reading monkeys, he realized. These caves could be connected to the ones where he and Cricket had seen the little monkey creature. Maybe there were lots of them living down here, like Cricket's science-project dream come true.

And then, a long while later, he heard a sound like distant roaring.

"What's that?" he whispered to Cricket.

"I'm not sure," she answered. "The smell is different, too, did you notice? Doesn't it smell like salt and . . . fish, maybe? Oh! Oh! I know what it is! Sundew, are we going to the ocean?"

Just then they rounded a corner of the tunnel — and there it was.

The ocean!

They were standing in an enormous cave that looked out onto the beach. It was early morning. Rivulets of water ran and branched and reconvened all through the sandy floor of the cave. Sea birds dove and wheeled in and out, visiting their nests near the rocky ceiling.

Cricket ran forward, her talons splashing in the wet sand, to the mouth of the cave. She opened her wings to the wind so they billowed out like pages flung into the sky. The waves roared cheerfully at her.

"Oh wow," Luna said, wading up beside her. She spread her wings, too, and they sat side by side for a moment, gold-orange-black and pale green, HiveWing and SilkWing, gazing out at the sea.

Blue sidled up beside them and looked out at the beach. It stretched away beyond sight in each direction, with tall cliffs overlooking the beach as far as he could see. Up at the top of the cliffs, long grass tossed and waved in the wind.

The ocean was *so big*. He'd never quite imagined how big it could be, or how noisy, or how active. It never stopped moving — charging up the beach, sprinting away, rolling and churning blue-green-gray with sprays of white.

"Have you ever been here before?" Cricket asked him. "I haven't, but I've always wanted to visit the sea. Doesn't it feel like a promise? Like the night before an exciting journey? The Distant Kingdoms are out there, Blue. I know it." She squinted at the tossing waves, as though she might be able to glimpse the far-off continent on the other side of the world. "Clearsight's home. We could learn so much if we could just figure out how to get there."

Luna gave a rueful laugh. "I'm afraid we have enough to deal with on this continent," she said. "I'm all for exploring new worlds, but I think we have to save this one first."

"Or we could just leave," Cricket said in a quieter voice. "If it's too dangerous here — maybe we'd be safer over there."

"Yes, we might be," Luna said. "But the dragons we left behind would still be in danger." She turned as Swordtail and Sundew came up to join them.

Blue realized it was raining. A quiet drizzle plip-plopped across the sand, turning the air misty in the pale dawn light. He held out his burning wrists so the raindrops could cool them down.

"Thank you for getting us out of there," he said to Sundew. "Where are your parents?"

"Sulking," she said. "They didn't want me to reveal the existence of the tunnel to the HiveWings, even though we'd already decided we can't use it. Also they're mad that I haven't given them this yet." She tapped one of her larger pouches and it made a thunking sound. "But they're not the boss of me, and I told them they could have it once you were free. I'll meet up with them tonight."

"And then what will you do?" Swordtail asked.

"Go back to the other LeafWings," she said. "Figure out our next plan. Since this one didn't go exactly the way we expected."

"Is that . . ." Luna started, pointing to the pouch. "Do you really have . . . ?"

Sundew reached in and drew out the Book of Clearsight. It looked even smaller and less mystical in the daylight. It just looked like a very old book that someone had sewn together a little crookedly.

But it holds the secrets of our future, Blue thought with a shiver of awe. *And we could read it . . . we could read it right now and know everything that's going to happen!*

"Can I show them?" Cricket asked Sundew. The LeafWing nodded, passing the book to her. Cricket found a flat, dry boulder and swept off all the sand on it with her tail. Blue sat down beside her, and Cricket scooted closer to him so Luna could sit on her other side.

"It's not what we thought it was," Cricket said. "It's . . . well, it's something else completely."

She opened the book to the first page.

Dear grandchildren, and great-grandchildren, and great-great-grandchildren, and all the many great-grandchildren to come,

How funny it feels to know you so well, when there are so many of you I'm never going to meet. I see you all the time, especially when I'm just on the edge of falling asleep. The future is so clear, suddenly, now that I won't be able to change anything. My time is almost up, and yours is just beginning.

I won't be able to control anything after this. I won't be able to use my visions to protect you, to keep you all safe.

But then, one thing I've learned over my long, strange, lovely life is that I never could actually control the future as much as I thought I could.

I should have learned that lesson with my first love, back home in Pyrrhia. But I kept trying anyway. And I did manage to keep you all alive. I battled the future for that much, and I won.

But the future will always win in the end, because it continues on forever, to where I cannot go.

So this is my last battle. The last thing I can do to try and keep my claws on the balance of the future — to keep you safe as long as I can.

In this book are my visions of what is yet to come. Some of it seems small, but I have included everything, even if I can't tell yet why it's important. I leave you this in the hope that it will make life better for both our tribes. I hope you will use it to protect the dragons around you, especially the ones who are the most threatened, regardless of who they are and how you think you feel about them.

There are some hard times ahead, as there always are, everywhere and for everyone. I'm sorry I won't be here to help you rebuild after the earthquake. I hope I've written down enough advice to get you through the famine.

But most of what I see is joy. Your futures are full of joy. What a miracle it is to be a dragon, alive right now and part of this wonderful world. Do you ever stop to think about that? About what an odd and lucky thing it is to be this soul inside this body. To live in a world with so many marvels in it. I am so grateful to have known and loved you all.

All the hurricanes and earthquakes and fires and storms cannot break you, if you remember a few things.

We are here to love with our whole hearts.

Lean into your kindness and empathy in the face of evil — but do not let evil win.

You are the only dragon who can decide who you want to be. Don't let yourself get stuck on someone else's path. Search for what's true, and think for yourself.

Over a hundred years ago, I thought my life was finished and there was nothing left to live for. I was so, so wrong. Keep going. The list of things to live for is limitless and it is possible to be happy again.

And — this one is going to sound ridiculous coming from me — don't worry about the future so much. Or else you might miss out on the extraordinary present.

Be happy, dragons of the future. You can change the world with your joy and your hope.

All my love,
Clearsight

Blue glanced up and saw Luna wiping away tears.

"This is exactly how I imagined Clearsight," he said.

"Of course you did," Luna said with a catch in her voice. "You have faith in other dragons. Whereas *I* thought she was a conniving manipulator who deliberately set up her descendants to be the most powerful tribe in Pantala." She shook her head.

"Yup, me too," said Sundew.

"Oh, no," Blue said, shocked. "She wasn't. She wouldn't."

"I see that," Luna said, waving her talon at the book. "But at some point that's what her descendants decided to do. Why didn't she see that coming and stop them?"

"Because," Cricket said softly, "it turns out she wasn't all-knowing and all-seeing, after all." She started turning pages, pointing to the dates up at the top.

After about two hundred years, the flow of visions slowed dramatically. A hurricane here. A tsunami ninety years later. A few more tiny notes, full of question marks.

And then, on a date marked about nine hundred years after the first, she'd written: *Take care of the trees. I think they might be in danger, but I can't see why. Help the LeafWings protect them.*

I love you. Good luck.

Cricket turned the page. The next spread was blank. And so was the next. And the next.

The last few pages of the book were empty.

The last vision from Clearsight was dated over a thousand years ago.

CHAPTER 26

Blue looked up at Cricket and Luna, blinking in confusion.

"Where's the rest of it?" he asked. "What about the Tree Wars? And us trying to steal the book? And everything Queen Wasp knows?"

"She doesn't know anything," Luna said furiously. "She was faking it the whole time. The power of the Book, everything that makes the HiveWings so superior — it's all *lies*."

"In case you're curious," Sundew interjected, "this is my 'not at all surprised' face."

Cricket was nodding. "Clearsight never saw this far ahead. She had no idea her book would be used this way."

"But —" Blue still couldn't wrap his head around it. "But Queen Wasp said Clearsight wanted the tribes to unite under her rule. That was the whole reason Queen Monarch gave up her throne. Because if it was in the Book of Clearsight, it had to be important."

"It was a lie, Blue!" Luna jumped up, and Swordtail came

over to stand beside her. "Wasp lied and used the Book to seize power."

"And to drive out the LeafWings," Sundew said. "Queen Sequoia wouldn't agree to step down without seeing the Book first, which of course Wasp wouldn't allow. Our queen said if she'd seen it in Clearsight's own handwriting, she might have considered it. Which I think is insane in the first place. We don't need anyone else to be our queen!"

"How *could* she?" Blue said, closing the book and resting his claws on it. "I don't understand. How could Queen Wasp read this and then decide to become the total opposite of what Clearsight says to be?"

Cricket put her talon over his on the book. "Some dragons care infinitely more about themselves than anyone else," she said. "Which I think is hard for a dragon like you to imagine."

"Well," he said, "I'm VERY ANGRY about this."

"Angry enough to do something about it?" Sundew asked. She lifted her chin challengingly.

"Like what?" Swordtail asked.

"We're going to take down the HiveWings," Sundew said. "We could use some dragons on the inside."

Swordtail snorted. "You may not have noticed, but we're not exactly on the inside anymore."

"We know dragons who are, though," Luna said, giving him a significant look.

"Wait, what does 'take down' the HiveWings mean?" Blue asked. "Are you going to hurt them?"

Sundew scowled at him. "That is sort of the point of a revolution," she snapped. She snatched the book away from him and stuffed it back in her pouch. "I thought you said you were mad!"

"Yes! But no," Blue said. "The HiveWings have also been lied to, and brainwashed and tricked. The queen is the problem. You have to fight *her,* not the whole tribe. I mean, we do. We have to stop her."

His wrists flared with pain, as though they were trying to remind him that he had slightly more urgent things to do first, such as for instance growing wings.

"Let's rest for a while," Cricket said, watching him with concern. "Everyone thinks better after sleeping." She hopped down to a dry patch of soft sand, in a sheltered corner of the cave, and dug a small hollow. "Blue?"

He gratefully slid down and sank into the hollow next to her. His wingbuds were really starting to ache. And his head felt strangely fuzzy, too. He sort of wished he could spin his cocoon now and shut out the whole mess and all the decisions they might have to make. But the thought also terrified him. He didn't want to be cut off from Cricket and Luna for five days, with no way to know what was going on.

And what if something went wrong with his Metamorphosis?

What could go more wrong than turning out to be a flame-silk? he thought.

"Well, *I* don't need to sleep," Luna said. "I'm going to test out my new wings! Want to come?" she said, bumping Swordtail's side.

"Obviously yes!" he said.

"Be careful," Sundew warned. "The HiveWings will be out in force looking for us. It would be safer to stay inside until dark."

"Just a little flight," Luna wheedled. "I finally have wings! And we're so far from the Hives. I promise we'll be careful."

Sundew shrugged. "You're not my tribe," she said. "But if you get caught, I'm not rescuing you again."

"Noted," Luna said, bounding to the cave entrance. "Be back soon, Blue!"

She soared up into the sky, scattering raindrops in all directions, with Swordtail in her wake. Blue sighed.

"I wish I were that excited about getting wings," he said. "I mean, I am. I'm just . . . nervous, too."

"That sounds normal to me," Cricket said. "But you'll be all right once it starts. How are you feeling? Do you have the same symptoms as Luna?"

He lifted his wrists and she held them gently while she studied them.

"Your silk glands look very bright," she said.

"So did Luna's," he said. "Kind of golden and fiery, just like this."

"Wow," she said. "I might be best friends with a real flamesilk!"

He couldn't squash down his smile. "Best friends?"

"Well, my circle of options is a little smaller than it used to be," she said, flicking her tail at the cave, and at Sundew, who was sorting through her pouches and grumbling. "But the truth is, I'd want you to be my best friend even if I knew every dragon in Pantala."

"Same," he said, resting his head on his talons. "That's how I see you. Best friend, best brain, best heart."

"Awwww," she said. She lay down and snuggled up next to him. "Are you totally asleep yet? Before you fall asleep, can you tell me about the flamesilk cavern? How does it work? How many dragons live there? What are they like?"

Blue drowsily tried to answer her questions, but sleep pulled him down inexorably, chasing away the pain in his back and wrists. It was peaceful with Cricket by his side and the rain pattering on the rocks around them. He felt calm again for the first time in days.

He didn't know how long he slept, but he woke suddenly to the sound of screams from outside.

Across the cave, Sundew dropped a handful of twigs and leaped to her feet.

The three of them ran to the cave entrance and looked out.

Up in the sky, a pair of HiveWings had Swordtail and Luna cornered. They circled like hawks, jabbing and feinting with claws and spears and stingers on their tails.

"Luna!" Blue cried, starting forward and immediately stumbling over his talons. Sundew caught him, pulling him back into the cave.

"No way," she said. "You can't fight in your condition. You can barely fight when you're not half-loopy on silk." She shoved him into Cricket's arms. "Make him stay here."

The LeafWing took off into the sky. It was raining harder than before, with a strong wind whipping up the seas.

Blue watched in a daze as Sundew smashed into the HiveWings, taking them by surprise. One wheeled around to grapple with her, and Swordtail broke away to tackle the other.

They struggled for several rain-soaked moments, talons slipping on wet scales. Blue had always thought of Swordtail as the best fighter he knew, but next to Sundew and the soldiers, he seemed badly outmatched. The HiveWing twisted to slash a claw along his side, and Swordtail roared with pain.

Alone in the sky, Luna flung out her front talons. Blue could see that she was trying to protect Swordtail — that she was trying to set his attacker on fire.

But her silk whipped out faster and wilder than she'd expected. The wind seized the golden strands and flung them together, weaving knots over Luna's head. In a sudden heartbeat, a sail of flamesilk billowed out above Luna — and then the storm roared in, snared the sail, and blew her out to sea.

"Luna," Blue cried desperately. His sister seemed to be struggling with the silk, but she couldn't break free. Lightning flashed, and a moment later, the clouds had swallowed her up.

Swordtail smashed his attacker in the face and flew after Luna, shouting her name. His wings beat frantically as he tried to catch up.

Then he was gone, too. Sundew was left grimly battling the two HiveWings alone.

"We have to — we have to go after them —" Blue said. His whole body was starting to shake, and his wrists felt like they were literally on fire. "Luna — Swordtail —"

"You can't go anywhere, Blue," Cricket said. She put her wings around him and guided him back into the cave, way to the back, toward the tunnels and secret passages. "It's starting. We need to hide you somewhere safe. Let's think."

"But —"

"They'll come back," she promised. "The storm will blow itself out and they'll fly back here and want to find you safe and sound. OK? You'll make things much worse if you go out there and get captured by HiveWings." She guided him down one of the passages, steering him around jutting spires of stone.

"Sundew . . . " he mumbled.

"Can take care of herself," she said. "In case you hadn't noticed, she's pretty fierce. Come on, I think I saw a cave this way — it's about as well hidden as we can get."

He couldn't argue. He couldn't think. Apparently his head was no longer connected to his body. The walls were shifting and rolling and kind of sparkling, too. He felt dizzy and sick and very hot.

It felt like an endless march before Cricket maneuvered him between two pillars into a small, curving cave with smooth walls. These ones really were sparkling, he thought, but actually, his eyes weren't to be trusted, so who knew.

"I wish I were in the Cocoon," he said, his teeth chattering. "I wish I were home."

"I know," Cricket said sadly. "I know, Blue. I'm so sorry you can't be."

He sank to his knees, and the silk started to pour from his wrists. It was bright and burning, flamesilk all the way through, and it wove swiftly around his tail and talons. Everywhere it touched him, his muscles relaxed, and a feeling of peace slowly swept over him, like a wave filling him up.

"I'll be right here, Blue," Cricket said. He lay down, looking up into her wonderful face, lit by the glow of his flamesilk. "I'll be here the whole time. I'll be here when you wake up. You'll be safe. I promise."

Blue was a dragon who didn't like change.

But in the last five days, he'd discovered that his whole

world was very different than he'd imagined. His queen was a controller of minds, the Book of Clearsight was a lie, and his father was a prisoner in a flamesilk factory.

And Blue was in love with a HiveWing.

He'd made it through all of those discoveries. He was stronger now; he saw things more clearly. Like Clearsight had written, he had to keep going and decide for himself what kind of dragon he wanted to be.

After everything he'd been through, he knew he could handle a little thing like growing wings.

The gold fire wrapped around him.

Blue closed his eyes and let the change begin.

EPILOGUE

Luna opened her eyes.

A seagull skittered away from her, cawing indignantly about dragons who pretended to be food and then weren't.

She was lying in wet sand. Wet sand was clumped between her talons and in her ears and in the cracks between her scales. Her face was half-buried in it. She was pretty much plastered with wet sand from horns to tail.

A wave rushed up from behind her, swooshing under her back talons and tail, soaking her underbelly, and whisking away again.

Luna pushed herself up to a sitting position with a groan of pain. She fanned out her wings to check them. One was badly bruised — she had a vague memory of being hit by a hailstone. And one of her back ankles twinged horribly when she tried to stand on it.

She dragged herself up the beach, away from the bustling waves.

Ow. Everything ached.

She squinted up at the aggressively cheerful sun.

How far had she been blown from Blue and Swordtail? This beach didn't look like the one where she'd started out. Instead of tall cliffs, the sand here rolled up into low hills with patches of shrubs. Luna could see quite far up and down the coast and inland, but she couldn't see any sign of caves or Hives.

She rubbed her head, trying to remember the map of Pantala. She'd been in the air for days, tangled in her silk balloon as the storm swept her along. She remembered nothing but white-capped waves below her.

Could she — she couldn't be — surely —

Talons landed on the sand slightly uphill from her. Luna started back, lifting one wrist to shoot fire if her wing was a HiveWing.

But it wasn't.

This dragon was pale yellow with light brown triangle markings on her wings. Only two wings — just one pair, like a LeafWing, but with her coloring, she definitely wasn't a LeafWing. And her wings weren't leaf-shaped either; they looked closer to bat wings, but covered in scales instead of fur.

The dragon took a step toward her, and Luna realized there was something odd at the end of her tail — a barb like she'd only ever seen before on scorpions.

"What are you?" Luna said fiercely.

"Oh, you speak Dragon," said the stranger. "That's lucky."

"What else would I speak?" Luna asked. "Who are you? Where am I?"

"I guess I thought your continent might have a different language," the yellow dragon said with a shrug. "I'm Jerboa."

"My . . . continent?" Luna echoed. She lowered her arm. "Do you mean . . . did I really cross the ocean?"

"It looks that way," Jerboa said wryly. "But not entirely unscathed, I think. Are you injured?"

"Just a little." Luna tried to take a step and winced. "Yargh. That's — *ow.* My name's Luna."

"My hut is just around that bend," Jerboa said, coming over and levering her wing under Luna's. "Hang on, we'll be there in no time." They started across the sand. Luna found it much more difficult to walk in than Jerboa did; her wing kept sagging unexpectedly under her claws or sucking around her talons.

"I have to get back," Luna said. "My friends are over there. They need me. Especially my little brother." She tried to guess how long she'd been up in the storm. She was starving, but that wasn't much of a clue. Blue must have started his Metamorphosis by now. Was he still in his cocoon? Was he all right?

"Well, you're not going far on these wings today," Jerboa said. "But help is coming. I have a feeling it'll be here soon."

Jerboa's hut was tucked into a cove, cozy and well built with a recently thatched roof made of palm fronds. Luna touched the wood of the door on the way inside. It was real wood, and she was startled to see it used for a house as small as this. Maybe Jerboa was wealthier and more powerful than she appeared.

Or maybe it's different over here, she realized. *Maybe there are still plenty of trees on this continent.*

Jerboa helped her over to a bed made of more palm leaves and Luna collapsed onto it, surprised by how exhausted she was. She was sure she'd slept on the beach for a while after crash-landing . . . but the walk to the hut had tired her out again.

"Sleep for a bit," Jerboa said. "I'll make fish stew."

Luna wrinkled her snout. "Um," she said, "that's all right. Do you have any fruit? Or honey?" she added hopefully.

Jerboa flicked her wings back with a thoughtful expression. "Not a fish eater?" she said. "What about crabs? Or rabbits? Or seagulls?"

Luna shook her head. "No animals, thank you," she said politely, and her stomach growled as if disagreeing with her.

"I'll see what I have." Jerboa glided off to another corner of the hut, and Luna felt herself slipping into a doze.

Sometime later, Jerboa shook her awake, talons gentle on her shoulder. "Luna. Our guests are here."

Luna blinked awake. The light had shifted outside, and there were quiet voices coming through the window.

"I'll go get them," Jerboa said. "Don't be alarmed. This is who you need to talk to."

She went out the door. Luna tried to think, although her brain felt overwhelmed and still muddled with sleep. Who was here? How could they help her?

"To who?" said a new voice, which was attached to a dragon ducking through the doorway. He was smaller than Jerboa, closer to Luna's size, but with the same kind of wings and tail as Jerboa. His scales were sand-colored like hers as well, and he wore a hoop earring in one ear.

But following him through the doorway was another dragon entirely. She was black from nose to talons, except for a few silver scales scattered under her wings and two tear-drop silver scales in the corners of her eyes.

A startled jolt ran through Luna, waking her up like a bolt of lightning.

This dragon looked like Clearsight.

Or at least, the way Clearsight always looked in pictures.

Luna sat up as the two of them came closer, with Jerboa behind them.

"Oh wow," said the one with the earring, noticing Luna.

"What —" said the Clearsight-looking dragon. "How — ?"

"I believe this is our first visitor from the lost continent," Jerboa said. "She blew in with the storm."

The little black dragon sat down and tipped her head as though she was listening to something far away. "I'm Moon," she said, "and this is Qibli. Are you really from across the sea?"

"I guess so," Luna said. "It was kind of an accident, coming here. I'm Luna."

"Hi, Luna," said Qibli. "This must be pretty weird for you, too. You have so many wings! I mean, that's cool. Is it hard to fly with all those wings? That's a silly question. I can't believe we're meeting a dragon from another continent! This is amazing!"

"Are you like Clearsight?" Luna asked Moon. "Can you see the future?"

Moon's eyebrows shot up. "You know about *Clearsight*?"

"I know some things about her," Luna said, thinking darkly of the Book and the lies Queen Wasp had told about it. "I know she came from here, and she had scales like yours. I always wondered if there were other dragons over here who could see the future, too."

"I can, sort of," Moon said. "Not as well as she could. But I had a vision about you. That's why we're here."

"Was it about getting me home?" Luna asked, sitting forward and flaring her wings. "Do you know how I can get back there?"

Moon shot Qibli an uneasy look. "Not exactly," she said, "although we can work on it."

"I have some ideas!" Qibli said brightly.

"Good," Luna said. She settled back into the palm fronds. She was suddenly sure that storm had brought her here for a reason. "Let's figure out how to get me home, and you can all come with me. Especially you, vision dragon."

"Me?" Moon said. "Oh, I don't know — I haven't seen anything about —"

"You have to," Luna said. This dragon could be the secret weapon the SilkWings and LeafWings needed. "My tribe needs your help."

Triumph sizzled through her veins.

We're coming for you, Queen Wasp. And now we have a dragon who can really *see the future.*

The reign of the HiveWings is over.